"Liza, for the last time, get out of here before it's too late,"

Dixon pleaded. "You don't even realize the kind of trouble you're up against."

"Maybe I don't. But whatever it is, Jilly's up against it, too, and I can't leave her," Liza told him quietly.

He gripped her arms and pulled her forward until they were nearly nose to nose. "You can't take care of her, either," he whispered. "Listen to me, damn it. You can't protect her, and you can't protect yourself. Not where we're going."

She looked at him, and he didn't need the light to see her eyes—indigo eyes, big and round, partly hidden behind the long, straight strands of her hair. She didn't believe him, and he had to make her believe.

"He's dangerous, Liza."

"More dangerous than you?"

Dear Reader,

It may still be winter outside, but here at Intimate Moments, things couldn't be hotter. Take our American Hero title, for instance: Paula Detmer Riggs's *Firebrand*. Judd Calhoun left his Oregon home—and his first love, Darcy Kerrigan—in disgrace. Now he's back—as the new fire chief—and the heat that sizzled between the two of them is as powerful as ever. But there are still old wounds to heal and new dangers to face. Talk about the flames of passion . . . !

Rachel Lee is on tap with the third of her Conard County series, *Miss Emmaline and the Archangel*. It seems the town spinster has a darker past than anyone suspects, and now it's catching up to her. With no one to turn to except Gage Dalton, the man they call Hell's Own Archangel, her future looks grim. But there's more to this man than his forbidding looks would indicate—much more—and Miss Emmaline is about to learn just what it means to be a woman in love. Marilyn Pappano's *Memories of Laura* takes place in the quintessential small town—Nowhere, Montana—where a woman without a memory meets a man who's sure he knows her past. And it's not a pretty one. So why does sheriff Buck Logan find himself falling for her all over again? In her second book, *Dixon's Bluff*, Sally Tyler Hayes mixes danger and desire and love for a small girl and comes up with a novel you won't want to miss. Harlequin Historical author Suzanne Barclay enters the contemporary arena with *Man with a Mission*, a suspense-filled and highly romantic tale linking two seemingly mismatched people who actually have one very important thing in common: love. Finally, welcome new author Raine Hollister. In *Exception to the Rule*, heroine Layne Taylor finds herself running afoul of the law when she tries to defend her brother against a murder charge. But with Texas Ranger Brant Wade as her opponent, things soon start to get extremely personal.

As always, enjoy!

Leslie Wainger
Senior Editor and Editorial Coordinator

DIXON'S BLUFF

BLUFF

Sally
Tyler
Hayes

Silhouette®
INTIMATE MOMENTS®

Published by Silhouette Books New York

America's Publisher of Contemporary Romance

SILHOUETTE BOOKS
300 East 42nd St., New York, N.Y. 10017

DIXON'S BLUFF

Copyright © 1993 by Teresa Hill

ISBN: 0-373-07485-9

First Silhouette Books printing March 1993

Printed in the U.S.A.

Books by Sally Tyler Hayes

Silhouette Intimate Moments

Whose Child Is This? #439
Dixon's Bluff #485

SALLY TYLER HAYES

lives with her husband and her two-and-a-half-year-old son. A journalist for a newspaper in her home state of South Carolina, she fondly remembers that her decision to write and explore the frontiers of romance came at about the same time she discovered, in junior high, that she'd never be able to join the crew of the Starship Enterprise.

Busy with a full-time job and a full-time family, she confesses that she writes during her son's nap time and after he goes to bed at night.

To my parents,
who always believed I could do anything

Chapter 1

Deke blinked twice, thinking there was no way the scum standing in front of him could have said what he thought he'd heard him say.

He froze for just one moment—a lapse he couldn't afford. It was a moment like this that might well get him killed before the whole thing was over.

He exhaled, long and slow, and by sheer force of will convinced his body to relax. Carefully, he schooled his features to show no emotion.

Because the man he was pretending to be wouldn't give a damn.

He couldn't afford to be surprised by anything he heard. He couldn't get upset. He couldn't change things. And he couldn't afford to care about any harm that might come to anyone caught up in this godforsaken mess, even an innocent child.

He simply stood there, under the sprawling oak whose branches shielded him from the surprisingly hot mid-October sunshine. Hands tucked into the front pockets of his ragged jeans, his T-shirt-covered torso curved against the base of the tree, he rested there, apparently at ease. No one would have guessed the struggle it cost him to appear relaxed.

Slowly, deliberately, he shifted his weight from one foot to the other, then straightened so that he could take out a fraction of his frustration on a nearby pebble. He kicked it and wished he could blast away at Nick Russell, wished he could watch *him* cartwheel over the steep embankment and down into St. Andrew Sound, never to be seen or heard from again.

"Got a problem, Deke?" Russell said with a smirk.

Deke. He hesitated only a fraction of a second now before responding to the name, a remnant of his childhood. He lifted his eyes to the man who stood before him. A man who years before had run a big smuggling operation in the Northeast. A man who wanted back into the business. A man who didn't care who got hurt along the way, even if it was his own three-year-old daughter.

But it didn't matter, Deke told himself. A conscience was a luxury he couldn't afford right now. He'd had a choice, and he'd made it. He'd seen a chance, and he was going to take it.

Deke knew how a man accomplished what he set out to do. It took a single-minded concentration on the goal at hand—concentration to the exclusion of everything else.

He'd believed he could do that, but damn, why did it have to be a kid in his way? It wasn't as if she were his concern. Yet somebody had to look out for the little girl, because her parents were doing a damn poor job of it.

Don't start anything with Russell, Deke warned himself. *Don't even think about it.*

Yet he smiled, barely, and shook his head in disbelief at the words he allowed to pass from his lips.

"I'm having a hard time taking all this in, Russell. I didn't know I'd agreed to spend the next few weeks with a damned idiot."

Russell merely raised an eyebrow.

"You'd be crazy to take a little kid along," Deke said, starting an argument he knew he had no business starting.

Still, the image of Jilly, smiling and laughing as only a truly innocent soul could, wouldn't leave him. She was just around the corner of the stately old house, playing in the tree house, singing a silly rhyme about a monkey who fell out of bed and hurt his head.

And he remembered Charlie, all grown up now, but in his mind still his baby brother, always his baby brother. Charlie had been that happy once, that innocent and carefree.

Deke remembered.

He could only remember, because Charlie would never be happy or carefree again. Charlie's innocence was gone, and Deke owed him. It was a debt that was proving to be hell to pay.

"How the hell are we going to keep her out of the way?" Deke said.

"No problem." Russell had an answer for everything, it seemed. "We'll take the nanny, too."

"We're taking Mary Poppins along?" Deke had a headache the size of Texas. "Great. We get into trouble, she can pull out her umbrella and fly us home."

It was too much. Too damn much.

At thirty-one, Deke MacCauley had always thought of himself as a man of principle, a man with scruples, an honest, hardworking man.

But nothing had ever before pushed him to the point where he was now.

Someone had put a price on his brother's life. He smiled bitterly at the concept, raged inside at the way someone had presumed to place a value on another man's life. His brother's life. Or what was left of it.

Deke was going to pay that price.

There had never been any question about it—that he would meet the conditions. But Russell had just upped the stakes. It was no longer just him and Russell and Russell's poor, drug-blind wife, Ellen, taking the risk.

Now Russell wanted to take his daughter and her nanny along, as well.

Deke settled back against the tree and ached to rub the cords of tension that stretched taut along the back of his neck.

Instead he looked out over the water to the opposite shore. He'd grown up about twenty miles from here, and his mother's family, the Dixons, had lived along the opposite side of the water about a mile down the sound, closer to the point where it spilled into the Atlantic.

He'd played along the shoreline as a boy—Deke, his brother and his cousins, all hanging out along the high bluff of the waterfront property that had belonged to his mother's family for so long that the area had taken on the family name. Dixon's Bluff.

And now here he was, back at Dixon's Bluff. God must have one hell of a sense of humor. Deke sighed and shook his head at the irony, at the strange way the past had of creeping up on a man when he least expected it.

A child's laughter brought him back to the present. Out of the corner of his eye he watched the three-year-old run headlong into the arms of a smiling young woman, watched the woman swing her up off the ground and around in a circle before they fell together, laughing, in the thick carpet of grass.

He cursed under his breath then, slowly and bitterly. *Anything,* he'd vowed. He was willing to do anything to save Charlie. He'd honestly thought he was willing. Surely he hadn't been wrong about that? Yet he still argued.

"This is no damned joyride we're talking about," Deke said, turning to face Russell again. "We're going down there to do business with some of the meanest SOBs alive, and it's going to be hard enough to keep our own butts out of trouble without taking Mary Poppins and the kid along."

"Relax," Russell purred, his voice as smooth and low as an alley cat's. "They're the perfect cover. Who the hell would take his wife, his daughter and a nanny along on a trip to buy a boatful of cocaine?''

And then he laughed, like the madman Deke knew he had to be. But if Russell was a madman, where did that leave Deke?

He'd never actually intended to go through with the trip; he hadn't thought he'd have to. But then, he seemed to be doing a lot of things lately that he'd never expected he'd do.

Strange, he thought, how the beliefs a man held on to his whole life could be abandoned in a flash when someone he loved was threatened.

He'd agreed to this while thinking that his end of the job would be over long before he had to set sail with Nick Russell. But more and more lately it appeared that, when the boat left in four days, he'd be on it with the rest of them. He'd helped prepare the special compartments in the sailboat that would hide the drugs. He'd mapped out the route they'd take, and, God help him, he might even be here to help distribute the coke once they smuggled it into the States.

He could have managed it all—but pulling off the deal with two innocent people involved was another story.

It made him no better than Russell. If anything, he was worse. Russell had been born without scruples, without any regard for good or bad. But Deke knew well the line between right and wrong, and still he was coming down on the wrong side of the line. He knew, but it hadn't stopped him—so far, nothing had—from agreeing to the trip.

Now Russell had thrown this at him, this condition he was having a hard time swallowing. What if the little girl got hurt? What if they didn't make it back? How would he live with himself then?

Every criminal Deke had ever met had had an excuse for the crimes he'd committed. He'd heard every reason in the book, and he despised the men who hid behind them. People had choices in life, and some people just made the wrong ones. Some people were weaker than others, some greedier, some more selfish, and some just didn't care that they hurt others.

Deke cared. He knew right from wrong. He fought as best he could within the constraints of the system, doing all he knew to crush the Nick Russells of this world.

He'd always made the bad guys pay.

Now it seemed he was no better than they were.

The evening sun sank lower in the sky, and at that angle its light was dazzling, blinding, as it danced across the sound. Deke squinted against the painful glare and then turned back toward the house. Jilly was gone, but Mary Poppins—he liked calling her that, because, for some reason, it riled her—was outside straightening up the toys in the backyard.

How much did she know about Russell's plans? Hell, how much did Deke, or anyone else, really know about Russell's plans? And they were all going to hop on a boat and sail out into the Atlantic with the man. Anything could happen. Inwardly he cursed again.

"What is this? Some kind of joke?" Deke scowled at Russell. "The last thing we need on this trip is an audience."

"Camouflage, Deke. We're just going on a little pleasure cruise. You, me, Ellen, Jilly and Liza."

Liza Snow, the nanny who'd mysteriously appeared out of nowhere a few weeks back. Deke saw her go suddenly still in the midst of gathering up the toys. She lifted her head cautiously and turned to look at them. He shot her a look that could have frozen hot coals, then turned his back to her and took a step closer to Russell so that they could talk without being overheard.

"Eyes and ears, Russell. She's got two of each," Deke said. "And a mouth. We don't need anyone with those attributes. Leave her behind. Leave both of them behind."

"I can't go without my Jilly, and Jilly doesn't like to go anywhere without Liza. Besides, Liza's looking forward to it." He'd raised his voice—apparently deliberately—so there was no doubt about the sound reaching her ears. "Aren't you, honey?"

Liza put down the last of the toys in the giant toy box beside the house, then turned to answer him. "I can't wait, Mr. Russell."

"Believe me, Liza, you can wait," Deke yelled back at her.

He thought for a second that Russell was going to slug him for that remark, and he wondered what had possessed him to defy the man so openly.

Desperation, surely. It was a powerful motivator.

He was still cursing himself a minute later, when Russell went inside to take a phone call. Liza went back to work.

Desperation had made him accept this job, he reminded himself. That, and his blind loyalty to his brother. Grimly he renewed his vow. He was going to do what he had to do.

No one had spelled it out for him, but then, no one had to. Deke knew enough about how the game was played to understand what might lie ahead for him. He would play his part in this sordid little affair. He would do whatever it took to get the job done, and if—it was, admittedly, a damn big "if"—nothing went wrong, he'd live to talk about it.

If everything worked as planned, he'd have his day in court, call in his reward and then disappear. He was realistic enough to know that there would likely be no other choice for him. Life as he'd known it might well cease to exist. He might never be able to see his family again. He might never even know if the price he'd paid had been enough to save his brother. Done right, the job would buy Charlie a chance, where now he had none.

Determinedly Deke overlooked the stark truth that, mission accomplished or not, should he survive, he would always have to watch his back, because there was no telling who would be after him.

He headed across the lawn, looking forward to the drive home, the twenty minutes of quiet, twisting, turning roads that wound around the rivers and the marshes to the duplex he'd rented on the other side of Brunswick.

Once in his pickup, he would give in to this urge that seemed to stay with him lately, the one that told him to run, fast. He couldn't run away, but he could drive, faster than he had a right to go on the curving old country road. And for a minute or two, he'd forget that he couldn't just keep on driving forever, away from Nick Russell, his boat and his cocaine.

He was making his way toward the truck, his mind on the journey ahead, not paying any attention to where he was going, when he found himself face-to-face with Miss Liza Snow. She stopped him with a hand on his arm.

"Don't try to make him leave me behind," she said quietly as Deke scowled down at the small hand on his forearm.

None of Deke's sources—and he had the best there were—had been able to come up with any information on her. He didn't like that, not one damn bit.

He didn't try to hide his anger as he ran his eyes over her from head to toe. She showed the good sense to back away from him.

Who was she? What was she? He didn't know what to think of her. She was slim, all arms and legs, in loose-fitting blue shorts and an Atlanta Braves T-shirt. Her hair was thick and straight, cut even with her chin and constantly falling into her eyes, instead of over to one side, where it was supposed to go.

She claimed she was twenty-three, but when he saw her in this getup he wondered if she wasn't younger. He wondered a lot about her—way more than he should. He wondered how she'd taste, how she'd feel pulled so tight against him daylight couldn't get between them. Sometimes, in his bed at night, when he couldn't sleep, he even wondered what it would be like to have her there beside him.

And it made no sense. A pretty woman turned his head every now and then, but he'd watched more than one walk away, watched with no regrets. He'd never met one who brought on this undeniable urge to chase her down the street and find a way to get to know her better.

Liza wasn't even the kind of woman who would normally have turned his head at first glance, but now he couldn't seem to keep his eyes off her.

Here he was, in the middle of the biggest damn mess he'd ever seen, and he had to fight to keep his mind on the job and keep it off a woman.

God, she was the last person he needed on this trip, and he wondered what he could do to keep her off the boat—not just for him, but for herself. He didn't want to see her hurt.

He took another step toward her, not sure what he was going to do, and she retreated a step in response.

Interesting. She was scared of him, at least a little bit. He could see it in those big eyes of hers.

"We won't get in the way," she said, evidently as stubborn as she was uneasy. "And I can take care of Jilly."

He had her trapped against the side of the house now, and he held her there with his gaze and two tanned, muscled arms stretched out on either side of her upturned face, his hands resting against the warm stone of the house.

"Maybe so, but who's going to take care of you, Liza?" he asked insolently.

"I can take care of myself."

"Can you?" Deke was closer to her than he'd ever been before, and getting angrier by the minute at the very idea she believed she could take care of herself in a mess like this. Hell, she didn't even know what she was up against.

"I've been doing just fine for years," she said. "And even if I hadn't, it's no concern of yours."

Point for her, he told himself. She was an adult. She could do as she pleased. He could do his job. She could do hers.

So why was it so hard to accept? Why did he find himself wanting to take some responsibility for her safety, as well as the little girl's?

Maybe because nobody else seemed to be looking out for them. Maybe because they had no idea what they were getting themselves into, and he did.

She kept right on talking. He realized she'd probably never stopped, and he had to fight to keep from interrupting and shocking the life out of her by telling her exactly what kind of trouble she was facing.

"...so just stay out of it, okay? Russell's decided to take Jilly, and if she goes, so do I."

He nodded, because she seemed to be waiting for some sort of response from him.

Deke wondered what she'd do if he just threw her over his shoulder and hauled her out of there. He could lock her up in his room until after the boat sailed.

He smiled at the thought. She wouldn't take that well. No one associated with this whole deal would take that well.

"So don't try to talk Russell into leaving me behind."

He wouldn't. He couldn't—not without risking arousing Russell's suspicions. He'd voiced his objections, and they'd been overruled. That was the end of it. Russell was the boss; Deke the employee.

No, he couldn't take it up again with Russell, much as he'd like to.

Deke looked down at her as she stood, stock-still, against the side of the house. He saw the defiance in her eyes, the confusion, and at the same time the confidence that the young wear like a shield before they figure out life will deal them some hands they can't possibly play and win, hands they can't bluff their way through, hands where they can't stop the game by simply throwing in their cards.

Life had certainly done that to him lately.

The frustration ate at him, and it must have shown.

"Are you done now?" he demanded.

Liza backed up a little more, although she was too close to the house to get much farther away from him.

She was afraid, no matter what she said. That was good, he thought. A little fear made people cautious, and she needed to be cautious.

He put his hands on her shoulders and pulled her body hard against his. Distractedly he noted that she was smaller than he'd thought, slighter, softer.

"So, you can handle yourself, huh? No matter what happens, right?"

She struggled in his unrelenting arms. "Right."

"Wrong." He held her fast. He wasn't about to let her escape. "A woman's always vulnerable, Liza, no matter who she is. She never knows what kind of man she's going to come up against, never knows what he might have on his mind."

He shook her a little, then tried to make himself let her go with just that, but didn't—because he wasn't sure he'd made his point.

"I could do anything I wanted to you right now—*anything*—and you couldn't stop me," he said, his voice dark and low.

His lips covered hers even as he said it, and now she stood as if frozen to that very spot. Grimly he thought that he could show her at least one way she was vulnerable.

He'd meant to kiss her hard and fast, do it and get it over with, but somehow it didn't happen that way.

He hadn't expected to feel anything, but he did. What caught him first was the utter stillness of her mouth and her body against him as he lingered over her lips.

Then he realized that she was trembling, and that her lips, so cool at first, were warming to his. She tasted so sweet, so clean, so inviting. Kissing her was a pure, simple pleasure that he'd never expected, and he was caught for good.

Suddenly it didn't matter that this was supposed to be nothing more than a rotten way of showing her that he could bend her to his will if he chose to.

For now, he needed this, this moment out of time, far away from the ugliness that his life had become. For just a moment, he let himself forget everything but the pleasure of kissing her.

He forgot about why he'd pulled her close, and simply concentrated on how nice it was to kiss her, to have her mouth open beneath his, to taste her, to feel her tongue sliding tentatively against his.

She stood absolutely still at first. Shock, he reasoned, feeling more than a little of it himself. But then she went to pull away from him, and he discovered he couldn't stand that idea.

He lifted a hand, and she shifted her left side away from him at the same moment, so instead of finding her arm, his hand brushed against the side of her breast.

That set her to trembling even more. Him, too, actually.

Deke knew he had no right to touch her this way. He put his hand on her shoulder, made himself keep it there for a moment so as not to spook her, but that hand had a mind of its own. It moved down to the center of her chest, until the racing rhythm of her heart was below his palm and beneath his widely spread fingers were the beginnings of each of her breasts.

No, he had no right to touch her this way.

But he wanted to. He needed to.

He meant to pull his hand away; he even lifted his fingertips from the edges of the soft curves. But then the resistance seemed to go out of her, and her body melted into his. Her breasts swelled against him, and, groaning inwardly, he rolled his palm slowly around one taut nipple.

How long it went on, he couldn't have said, he was that lost in her. For certain he knew he'd held her much too long, but he found it difficult to stop. It surprised him. Worse than that, it shocked him to think of how much he wanted to go on kissing her.

Much too soon, he forced his hands to his sides and eased his body away from hers. But his mouth lingered over hers in one last slow, sweet kiss.

Finally his lips left hers.

She gasped.

He groaned.

They stood there in the shade beside the house. Her eyes downcast, she stared at a spot four inches west of his right shoulder. She refused to meet his gaze.

He watched her and wondered again who she was, what she knew about the boat trip, and how in the whole damn world she could make him feel such yearning with a simple kiss.

They were both breathing hard, both trembling in the aftermath.

He hated himself for pushing himself on her, but he cursed her for making him want her, for making him forget the purpose behind the kiss. And he wondered what he could do to salvage the situation.

Reluctantly he took a small step backward. He leaned against the hand he'd rested against the wall and tilted his body toward hers, crowding her back against the wall. Using his other hand, he lifted her chin to make sure she was watching when he let his gaze linger at her breasts, then on her lips, as if he had every right to do so.

"Now, you want to tell me again about how you can handle anything that comes along on this trip?" he said, the words harsh and quiet.

Her eyes came up then. Wary eyes. Suspicious eyes. Eyes that were much too old for someone her age.

Heat was burning her cheeks, and her lower lip was trembling, but she wouldn't let herself turn away from him. Inwardly he smiled appreciatively. He was face-to-face with one gutsy woman.

He let his eyes rake her body up and down once again, as if measuring its fit against his, as if he liked what he saw, as if he believed she was his for the taking.

She decided she'd had enough then, and she surprised him with how fast she could move and how hard she could hit. His cheek stung from the impact of her open palm, but he knew it wasn't nearly the punishment he deserved.

In the ensuing heavy silence, they stared at each other. For a second she looked as if she regretted it, just for a second, before she got mad all over again.

She wasn't fast enough the second time, and he caught her hand before it connected with his face, then caught her hard and fast in his arms in a hold that had nothing to do with desire.

"Stop it," she said, panic now evident in her voice. *"Let me go."*

Deke held on for just a moment, just long enough to let her know that the only reason she was getting away was that he'd decided to allow it.

"Fine, for now." He let her pull out of his arms. "Just remember, out there on the water, you'll have nowhere to run."

Chapter 2

Liza ran across the backyard as if the hounds of hell were bounding after her. She made it to the twisted old oak in seconds flat and leaned back against its massive trunk.

It was quiet here, so quiet she could hear the runaway beating of her heart and feel the blood pulsing through her veins, marching in time to her heart's pounding rhythm.

She waited there, pressed against the old tree, to hear the slam of a truck door, the roar of the engine as a truck started, the rumble of its motor as it gradually faded into the distance. She needed proof of the distance between them.

Standing there, finally alone, surrounded by the still, silent, darkening sky, Liza was very much aware of how her body had betrayed her.

He'd reached out and touched her, as if he'd had every right in the world to do so, and her breast had swelled into his palm as if to welcome him. He'd kissed her parted lips, his tongue had swept through her mouth, and that, too, she'd welcomed.

She closed her eyes, still feeling the heavy imprint of his body against hers, his broad, firm chest, the flat wall of his stomach, the muscles of his thighs. She felt the ease with which he'd pulled her to him, the bold confidence of his knowing touch, the delicious warmth that had radiated from his body.

He'd touched her, boldly but briefly, and she'd simply melted against him, so completely that she hadn't known where her body started and his ended.

Liza had felt the steely muscles of the arms that had held her close, and was ashamed to admit that it had taken none of his considerable strength to keep her in his arms. She'd clung to him; she'd be clinging to him yet, if he hadn't decided to pull away from her.

She remembered, oh, so well. Her body remembered, too much. The heat came, like a fever, flooding her senses.

The screen door slammed, its sound ricocheting through the quiet of the coming night. Liza jumped at the noise and wondered who had left the house. Whoever it was, she didn't want to see him. While she still had the opportunity, Liza scrambled up the rope ladder to the rough-hewn platform of Jilly's tree house.

It was a silly place for a grown woman to hide; in her scramble to get there, she recognized that. But after two months in the Russell household, Liza knew this was one of the few places where she could count on being alone. No one came here except Jilly, and the little girl couldn't get up here without help. And it was impossible for anyone to get there once Liza pulled up the rope ladder.

With her heart pounding, and not because she'd run across the yard and climbed up into the tree, Liza simply stretched out on her back and stared through the canopy of branches into the twilight sky. She waited for the heat inside her to subside and watched as the sky went first gray, then blue, then purple—the final burst of color—before fading to black.

The world faded to black, and a miserable Liza wondered when running and hiding, both literally and figuratively, had become second nature to her. It had been her first instinct. Once Deke had let her go and some semblance of order had been restored to her world, the first thing that had occurred to her was to flee. Like an animal spooked by a noise, she'd run; she'd always run from her troubles.

Until now, she'd done it without asking questions. At the first hint of any danger in her life, something inside her, a sixth sense of sorts, had always told her it was time to get her things together, time to make plans, time to be ready to move at a moment's notice. Others might stand and fight— even win on occasion—but it seemed that Liza was doomed to spend her whole life in flight.

It was tradition, after all. She'd lived her whole life this way, while her mother had run from one man to another, each seemingly worse than the last, but all of them bearable for her mother with the help of an understanding doctor and a little pill every now and then to calm her nerves.

Running was an instinct she'd inherited from her mother, one that had served her well so far, but it wasn't that anymore. She had a reason to stay now, someone who needed her, someone she loved. Before, it hadn't mattered when she'd run, because there had been no real reason to stay, no strong attachment to any one person or place.

She'd never been in any kind of trouble she couldn't run or hide from.

But Deke was right. He'd made it painfully clear that on the boat she wouldn't be able to run, and there would be woefully few places to hide.

Deke.

Liza could only shake her head in wonder over what had happened this evening. She trusted her instincts, but her instincts just didn't know what to make of him.

He'd never been overly friendly to her, but she'd thought that he just wasn't a friendly person.

He'd watched her; she'd felt his guarded eyes on her when she was doing the simplest of things. But it had never been the look of a man interested in a woman, or a man intent on taking advantage of one. She knew how that felt, and she'd have sworn that wasn't what she'd seen in him.

It wasn't so much an interest as a curiosity of sorts, as if he were sure that if he looked long enough he'd be able to see inside her. Deke looked at her as if he wanted to discover every secret she'd ever had, as if he could do so simply by watching and waiting.

Liza had her secrets, and she didn't care for the idea that anyone was trying to discover what they were.

He had perplexed her as few people ever had. And he honestly frightened her. There had been a recklessness to his anger today that she hadn't seen in him before.

Liza judged people quickly as friend or foe, disregarding the people who fell somewhere in between. To her, people were either a help or a hindrance. Either they gave her a hand along the way or they blocked her path. She had few friends, and she tried not to keep count of her enemies.

She'd categorized this entire household within hours of coming here two months ago.

Jilly, more than a friend, was a kindred spirit, a soul mate of Liza's who'd happened to be born twenty years after her. On a good day Jilly was a slight, soft, apple-cheeked, curly-haired bundle of love, a pure joy to behold.

And Liza loved her. It was as simple and as complex as that. She loved her, and she was going to protect her.

They'd met on one of Jilly's bad days. Liza had spotted her on the floor in the middle of the mall one afternoon. Jilly had been screaming bloody murder, had been for so long that Ellen Russell couldn't even remember what had caused the tantrum in the first place. Liza knew now that Jilly wasn't a terribly difficult child. She just hadn't ever received the attention and discipline she desperately needed.

She'd lost her heart to the little girl in a matter of minutes, and because of Jilly she was still here, today, in the middle of God only knew what kind of trouble. She was staying, too, no matter what.

"Liza?"

Nick Russell's arrogant voice boomed through the night. "Liza?"

She wouldn't have answered him, but he wasn't the only one looking for her.

"Wiza, where you go?"

Jilly, sounding so grown up and so babyish, all at the same time. She had trouble with her *l* sounds, so Liza came out more like Wiza. Liza smiled and shook her head.

"Coming, Jilly."

She lowered the rope ladder and carefully descended from her hiding place. Russell's hand, cold and clammy as a fish out of water, met her halfway down. The hand closed around her ankle and then smoothed over the back of her lower leg, and she felt as if a bug had crawled on her.

"Don't stop now, honey," he said, laughing as he felt her shiver with distaste. "Come on down."

Liza kicked her feet off the rope ladder and jumped to the ground. The distance was too much for her; her knees buckled, and she landed in a heap on the hard ground. Winded but satisfied with herself for having evaded his loathsome hands, Liza glared at him in the darkness.

"So he can touch you, but I can't?" Nick Russell chuckled slyly. "You didn't seem to mind so much a minute ago, when it was his hands on you."

She had a feeling that before she was through she was going to loathe Nick Russell even more than she did now.

It was no wonder Liza had such a low opinion of men. Most of the ones she'd met had been no better than Russell. She hated the way they felt they were entitled to take whatever they wanted from a woman, just because they were stronger, bolder, richer, just because they could get away with it.

More than once she'd turned her back on a good job or a decent place to live because some man had decided she was his for the taking. It frightened her, it always had, the things women were forced to endure because of some man who lorded it over them.

And, deep inside, she hated herself for allowing herself to be vulnerable to any man.

At this moment, she hated Nick Russell more than most, and part of the reason was his knack for finding her weaknesses. Like arrows finding their marks, his insults always zeroed in on her weak spots.

Leave it to him to notice. She'd already admitted it to herself—God help her, she hadn't minded having Deke's hands on her. Of course, she wasn't about to admit that to anyone, let alone Nick Russell.

"Wiza!" Jilly came running into her arms. "You fall down?"

Liza bent down so that the little girl could throw herself into her arms. She let the momentum carry them both backward until she was flat on her back in the grass with Jilly sprawled on top of her. She hugged Jilly tight, wishing her arms were enough to shield the little girl from whatever hurts her father might inflict upon her.

Jilly was the reason she was here, the reason she would remain here, and she was worth whatever trouble Russell and Deke tried to dish out.

"Yes, Jilly." She forced herself to loosen the embrace and then, somehow, to smile. "I fell down."

The girl giggled and then turned serious. "You hafta be careful, Wiza."

She said it like a schoolmarm scolding a pupil.

"I promise, Jilly. I'll be careful."

"You'll have to be very careful," Russell said. He offered her a hand up, which she ignored. "Deke's no fool. If you don't handle him just right, he'll know what you're up to."

Liza stood, then picked up Jilly. The girl's arms closed around Liza's neck, her head rested on Liza's shoulder.

"It time go night-night, Wiza?" Obviously, even to the child bedtime was preferable to enduring her father's presence.

"Yes, sweetie." Liza squeezed the child close and bit her tongue. She could handle this. She'd handled worse. Besides, this was for Jilly.

"Remember, Liza—" Russell's voice continued to taunt her "—whatever he does, whatever he says, I want to know about it."

He followed a scant step behind them as they made their way across the backyard and to the house. Liza was afraid he'd always be just a step behind her, but she walked without slackening her pace, without so much as looking over her shoulder.

"I understand, Mr. Russell."

Bitterness welled up within her. It seemed that wherever she went, whenever she showed an interest in settling in, there was always a man waiting to ruin it for her. This time, though, it would be different. Because if, in the end, she couldn't make it here, if she ran the way her senses urged her to, it would just be one in a long list of places she'd fled in fear of some man.

She couldn't spend her whole life running, and she couldn't bear to leave this child alone with no one to protect her from the people who were supposed to love her and care for her.

"I told you," Russell whispered, "if you just waited, he'd come running. It didn't take him long."

Liza tried to open the screen door, but his arm stretched over her shoulder, his hand holding the door shut.

"You take real good care of my girl, Liza. I'd hate to see you have to move on after my Jilly's gotten so attached to you."

Hearing all too clearly the unspoken threat, Liza closed her eyes and squeezed Jilly tight. "I understand, Mr. Russell."

"That man wants to kiss you, you can't afford to go slapping his face, honey. At least not more than once. You try that next time around, and he's liable to think you really aren't interested."

"I'll remember." Liza forced the words out between clenched teeth.

Russell paused there for another moment to let his point sink in. He was in charge, and she was powerless to change that. So the question was—was she going to do as he asked? She wasn't sure yet. But, for the moment, she would let Russell think she was.

He stayed outside, and they went in. As she went through the ritual of putting Jilly to bed, Liza eventually calmed down.

They had to find PJs, had to wrestle until Liza managed to get Jilly undressed, washed off and dressed again. They had teeth to brush, hair to smooth down and cheeks to kiss. Jilly needed her stuffed monkey, her polka-dot blanky and her Bambi book, all beside her on the crowded little bed, before she could go to sleep. The stuffed monkey was closest, right beside her on the pillow. The little blanket was spread out on the bed, with Jilly stretched out on her belly on top of it and the Bambi book placed under the pillow.

Liza suspected the little girl craved order and quiet because she'd found so little of it in her own life before her nanny had come. A little peace and quiet, a little predictability in her life, and Jilly could be happy. She'd found none of that with her parents.

Liza hadn't seen much of it, either, when she was growing up, except for the few brief years before her big sister had left home. She knew what it meant to a lost little girl to have someone to anchor herself to, because, for a while, Liza had done that with her sister.

She rubbed her hand in slow circles on Jilly's back, soothing the child with her touch and her words. It was so sweet, being here with her, holding her close. In a way she wished that Jilly were her own.

It was a dangerous thought, fueled by a dangerous emotion, Liza knew that, but she couldn't help feeling that way. And she didn't know what she was going to do, because she couldn't stay here forever, and she couldn't leave Jilly here, either.

The little girl quieted—down but not quite out. She was so adorable now, so sweet and cuddly, so helpless when it came to her parents. Jilly loved them—all children loved their parents, no matter what they had to put up with from them. Jilly wanted to please them, but Liza knew she'd never be able to.

The thought left her incredibly weary. She walked across the hall to her own bedroom and suddenly found herself so drained that she just collapsed on the bed, stretching her arms above her head and staring at the ceiling.

Ellen and Nick Russell should never have been allowed to have a child. Russell, she feared, was a truly dangerous man, and Ellen was simply no match for him. Liza would never understand how Ellen put up with him, but the meek woman would never put herself between her husband and her child, no matter what price the child paid.

Liza remembered the way the simple tantrums at the mall that first day had been too much for poor Ellen. As usual, she'd been lost when faced with Jilly's disobedience.

Motherhood, for Ellen, had somehow turned into an endless maze that she was totally unequipped to handle. Idly Liza wondered how Ellen had stumbled into mother-hood, and wondered that Ellen, once there, hadn't known how to get out. Now what little time she chose to share with her daughter was spent practically bumping blindly into walls, turning this way and that, stumbling helplessly, deeper into the hole she'd dug for herself.

It wasn't that Ellen was a bad person; it was just that she should never have been a mother, not in the shape she was in. She didn't have the patience, wasn't willing to commit the time and lacked the energy she needed for a little girl like Jilly. Ellen loved her, as best she could, but that wasn't enough.

It was the drugs, mostly, Liza believed, that kept Ellen from ever being the mother Jilly needed, the one the girl deserved. Ellen was fighting against her addiction still, as much as she could, but it didn't seem likely she would ever win. How many people ever did against that seductive, all-powerful enemy?

And the drugs took their toll—not just on Ellen, but Jilly, as well. Ellen Russell wasn't physically abusing her daughter, but Liza knew that words could easily carry a sting as sharp as a slap.

Seeing the two of them together was like stepping out of her own body, traveling back in time and watching her own family—a generous term to apply to the group of people in which she'd grown up.

She should have run from it right then, as soon as she recognized the resemblance. She didn't need any help remembering the past. The past, after all, was what she'd been running from that day at the mall, what she ran from every day. She'd been afraid she'd spend her whole life running, and now it seemed she'd run so fast that she'd caught up with her very own history.

Liza had often wondered what she'd done, which guardians of the universe she'd slighted, to land herself in the life she was living. But it had been ages since she'd done so. In the past few months she'd believed she'd made some sense out of it.

She now believed that she'd been given the life she'd lived because she was meant to be in this place, at this time, with these people, to save Jilly from the people who should have loved her the most.

Her destiny was staring her in the face, and she was afraid to face it. She didn't know if she could see it through, but didn't know how she would manage if she came up short of what life was asking of her now.

A victory here would prove to her that she was stronger than she'd ever imagined. That the fight she'd fought against her past hadn't been in vain.

A victory would last a lifetime.

A defeat would be a blow from which she'd never recover. She'd run from trouble forever if she failed at this, the most important challenge that had ever been placed in her path.

Liza took a deep breath and rolled over onto her stomach so that she could look out the window at the water, now a shimmering inky-black trail that curled like a ribbon through the marsh.

She believed she'd found a purpose for being here, a more important reason than she'd ever had for staying in one place. She wasn't about to let a man or two change that.

Liza wasn't sure what Nick Russell had in mind. For the most part, she'd ignored him and Deke the past few months as they'd planned their trip. A pleasure cruise, Russell called it, just a little vacation down to the islands, a chance for him to learn to handle his new boat. Supposedly he'd hired Deke to teach him to handle the sailboat, which Russell claimed he couldn't even steer away from the dock without help.

But Russell was becoming more and more agitated as the time to leave grew closer.

Yesterday he'd decided that he wanted Jilly along. That made no sense, because he never wanted the child around unless they had company. Then he played the devoted father in a performance that never failed to sicken Liza.

Ellen was nervous, too. Liza had picked up on that right away. Not that it was hard; whenever life was too much for Ellen, she fluttered back and forth like a flag in the wind, alternating between a state of depressed lethargy and one of nervous energy. It was the only fight she put up, and it was one that never lasted for long.

Then Nick Russell—loving, caring husband that he was—would take his wife to the doctor for her medication. She had a half-dozen doctors in three towns who were more than willing to write her a little prescription every now and then to "help her over the rough spots of life."

Russell encouraged it. "It's so hard," he would croon to his wife. "Jilly's so demanding." He was so demanding himself. It was hard to be a woman, to deal with the pressures of a husband, a home and a child. It was no sin to need a little help along the way. And then he'd hand her the pills, just a few tranquilizers to take the strain off, then a few more to ease the tension altogether.

And for the next few weeks Ellen would walk around in a pleasant haze. For her it was as if life really were just too much for her, as if the pressure had built up until she had to have a break. She used the pills like someone who needed a vacation from reality. Afterward she would always "come back," a grim, silent, shell of a woman.

Guilt ate at her. Liza could see that. Ellen wasn't so far gone that she didn't struggle with misgivings. She hadn't yet sunk so far into the chemical haze that she didn't know that what she was doing was wrong. But without anyone's help, and with her own husband to push her down into the mist again, Liza knew, Ellen would never surface for long.

Lately, Ellen had been under the influence more than she'd been sober. She'd been even more uneasy when Russell had made his decision about the three of them—Ellen, Liza and Jilly—accompanying him and Deke on their trip.

Yesterday, while Liza had been doing the laundry, Russell had come to her to ask her to keep an eye on Deke for him. He wanted to know everything Deke said and everything he did.

Russell said he wasn't sure he could trust Deke. But to run the boat, or what? Liza couldn't understand. Why didn't he just find another boat captain? Why come to her? Why not ask some of the other people Deke had worked for whether he was trustworthy?

Worst of all, Russell hadn't just asked for Liza's cooperation. He'd implied, just as he had today, that her job depended on it.

Then there had been the scene tonight with Deke. What had that been about? He frightened her and confused her all at the same time, mostly due to the strong reaction that he'd so easily drawn from deep within her.

She wasn't even sure she liked him. She surely didn't trust him. And at times, like today, she felt there was so much anger in him that it frightened her.

But there was no escaping the fact that he was the sexiest man she'd ever known.

Oh, Lord! There, she'd admitted it. She hated to do even that, but there was no other way she could explain it. And he got to her, to some part of her that she'd never even been aware of before.

Deke made her mouth go dry, the way he sauntered across the backyard on his way down to the boat, wearing nothing but a ragged pair of cutoffs and a gorgeous tan.

He made her hands tremble just thinking of touching those muscles that she'd watched stretch and contract as he worked under the sun getting the boat ready.

And it frightened her to want him that much. She'd watched more than one woman make a fool of herself over a man. It was as if some hormone clicked in and suddenly a perfectly sane woman found herself ignoring every lick of sense she had the moment some grown-up bad boy showed up.

Liza wasn't a foolish woman. At least she hadn't made a fool of herself yet over a man. She didn't want to start now.

So what *had* Deke been trying to do today?

She couldn't believe he or any man would be overwhelmed with passion for her. A man who couldn't do without her? The very idea made her laugh.

But for just a moment it had felt like that, like he was starved, hungry for the taste and feel of her. Like he needed something only she could give.

And what about the way he'd pulled away from her in the end? Was that reluctance she'd felt in the way his lips had lingered over hers? Was it regret she'd seen in his eyes? Because he'd kissed her? Because he'd found some genuine pleasure in it? Or because of the way he'd pushed himself on her?

Why in the world would he come on to her like that? It was true that she hadn't had a lot of experience with men, but she was sure that if Deke truly wanted to put the moves on a woman he'd know just how to go about it.

She knew what he'd said to her, but what had he really meant?

Liza had always been able to spot a liar a mile away, probably because most of the people she'd known had lied to her. Most people always gave themselves away in some small way.

With Russell there was no question about it. Liza suspected he was one of those people who found it as easy to lie as to tell the truth.

But Deke? He held himself away from everyone, and he could close down his features as easily as a stagehand closed the curtains on a play. He held back, held himself away. As a means of protecting himself, or a means of deceiving others? she wondered. She couldn't be sure.

The only thing she *did* know was that she was caught there in the middle of them all; Russell who frightened her, Deke who puzzled her, Jilly who needed her.

And she was staying, because no one had ever needed her before, at least not anyone she had had the power to help. No. She wouldn't let Jilly—or herself—down.

Chapter 3

Liza stood absolutely still at the top of the outside steps, Nick Russell behind her and Deke in front of her.

It was a telling arrangement. She'd been caught between them this way for what seemed an eternity, although it had actually been only seventy-two hours.

And she didn't like it one bit.

Russell was leaning against the back of the house, watching her to see whether she would do as he'd ordered.

Deke, as always, was on the boat.

Liza had been standing there long enough to count how many steps stood between her and Deke. There were fifteen actual stairsteps leading down the steep embankment to the sound, and then there was about a hundred and fifty feet worth of deck leading out to the boat.

Russell, for some reason that Liza failed to understand, worried more every day about what Deke was doing. He'd apparently decided for certain now that she was his only way of finding out. And he'd been applying more pressure than ever.

That was why he was standing where he was, waiting to make sure she walked down the dock, got on the boat and spent some time with Deke.

Liza turned to look over her shoulder at Russell, and hoped she was too far away for him to make out the scowl on her face.

Resentfully she considered her options. She disliked Russell more every day. She was uneasy around Deke, a little scared of him, but she was truthfully more scared of her response to him than anything else.

That made her decision a little easier. She would do what Nick Russell had ordered, or at least make it look as if she were. She would decide for herself, later, how much, if at all, she would tell Russell.

Liza walked slowly down the wooden stairs and out to the end of the dock with thoughts of rebellion.

She made it a practice to mind her own business, to never go out of her way to call attention to herself, to ask little of life and expect little in return. These were habits that had always served her well, and she'd followed those habits faithfully in the past three days. But lying low hadn't been enough to keep her out of the turmoil that had overtaken the household she worked in.

Deke was at the house constantly. He was forever doing something to the boat, a weathered but, she believed, sturdy sailboat that was docked in the sound, behind the house.

He and Russell had taken the boat to Florida for a day and a half for some repairs, but hadn't seemed happy with the work once they'd returned home.

So they worked, pounding, pasting, painting, pulling at things deep within it.

Russell was impatient, with the boat, with Deke, and with Liza, because he didn't think she'd been trying hard enough to get whatever information it was that he wanted out of Deke.

The boat was rocking gently with the incoming tide as she approached and stepped aboard, and Liza wondered how well she'd handle the rocking motion that was forever present on a boat trip.

She'd never sailed before. In fact, she'd never been out on the water on a vessel larger than a rowboat. Liza, who had often wondered in the past two years where her next meal was coming from, was about to leave on a three-week cruise of the Caribbean. Imagine that.

Her transportation, the *Loralei,* was much bigger and much grander than a rowboat. Liza knew from Russell's boasting that it was a fifty-eight-footer. It had a small kitchen, a dining area and two staterooms, one in the front and one in the back, and two bathrooms. Liza couldn't remember the proper terms for those parts of the boat. She did know that the bathrooms seemed minuscule to her, but according to Deke they were spacious by boating standards.

She stepped down into the pitlike seating area at the back of the boat, then climbed down the ladder that led below.

Deke was cursing, long enough and loud enough that he didn't seem to be aware of her presence on the boat. He was lying on his back, buried to his waist in what she thought was the engine compartment. He was sweating. Little beads of it glistened as they clung to the short, curling hairs on his legs, bare beneath the ragged denim cutoffs he wore.

Liza almost lost her nerve at the sight of his bare legs. Looking at them did funny things to her stomach. It left her warm all over and a little dizzy, filling her with pleasure, and yet, at the same time, it left her feeling uneasy.

A lot of things left her uneasy these days, and she wasn't sure what she was going to do about it.

Deke was so caught up in the job he was trying to do that he wasn't paying attention to his surroundings. He was six feet tall and weighed one-ninety, and he was twisted up inside a space meant for someone half his size. He was trying to find a spot to plant a tracking device on the boat. Just in case his old buddy Nick Russell decided to double-cross him, Deke wanted someone else to know exactly where they were.

The tracker was small but powerful, enough to last for weeks and send a signal that could be traced for miles. Deke hoped that was enough, because the ocean was no fish pond. There were plenty of places to run and hide, if that was what Russell wanted. Grimly he wondered if he'd be able to find one himself if he needed it.

He thought about the trip as something inevitable now, even though he'd never believed that it would actually come to this. There was supposed to have been a way out long before he got this close. But in the past few months it had been like finding a way out in a fun house full of mirrors. When he *hadn't* wanted one, it had seemed as if there were an exit at every turn. Now that he was desperately looking for one, there wasn't one to be found. He was doing nothing but bumping into walls at every turn.

Time was running out, and at this moment he didn't see any way out.

He was conducting a final check on the placement of the tracking device when he thought he heard something.

Adrenaline shot through his body, sending it into overdrive. He lay perfectly still in the cramped space and felt a surge of nervous energy sweep through him.

Someone was on the boat. He didn't know how he knew, he just did. And he cursed himself for not knowing how long they'd been there or what they might know about what he'd just done.

He was playing a dangerous game, a potentially deadly one, he reminded himself. He couldn't afford a lapse like the one he'd just made.

Placing his hands on the edge of the engine compartment, he used the leverage to lift his body a fraction of an inch off the bottom of the boat and ease himself out of the engine compartment. His head cleared the top, and his eyes quickly swept through the back cabin, the hallway and then forward to what he could see of the kitchen.

Someone was in the kitchen, around the corner to his right, and leaning against the back wall.

Deke didn't even breathe. Without making a sound, he got to his feet. He could see the countertop now, and the big kitchen knife he'd tried to use to slice the tomato he'd put on his sandwich. He was lucky. The knife would look good, even if the blade was too dull to break the skin of a tomato.

Not giving himself time to think about what he might be up against or who might be waiting for him, he crept forward, rounded the corner and then lunged for the knife with his left hand and the intruder with his right.

He threw his nemesis to the floor, covered the stranger's body with his and had the dull knife to a throat before he realized he recognized the wide, frightened eyes staring back at him.

Her mouth was slightly open in shock. No sound came out, but her eyes were pleading with him.

Deke cursed himself, his life, the whole damn world. He closed his eyes for a moment, hoping that somehow, when he opened them again, he'd be somewhere else entirely. But when he opened his eyes, he was still on the boat, and Liza was still beneath him.

"Please."

He read the word on her lips, heard it on the slight breath that left her body as she tried to speak. But she still couldn't get any other words out.

Until that moment he hadn't realized that he still had the knife at her throat.

And he had to keep it there. He had the presence of mind to remind himself of that before he made the mistake of easing up on the pressure.

He had a job to do, and this was part of it. One way or another, he had to keep Liza Snow from getting on this boat again. And here he was lying on top of her with a knife at her throat. It wasn't a situation he would have chosen himself, but now that it was here, he needed to take advantage of it.

"Please," she barely managed to whisper again. "Don't hurt me."

She wasn't watching him any longer. She was looking down, trying to see the blade.

Deke felt he'd damned his soul to hell for sure even as he forced himself to hold it there for another moment, letting her feel the edge of the blade against the side of her neck, there against her pulsepoint, where the blood vessels were so close to the surface.

Scaring Liza had started out as an impulse that day when Nick Russell had first told him of his plans to take both her and Jilly along on their trip. Deke didn't want them there. They would prove to be nothing but a complication, and he didn't need any more complications.

And the more he'd thought about it, the more convinced he'd become that they had to stay behind. He could handle the risk he was taking with his own life, but he couldn't stomach risking Liza's and the little girl's.

Convincing Liza to stay behind might take care of Jilly, as well, because the little girl was pure hell with just her parents to look after her.

Well, Deke thought grimly as he looked down at the frightened woman lying motionless beneath him, his task had been clear from the beginning—do what he had to do to make the trip a success. Lie, cheat, steal—whatever it took. And he'd be damn lucky if this was the worse thing he had to do before this trip was over.

The knife was still there, held against her throat. Ever so slowly, he slid it sideways, stroking the blade menacingly against her skin.

"Please." She was begging him now.

Deke recalled the times he'd been inside a prison, remembered the most threatening voices he'd heard in that place. The ones who'd truly had the power to scare had never raised their voices. They'd threatened, but almost with indifference, with a calm, almost careless manner, with no emotion behind their words. He imitated them now, grimly congratulating himself when he heard the soft, deadly tone escaping him.

"I don't like surprises, Liza."

He stared at her for another long moment, and then at the knife, before he slowly pulled it away from her throat.

He glared menacingly at her. "Don't surprise me again."

Liza simply stared up at him, eyes as big as the moon. They were the most unusual color. Not blue, not brown. Deeper. Bolder. The color so pure and bright...indigo. She had indigo eyes.

And he had no business noticing their color, especially now, when he could clearly see that she was scared to death.

But that was good, he told himself. He wanted her scared. He didn't want her anywhere near this boat when it sailed tomorrow, and this might be his last chance to convince her to stay.

Her lips were moving again, but she was having trouble getting the words out. He couldn't make out what she'd said.

"Come on, Liza," he said impatiently. "It's not like I cut out your tongue. Say whatever you have to say."

"I can't breathe."

Immediately he braced himself on his elbows to take some of the weight off her chest, but the move settled his lower body more intimately against hers.

He knew it instantly for the mistake that it was. He didn't want to hurt this woman, and he certainly had no business being this close to her again, but the soft cradle his starving body was locked into was heating him up fast.

He'd tried his best to forget the long moments out of time when his lips had moved freely over hers and her body had been so close he'd felt every breath she took.

Now he was flush against her again, the way he'd been before, right where he had no right to be. For a moment his face remained an inch from hers, their mouths only a breath apart, and he wondered hazily whether, if he kissed her again, he'd feel that same incredible pleasure he'd felt the first time.

He stared at her mouth for a long moment, remembering how the curves of her soft lips had fitted so perfectly against his, and then he looked up into her eyes.

She felt something, too, he could sense it, some emotion that for just a second kept her frozen there against him, but she turned her head away.

They were closer than they'd ever been, and he had to admit that he'd wanted this to happen, though he knew he had no right to. He'd wondered, too often, what it would be like to have her lying beneath him like this, wondered whether his weight would be too much for her to take. He'd wondered, and now the wondering was over. He felt his body harden in response to the closeness he'd only imagined before.

She must have felt his reaction, because her eyes raced up to his, and he recognized the emotion in them instantly. Pure fear.

"Oh, hell," he said as he rolled over onto his side, then eased up onto his feet. "I'm not so hard up for a woman that I have to take one at knifepoint."

She stayed where he'd left her, lying on the cabin floor, all the while looking at him, her indigo eyes big and round, partly hidden behind a few long, straight strands of hair that fell over one eye.

"What are you and Russell up to?"

He stared at her, amazed that she had the nerve to ask, wishing that she hadn't. "You don't want to know, Liza," he answered tersely. "Believe me, you don't want anything to do with it."

He picked up the knife, turned it in the thin line of light shining through the open hatch. It was big enough to look menacing, especially with the light glinting off the blade. He watched it instead of her.

"I'd use it if I had to, Liza. Don't doubt that. I don't want to hurt anybody, especially not you, but I may have to. I may not have a choice."

She turned to go, and he stopped her when she was on the steps leading to the deck. Liza looked down at the hand that held her arm, the one that a moment ago had held the knife.

"Don't get on this boat again, Liza. Get off it for good. Get out while you still can."

The sunlight, glinting off the water, was blinding, but it couldn't block from her mind the sight of the knife blade in his hand as he'd slowly pulled it away from her throat.

Liza sat on the steps leading from the dock up the steep bluff to the Russells' yard.

Deke had stayed on the boat, and Russell, no doubt, was waiting for her at the top.

She was trapped again, only this time she wasn't at all sure of her ability to cope with the situation.

Until today, she hadn't truly been scared. Not until she'd felt the blade at her throat, felt the strength in the hand that held it, understood the ease with which Deke could have pushed the blade through the soft skin to the blood vessels lying beneath it.

Liza hadn't truly understood how dangerous Deke could be until this moment. And she wondered, now, just how dangerous the man waiting for her in the yard could be, as well, and just how dangerous this trip was going to be.

But she knew she couldn't leave. She was frightened, but she wasn't going to run this time. She'd made a promise to herself. She'd made a promise to Ellen, and one to Jilly.

And a promise wasn't the only thing that bound them all together. Not when she wasn't just anyone, not just a nanny to Jilly and a concerned bystander to Ellen.

She was Ellen's *sister*.

Years ago, when Liza had needed someone so desperately, Ellen had been there for her. Now she would be there for her sister and her sister's child.

Chapter 4

Twenty minutes later Deke was roaring along the narrow country road that led to his apartment. His tires screeched out a protest as he recklessly took the last curve at nearly twice the posted speed limit.

He was going much too fast, he knew, but he still enjoyed the brief freedom of having the steering wheel in his hands and the accelerator and the brake beneath his feet and taking the road of his choosing.

How long had it been since he'd been able to choose his own path, his own speed, pick his own stopping place? Only six months ago? It seemed more like a lifetime.

He had little more than a semblance of control over the truck, just as he had over his life at this point. It was taking him places he didn't want to go, and it looked like he was going to get there much too soon.

The boat was leaving tomorrow afternoon. With a number of stops along the way to gather supplies and reinforce their story of being on a pleasure cruise around the islands, they just had the time they needed to arrive at the meeting place off the South American coast in ten days' time.

They wouldn't take such a leisurely approach to the trip back—a week, tops.

Deke wondered what his chances were of making it back alive, and he wondered, if he survived, whether he'd be able to live with whatever he was forced to do to survive.

He took the long way back to his apartment, but it was still only a twenty-minute drive, not nearly enough to satisfy him. He pulled up at the run-down two-story cinder-block house, now cut into two apartments. The place was so different from the one he used to call home, just as his life was so different from what it had been before.

Deke eased out of the old pickup and slammed the door, unsettling the birds in the trees and the squirrels that had been scampering about at the edge of the winding creek that meandered past the right side of the old house.

The animals scattered, and then the night went quiet— unnaturally quiet—just as the boat had the minute he'd realized someone else was aboard.

He stood there, one foot on the front bumper, his forearms resting on the hood, while he watched and waited— for what, he didn't know. He just knew he didn't like it— not one damn bit. His mind mulled over the past, resentment within him for the way things had turned out.

Things had always worked out for Dixon MacCauley— Deke, as he'd come to be known when he was growing up. It wasn't that life had been easy for him, or that he hadn't worked hard. He had. But still, until now, he'd managed to get most everything he'd ever wanted.

Jackson MacCauley had walked out on his family for the first time soon after his son was born. He'd left and come back a half dozen times over the next ten years, until he'd disappeared for the final time, shortly after Deke's younger brother, Charlie, was born.

At first Deke's mother, Rose, had scraped by on the generosity of relatives and occasional guilt-tainted money from her husband. She'd given up on ever seeing her husband again by the time Charlie was two and Deke was twelve. And then Deke was no longer a child; he was the man of the family, according to Rose. He would have to look out for himself and for Charlie.

It was a responsibility that Deke took seriously. He missed out on a lot of lazy afternoons playing with his friends because he had to be home right after school to take care of Charlie.

His mother had to take work where she could find it. Until Deke was sixteen, she worked the four-to-midnight shift as a checker at the local grocery store. Deke was on his own with Charlie during that time, through the storms, the high winds, the deep dark of starless nights. They were simple things that might frighten a child but couldn't scare the man of the house, no matter how young he was.

Later he'd pulled Charlie out of childhood scraps, helped him with his homework and tried to convince him that pulling a girl's hair or calling her names was not the best way to get her to notice him.

Deke never expected to make it to college. He had grades that were good enough to get him some scholarship help, but not exceptional enough to put him through school completely. Colleges just didn't shell out academic awards the way they did athletic scholarships.

Besides, he didn't have the time for four more years of school. He'd been letting his mother support the family for years, and it was time he eased the burden on her. He needed to go to work.

Then, when he started his junior year in high school, his mother finally got a day job. Money wasn't so tight now. Charlie was in school, and his mother was home in the evenings.

Deke planned to go to work right away, but jobs weren't that easy to find in his rural corner of southeast Georgia. Before he could find a job, he earned a spot on the high school basketball team. No more sandlot pickup games. He made the varsity. He was good, and so were the other guys.

He felt selfish, even guilty, about spending so much time doing something he thought of as fun when he should be out earning money to help his family. But his mother insisted that he'd earned this time to enjoy himself.

He did more than enjoy himself. He wasn't tall enough or strong enough to be a superstar, but his speed and his ability to think on the court won him a pivotal role on a talent-charged small-town high school team. Deke was the brains of the squad. On the floor he called the shots and set up the plays. He was the glue that made four talented individual players come together as a winning team.

And it all paid off in his senior year. His team got knocked out of the state tournament in the quarter-final round. Deke was disappointed, but not for long. As he was leaving the floor, a coach from North Carolina State University offered him a basketball scholarship.

It meant leaving his family—deserting them really. And when he looked back on it now he knew that was exactly what he'd done. Oh, at first he told his mother that he would turn the scholarship down, that he couldn't go live five hundred miles away from her and Charlie, that it was time he started helping support the family.

He said all those things, all the while hoping desperately that his mother would say what she did, that she was all right, and so was Charlie. She was still working the day shift at the grocery store, and while the money wasn't all that good for a single parent with two growing boys, it was enough. They could get by, as they always had, and she wanted Deke to take advantage of this chance.

Now Deke leaned his head back and stared at the starlit night. He didn't want to remember—how, in going after his dreams, in turning his back on his obligations to his family, he hadn't been around when Charlie had needed him most.

He'd dismissed Charlie's problems. A little drinking, a little rowdiness, some marijuana and once—only once that Deke found out about—a little cocaine.

Deke had seen the problem, but he hadn't recognized the seriousness of it. He'd failed himself, his mother and his brother. And now he was doing all he could to make it up to them. That was where his loyalties were now, with his family, not with Liza or Jilly.

Or, at least, that was what he'd told himself when this whole thing had started—that he desperately wanted to save Charlie, to give him another chance to straighten out his life, that Charlie's big brother owed him.

But that was all before he'd come to know the innocents involved. Now he knew he couldn't stand by and let someone hurt Liza or Jilly, no matter how much he wanted to help Charlie. It seemed he did have something of a conscience left after all.

He wasn't as worried about Ellen Russell. When it came right down to it, he despised the woman for ever allowing her child to come into contact with the likes of Nick Russell. But if push came to shove, he'd probably stick up for her, too.

And what were the odds of making it through this without one of them being harmed—or at least threatened enough to make Deke blow his cover and come to their rescue?

Not good. Not good at all.

Deke looked the house over one more time and saw nothing amiss. He was just spooked, he decided. He didn't have the nerves for the kind of games he was playing.

He walked up to the house, unlocked the door and walked in the back way, which led straight into the kitchen.

It took him three precious seconds, maybe four, to realize that someone had been there. There was coffee in the pot, hot coffee; he could smell it.

Deke didn't even have time to curse his own stupidity before he felt, more than heard, footsteps coming from the living room. He whirled around to find someone in the doorway. He would have tried to figure out who before he struck if it hadn't been for the man's right hand. He was holding something out in front of him.

Deke could only react and hope he wasn't too late. He had his own gun close this time—as he should have, since it was the second damn time today someone had tried to sneak up on him.

Pulling it out of its shoulder holster, Deke used his other shoulder to slam the guy against the kitchen wall. He used the barrel of his gun to knock the other guy's piece away and had his own weapon to the man's head before he stopped and listened to what the intruder was saying.

"It's only me, Dixon."

Chapter 5

Dixon. It had been a long time since anyone had called him Dixon. He didn't think of himself as Dixon anymore. He couldn't.

Deke exhaled softly and slowly as he waited for his system to ease out of overdrive, a reaction brought on by the rush of adrenaline that had kicked in the moment he'd smelled the coffee. Then he looked up at the man who'd been more of a father to him than his own father ever had.

As usual, he was impeccably dressed in a crisp white shirt, silk tie and tailor-made suit. There, up against the kitchen wall, with a gun to his head and a muddy-colored liquid staining the shirt, dripping off the suit, he still managed to look as unruffled as he did in the courtroom when he was waiting for a jury to deliver its verdict.

Coffee. Deke could smell it. He hadn't knocked a *gun* away from his friend's hand. It had been a *mug*. Now it was in four or five pieces, scattered across the floor.

"Sorry about the coffee," Deke said, putting away his gun.

Thomas Merriwether, chief U.S. attorney for Virginia, didn't sweat the little things. Coffee on his suit wasn't nearly as bad as having a gun to his head, which wasn't nearly as bad as surprising a man with a gun and losing his head as a consequence. And Dixon was an old friend. Tom just smiled.

"Not bad, Dixon."

"Not good enough."

Tom only shrugged. "Not fast enough to keep you alive out there, but it looks like you'll have a chance—more of one than I thought."

"Oh, hell. You're the second person today who got close enough to blow me away before I even knew you were here."

Tom looked down at his ruined shirt and smiled. "What did the other guy look like when you got through with him?"

Deke didn't have to close his eyes to see Liza lying on the floor of the boat with a knife at her throat—an image that would haunt him for some time to come. Had he convinced her not to make the trip? He doubted it.

"She," he said, and shook his head. "And I'm more afraid of her than she is of me."

Tom shook his head. "Not going well?"

"No." He turned back to the sink to find a clean dishrag for Tom to use to clean up.

"Dixon, you don't have to go through with this."

"I don't have a choice. You know how the damn game is played better than I do. They've got Charlie cold. The only way he's going to walk is if I get enough to send Russell away for three or four lifetimes."

Deke found a cloth, ran hot water over it, then handed it to Tom. "I really am sorry about the shirt."

"At least it wasn't hot coffee." Tom took the wet cloth and blotted the mud-colored stain. "Look, I don't care about the shirt. I can get more. But I'm not going to find many more prosecutors like you."

"Tom, we've been through this...."

"Well, we're not done, because I still haven't heard an answer I like. I need you, Dixon. I've got twenty assistant attorneys in that office, and you're better than all of them put together. I didn't waste five years of my life turning you into the best assistant prosecutor around to lose you now."

Tom had trained him well, and Deke knew by now that there was no way to win a shouting match with him. So he stayed as quiet as he could while his friend's anger burned itself out.

"It was bad enough before, just trying to get enough on tape to nail him, but now I hear you're actually going on that damn boat trip Russell's been planning. Tell me you're not that stupid, Dixon."

"We don't have enough to make a conviction stick. The man hasn't been stupid enough to say what we need on any tape we've got," Deke answered shortly, his jaw tightening.

"They double-crossed you, didn't they?" Tom bellowed. "Those bloody bastards never intended to let it end with just the setup."

Deke couldn't help but laugh at that characterization of Buddy Morris and his crew. "You're forgetting, my friend. Those 'bloody bastards' are on our side. We're supposed to be the good guys, remember?"

"Oh, hell." Tom's impatience was showing through. "Don't you go lumping us together with them. You and I never would have authorized a deal like this."

Deke would like to think that they wouldn't have. In his mind, two wrongs didn't make a right, although a lot of justice systems operated that way these days.

As far as the Georgia prosecutor was concerned, Deke wouldn't be breaking any laws. He would be cooperating with a federal investigation. And in exchange for his cooperation—no, he thought grimly, the real price was a conviction against Nick Russell—Charlie would serve what little sentence he received in a drug treatment facility and then be on probation as long as he stayed clean.

Two wrongs committed. One man punished, and one rewarded for doing the job federal agents should have been doing themselves.

What kind of a judicial system relied on people picked up off the streets to put the crooks away because the cops didn't have the brains or the knowledge or the time and energy to do it themselves and get two crooks off the street instead of one?

It wasn't the kind of justice Deke had been taught to uphold, although it wasn't all that unusual in an overburdened criminal justice system with overcrowded prisons. Trials were time-consuming, expensive and chancy, and few prosecutors took that kind of risk these days, when plea-bargaining was the norm.

But Deke had always believed that justice was justice. A criminal was still a criminal, even if he could help the authorities get a conviction they wouldn't otherwise have gotten. It didn't make a criminal any less guilty.

He'd believed it. He'd upheld the law that way, until the criminal in front of him had been his own brother. A deal had been—was—the only way he could help Charlie now.

"It's crazy for you to go along on this trip," Tom protested. "Hell, it's practically suicide. You're not trained for anything like this, and you know it."

Tom was pacing now. Deke was sure he'd be pounding his fist soon.

"Damn it, Dixon. I can't let you trash your whole life for some two-bit drug dealer."

"He's my brother." Deke gritted his teeth to keep from saying more.

"Do you realize that? Sometimes I think you see yourself as his father. You're not. You're just his brother, and even that doesn't make you his keeper."

Deke poured himself a cup of coffee and handed one to his friend. "I owe him, Tom."

"For what? Because you jumped on an all-expenses-paid trip to college? Because you somehow managed to work your way through law school, then took a damn good job

with me? Don't you dare blame yourself for making something of your own life!''

Deke was barely hanging on to his temper. He put twice
as much sugar in the coffee as it needed, because the
smooth, repetitive stirring motion gave him something to
concentrate on. "I owe him."

"Some help. Some support, sure, but not your life."

"I made a deal," Deke said.

A dangerously simple deal—put Nick Russell behind bars
and Charlie would go free.

"No." Tom slammed his coffee down so hard it sloshed
over the rim of the mug and onto the countertop. "A poor,
stupid cokehead named Charlie MacCauley made a deal to
save his worthless butt, and when he couldn't pull it off you
charged in to save him like a one-man cavalry."

"Okay, you've made your point—"

"No, I haven't. Your brother's a crook. You remember
what they're like, don't you, Dixon? You used to help me
put 'em away. This kind of deal-making you're doing used
to make you sick. More than once I heard you call it out-
and-out blackmail."

"It is," Deke shouted back. "But he's my brother."

Tom was silent at last, but it was obvious he still wasn't
satisfied with the answers he'd received.

Deke couldn't help him. He didn't like any of the answers he'd come up with, either. Nor was he ready to look
too closely at his own distaste for his or his brother's actions.

The two men stood there, both knowing they'd never
agree on this, no matter how long they argued.

"Oh, hell." Tom was clearly still mad, but he seemed to
be giving in. "If I can't talk you out of it, I can at least do
what I can to help. I got Charlie out of Georgia for you."

"You what?" Deke had never expected that.

"He's in our district now, and I'll take care of him. So
when you're out there on that damn boat, you concentrate
on your own problems and let me worry about Charlie."

"I don't know what to say, Tom. I never—" Deke laughed for the first time in days. "Buddy Morris must have had a fit. How'd you manage that?"

Tom laughed, too. "I can pull twice as many strings as a lazy, two-bit prosecutor from nowhere like Buddy Morris. He didn't even know where Charlie was going until after we crossed the Georgia state line with him."

Deke was still laughing. The relief of knowing Charlie was safe in Virginia was incredible. This was the first thing that had gone his way in months.

Coming up against a problem he couldn't solve was a new experience for him. There had been a way around every obstacle that dared to try to block his path. They never stood in his way for long. He didn't think of them as obstacles so much as challenges. And he loved a challenge.

So far Buddy Morris, a U.S. attorney in Georgia, had been a formidable obstacle. Deke had found himself in the uncomfortable position of being across the table from Morris while defending his own brother, with his hands tied by Charlie's own confession.

It hurt more than Deke cared to acknowledge to know that when Charlie was in trouble with the law he wouldn't even call his own brother, who had a law degree and an insider's knowledge of the federal court system.

Because he was a federal prosecutor himself, Deke couldn't have been the attorney of record on Charlie's case. But he would have made damn sure Charlie got a good attorney, and he would have watched that attorney's every move as if the man were defending Deke himself. He sure as hell wouldn't have let Charlie make a confession before Deke was certain that he had a deal with the prosecutors and that Charlie could deliver the information he promised when negotiating the deal that was supposed to get him off with a suspended sentence.

The information Charlie had offered the agents hadn't panned out, and Charlie had been left with nothing but his own confession of possession of cocaine with the intention of selling it.

It never would have come to this if Charlie had just called Deke and kept his mouth shut until Deke got there.

But when it came right down to it, Deke seldom looked at the situation that way. More often than not, he told himself that none of this would have happened if he'd been around to look out for Charlie over the past thirteen years.

Oh, he'd gotten his precious college education, his law degree and a great job right out of school under Richmond, Virginia's, head prosecutor, Thomas Merriwether. And though Deke had been overworked and underpaid— at least compared to his law school colleagues who'd entered private practice—he'd gotten an education under Tom that was unmatched by any he could have gotten in any private corporate practice anywhere.

And when Tom had been appointed U.S. attorney for Virginia—the federal government's chief prosecutor in the state—he'd taken Deke with him.

At thirty-one, Deke was Tom's top assistant prosecutor. Throughout the years, no criminal had wanted to end up across the table from him. Then Deke had found himself on the other side of that bargaining table with Charlie beside him, while they both stared at Buddy Morris. Morris had relished the idea of taking down the brother of a hotshot prosecutor from Virginia.

Until now, Morris had won every round.

Deke smiled again, just thinking about Tom besting Morris by getting Charlie out of Morris's jurisdiction. "How'd you pull it off?" he asked again.

"I've got an old buddy from Nam in the U.S. marshal's office down here," Tom said.

U.S. marshals were responsible for the safekeeping of people in the federal witness protection program, and Charlie was hidden with the marshal's office for now, but Deke knew that just involving someone from the Virginia offices wouldn't have guaranteed the miracle Tom had worked.

"And?"

"Well—" Tom's grin was wicked "—my old friend and I may have misled Mr. Morris a little. As far as he knows, someone got damn close to your brother, close enough to blow him away. So my old friend convinced Morris to move him, conveniently forgetting to mention that Charlie was going to Virginia for a while. We got him about ten days ago. He's safe."

"In the mountains?" Deke thought the isolation of the Appalachians would be the best place for Charlie. There were dozens of roads through sparsely populated areas that still hadn't made it onto any map.

"Well, we—"

"What?" Deke jumped in, not liking the look on his friend's face. "Something happened?"

"Dixon..." Tom paused, evidently not wanting to break the news to him. "You know Charlie's an addict."

No! Deke told himself, he couldn't, *wouldn't* accept that. "A lot of people dabble in drugs."

"And a lot of people drown in them. Charlie's an addict. Don't kid yourself about that, especially if you're going to throw your own life away for him. He's addicted to cocaine."

"No." Deke's jaw tightened, and his eyes darkened, even as the stark truth in the words, a truth he'd been avoiding for too long, hit him so hard he felt as if he were dying inside.

"Yes. He is."

They stared across the kitchen at each other, and Deke got this terrible sinking feeling. He had known. Of course he had. He'd seen enough addicts moving through the courts. But not Charlie. Not his baby brother.

"We had him up in the mountains," Tom said softly, "and there was an early snow—and he freaked. He was convinced he could snort it and get high. The doctors said it happens. An addict sees something white and powdery, a pipe, maybe a syringe—anything that reminds him of doing coke—and it triggers some chemical reaction in his brain, making him crave the drug the way a man lost in the desert craves water. It just pushed everything else out of his head."

Silent, and hurting like never before, Deke stood there against the countertop and wished he could hit something. No, break something. Shatter it, and watch the pieces scatter.

The image of Charlie trying to inhale snow in a fevered and desperate search for a fix burned within him. How could he make up for that? How could a life like that be put back together?

Charlie! Deke closed his eyes and saw the little boy his younger brother had once been. He remembered that when Charlie was about two, he'd had to watch where he stepped, because Charlie was always underfoot. He'd trailed after Deke like a puppy dog. When he'd skinned his knees or bumped his head, Deke had held him close and promised that he would always take care of Charlie.

Why couldn't he have kept him safe?

Deke shook his head and swore.

"I'm sorry," Tom said. "But don't kid yourself about the kind of second chance you're buying your brother with this foolish stunt. You know what the odds are of somebody kicking a cocaine addiction?"

Deke had a feeling he didn't want to know.

"Worse than ten to one that he won't be able to stay clean for two years," Tom said. "And that's if he *wants* to stay clean *and* if he gets good help."

"So we'll just have to buck the odds," Deke said. Suddenly he found he was madder than he'd been in a long time.

"I hope to hell you both do," Tom shot back. He opened his mouth to start all over again with his argument against the deal that had been made to free Charlie, but Deke cut him off.

"He's safe?"

"Yes. Don't ask me where. It's better that you don't know," Tom said. "He's safe, and I'll make sure he stays that way."

"Thanks, Tom."

"Thank me by coming back in one piece."

Deke would have loved to make that promise, but it would be a rash statement. "We need to talk about that. You know there's a chance that I can't come back."

It was Tom's turn to swear, and he did so with a flair that came from being an ex-marine and from spending his life around hardened criminals.

"It's a possibility, Tom."

"So don't go—"

A high-pitched beeping erupted from Tom's pocket, the noise quieting Tom more quickly than Deke ever could. As he shut it off, Tom scowled at the beeper.

Deke just smiled, recognizing a savior when he saw one.

"Phone's in the living room," Deke said, then turned, looking at the four walls surrounding him.

He wouldn't come back, not to this place or to his mother's, maybe not even to his town house in Richmond.

He could end up dead, in which case Nick Russell would be held responsible for it.

Or he could make it back to testify against Russell—but that was a move that could effectively put a noose around Deke's own neck. Russell had a lot of friends who wouldn't sit idly by and watch him go to prison. There was a chance—Deke didn't want to dwell on how much of a chance—that he would be safe, but the price of his safety might be entering the federal witness protection program, being given a new identity, a new town and a new career.

For now, though, Deke refused to think about that. He concentrated on one thing, and one thing only. All he had to do was get Russell put away, and he'd have fulfilled Charlie's deal with the prosecutors.

Deke still wasn't sure of the whole story regarding Nick Russell and his baby brother. He knew Russell was a retired cocaine smuggler who was finding his life-style a little hard to support now that he'd given up the business. Obviously the man hadn't planned carefully enough for his retirement. So he had no choice but to go back to work.

And for the job he had planned, Russell needed some-body to steer his boat.

Charlie knew his way around a boat like few people Deke had ever known, and it was painfully clear now that Char-lie hadn't been shy about using those talents to help people bring things they shouldn't into the country.

Full of all sorts of nooks and crannies, barely known rivers and creeks running through nothing but acres of marsh, places where you didn't pass a house for miles, the Georgia coast was much too much coastline for any law enforcement agency to patrol adequately. It was perfect for smuggling whatever a crook had in mind.

Charlie had worked with Russell before—before Russell had retired and before Charlie's nerves had gotten the bet-ter of him and he'd turned to some of the products he was bringing into the country to help ease his mind.

Funny thing about drug smugglers and dealers. They knew better than most the kind of stupid, irrational things a man could do when he caught a buzz. A smuggler wouldn't tolerate a user in his midst. It was too dangerous in a business where one wrong move could send the whole crew to prison—or worse.

Russell had fired Charlie two years ago, when Charlie had started using, but somehow, in the past few months, Charlie seemed to have wormed his way back into Rus-sell's good graces by convincing him that he was straight.

Well, Deke's little brother wasn't straight. That had be-come painfully obvious to everyone.

A few weeks after he'd started working for Russell again, Charlie had gotten caught bringing in some drugs for a small-time dealer. The way Deke heard it was that the op-eration busted had been just nickel-and-dime, but one the cops had decided they wanted to crow about to try to win some brownie points with the community. Only they'd done a sloppy job on the collars, and no one liked to admit that once they'd bragged to the press about their victory.

Most all the other defendants had gotten off because of insufficient evidence. Charlie probably would have, too, if he hadn't panicked and the cops hadn't been caught in a corner, trying desperately to make themselves look good.

They'd played the charges they had against Charlie for all they were worth, and then some.

And Charlie—who knew what Charlie had been doing or thinking. Had he truly panicked, or had he just gotten too cocky for his own good? Had he been sure he could get out of this, because Deke had always managed to get him out of his scrapes before?

Whatever the reason, Charlie had decided to handle this mess on his own. With scant help or protection from an overworked, underpaid, assistant prosecutor, Charlie had attempted to cut himself a deal, the kind that usually turned Deke's stomach.

In today's incredibly overburdened criminal justice system, any crook who had enough information to help the cops catch a bigger crook could get himself a shortened or even suspended sentence. All he had to do was confess to his own crimes—thereby saving the prosecutors and the cops the time and expense of a court hearing, as well as the uncertainty of winning a conviction before a jury—and give the state enough evidence to put someone else in jail.

The trick lay in the value of the information someone like Charlie had to offer. And as Charlie had discovered, his wasn't good enough to convict anyone, but by the time that had been determined it had been too late. Charlie had already gone to court and pleaded guilty to charges Deke was sure Charlie never truly understood.

All of a sudden Charlie had gone from looking at a suspended sentence to facing years in a federal prison.

Then he'd really gotten himself into trouble. He'd cut another deal. He'd agreed to deliver to the authorities a conviction against Nick Russell, when he had no idea of the severity of the crime Russell was planning. He planned to smuggle a boatful of cocaine into the United States.

It was arranged that Charlie would, in exchange for immunity, work undercover for the feds, who wanted to follow Russell through every step of his smuggling scheme, from Georgia to Colombia and back again.

But not long after Charlie had cut that deal it had become clear that he'd never be able to go through with it. He was too unstable. He was hooked on drugs. He twitched and shook, ranted and raved, all the while craving cocaine. He begged and pleaded for it like a kid after some candy.

Finally he'd given in and contacted his mother, allowing her to call Deke to come to the rescue.

But there had been nothing Deke could do. Nothing except wheel and deal with the law as he'd never done before, to sell the authorities on an outrageous plan for Deke to take his brother's place. It was crazy. Only the feds' desperation to catch a crook like Nick Russell had made them agree.

That, and the fact that they had little to lose. Charlie MacCauley meant next to nothing to them, as did Deke. And the only thing that was really on the line was a good bit of money for the investigation, a few agents' time, and Deke's life.

If he was willing to risk it, they were more than willing to let him.

Deke had been certain, and the agents had reassured him, that it would probably never come to his going on the trip Russell planned. They were confident that he'd be able to get what they needed for a solid charge of conspiring to smuggle a controlled substance into the United States.

So Deke had let his hair grow, had taken to wearing ratty jeans and T-shirts, and had let the worrying he was doing destroy his appetite to help him lose twenty pounds he hadn't needed to lose. Now he certainly looked more like a crook than a federal prosecutor.

As far as anyone knew, the charges against Charlie had been dropped, although the arrest had made Nick Russell nervous. He'd just rehired Charlie, but no way was he going to risk his coming operation with someone fresh from the cops' eyes. And when he'd discovered Charlie was "using" again, the decision had been final.

When Russell had been ready to drop Charlie, however, Charlie had offered up his big brother, Deke. The name had taken a little getting used to now that he was an adult. Charlie was the only person who had ever called him that, but now everyone did. And "Deke" had spent the past three months helping Nick Russell plan the biggest drug deal of Russell's life.

While they'd been on solid ground, Deke hadn't felt that threatened. But come tomorrow they were sailing. He'd be on a little boat in the middle of a big ocean with not much more than his wits to get him through.

Oh, there'd be about ten different state and federal agencies watching over them along the way, but it was doubtful they'd be close enough to save him if he slipped up and gave himself away. Or, for that matter, if the transaction between Russell and his buddies went sour, as drug deals so often did.

Deke believed in himself, in his ability to at least outsmart Nick Russell, even if he couldn't fool him. He thought he was going to make it through this. So it wasn't a feeling of impending death that made him want to talk to Tom now, make any arrangements necessary for that eventuality. It was more the feeling that he *wasn't* about to die.

But then again, he also knew that he would be foolish not to plan for the other possibility, which meant he *really* needed to talk to Tom.

Deke's coffee had grown lukewarm, so he poured it down the drain and made a fresh pot. Filling up two new cups, he took them into the living room, where Tom was finishing up his call.

"Trouble?"

"No." Tom looked grateful for the coffee. "At least not this time. That was Benning from the marshal's office. We've decided we need to get Charlie into a treatment place, and he thinks he's found one. Nice and low-key.

We'll move him Thursday or Friday, once you all are on your way."

Deke nodded and sipped while he thought. It would be a chance, and right now that was the best he could offer Charlie. "We need to talk about later."

Tom merely raised an eyebrow.

"You know, later?" Deke said.

Tom was going to make Deke say it himself.

"If I don't come back. If I can't come back—"

"So you do understand that's a real possibility?" Tom asked. "You know, it's still not too late. You do still have choices."

"You want to read me my rights, counselor?"

"Okay." Tom threw up his hands in surrender. "I'm beaten. What more do you want from me?"

"A promise."

"Sure."

"That you'll see to it that Buddy Morris sticks to our deal. If I get him enough to put Russell away, Charlie walks. At least out from under Morris. I guess he should stay in the hospital for a while, no matter what."

"Done," Tom said.

Knowing the man behind the promise, Deke could be confident that it *was* as good as done.

He smiled and wondered how to say goodbye to a man who'd been so much more than a friend to him.

"I'll miss you, buddy."

Tom's stare was level and steady for a long moment. He looked at the ceiling, cursed, then put one arm around Deke. A pat on the back became a quick hug, which turned into a desperate embrace.

"Damn," Tom said hoarsely, reluctantly letting him go. Finally he cleared his throat and said, "I'll take care of Charlie."

"I know you will, and that helps."

Then Deke watched his friend walk away, wondering if he'd ever see him again.

Chapter 6

Liza lingered in the kitchen long after dinner was over.

Russell had been more agitated than she'd ever seen him. He'd snarled and snapped at everyone throughout the meal.

The louder Russell had been, the quieter Deke had become. Deke was there for the night, apparently, and he'd brooded in silence as he watched Russell's every move—as if Deke expected disaster to strike at any moment.

Ellen had escaped early, using the excuse of wanting to get Jilly to bed—a curious move, since she almost always left the chore to Liza.

Liza welcomed the solitude once the meal had finally ended and the men had left. She'd cleared the dining room table, scraped the dishes, wiped the countertop and the stove, then had turned back to the dishes.

Rather than load the dishwasher, she did the dishes by hand. It was soothing to stand there at the sink with her hands in the warm, soapy water, making slow circles on a dinner plate with the bright pink sponge. She lingered over the chore, because here, safe in the kitchen, she could almost believe that everything was going to be all right.

Almost.

The truth was, she had to fight even now to keep her breathing even, to keep her hands from shaking and her heart from running wild in her chest.

She was well and truly frightened of what was ahead, and she didn't know what to do about it.

So there she stood with the dishes, rinsing them one by one under the slow stream of water trailing out of the faucet before setting them out to drain.

The slow, rhythmic motions eventually soothed her. She was lulled into a false sense of security, one that was shattered after a few seconds.

She'd finished putting the last of the silverware away and had turned out the lights to leave when she'd seen the butter dish and the knife sitting on the windowsill above the sink. Her already skittish heart had kicked into overdrive at the sight of it.

Liza laughed weakly as she looked down at the harmless little butter knife and saw the big butcher knife instead. She'd gotten distracted by some other chore before putting the butter back in the refrigerator and cleaning the dull little knife. It was right there under her nose—well at least just to the right of her nose—the whole time she'd been doing the dishes, and still she'd forgotten. Where was her mind these days?

But as she continued to look down at the knife, she knew. She'd been able to think of little else all day, save the feel of a certain blade against the pulsepoint in her throat.

She knew just the spot where he'd pushed it against her neck; she could still feel the blood throbbing heavily past that point. She could imagine so easily, even now, how simple it would have been for him to push the knife through her skin, through the vein, sending the blood out in spurts timed to the beat of her heart.

Funny, but of all the places she'd been since she'd run away from her mother's house when she was seventeen,

she'd felt safest here—or at least she had, until a few days
ago.

She could do nothing more than shake her head in wonder at the irony of it all—there had been times when she'd
wondered where her next meal would come from, where
she'd sleep at night and where she could turn for help.

She'd gotten through them, amazingly unscathed by it
all, only to land here, in her own sister's house, scared for
her own safety, her sister's and her niece's, scared of what
her sister's husband was going to do.

And she was scared of Deke, too.

She couldn't forget how utterly helpless she'd felt, lying
there under the blade he held to her throat.

And then her attention was caught by movement outside the window. She saw a light. It jerked, then swayed,
jerked, then swayed, back and forth, across the backyard.
A long shadow followed it—a man, she decided, one with
a flashlight.

Who was it? But she couldn't tell—there was barely
enough light to throw a spooky series of shadows across the
backyard. That was wrong, Liza realized suddenly. There
should have been more light. The house had security lights
along the back, there was one on the storage shed and another on the dock, but none were shining tonight.

She might not be able to tell who was out there, but
whoever it was, she could see that he was coming from the
direction of the shed. He was carrying something in his
right hand, something long and skinny. A gun? She
couldn't tell that, either.

Liza jumped back from the window, afraid that the man
might look toward the house and see her. Then she remembered the inside lights. She'd turned them all off because she'd been ready to leave the kitchen. If the man
looked in the window, he'd see nothing but darkness. She
went back to the window and worried about the gun.

There was some comfort in the fact that he wasn't coming toward the house. He was moving parallel to it, searching for something on the ground. Why would anyone be

searching for anything outside now? What could he be
looking for that he couldn't find so much easier in the light
of day?

The man zeroed in on one spot a few minutes later. At
least that was what Liza thought, but then the man didn't
pick anything up. He put down his flashlight and started—
digging? The motion fitted, and the shape she'd taken for
a gun could be a shovel.

He was digging, she told herself, not coming at her with
a gun. But digging suddenly seemed so much more sinis-
ter.

Oh, Lord! Was it Russell? Or Deke?

Digging?

Her stomach lurched. Her nerves must be raw, she decided, because all she could think of was a grave. What if
the man had hurt someone? Or, even worse—what if he'd
killed someone? What if the man was digging a grave?

Ridiculous, she told herself. Sheer nerves. Yet the man
dug on. The hole got deeper and deeper, longer and wider,
the dirt piling up on the side.

It was big enough to be a grave—at least it would be
soon.

Who was it? And what was he going to put in that hole?

Finally the man turned to one side and stepped into the
light of the flashlight, which he'd set on its end, the beam
of light shining up into the night sky. It lit his profile, and
then it was clear. The darkness and the angle of her view
had disguised the thickness of his figure. Now she could see
his big nose, his wide belly. It was Russell.

The hole got deeper and wider still; all of a sudden it was
definitely much too big. Big enough for a man?

She gripped the edge of the sink hard and tried to be
calm. What was he going to put in that damn hole?

It seemed that she waited there forever while he dug,
deeper and deeper, until he was buried up to his waist in the
hole.

She looked around in the darkness, but she couldn't see anything he might be planning to bury. Maybe it was in the house. A body, in the house, with her.

Liza waited, listening to her heart beating in the silence in the dark house. And then it wasn't so silent anymore. She heard footsteps in the hall, or perhaps they were coming from the staircase. Those were the only two areas of the house that weren't carpeted, and the footsteps seemed to be moving across a wooden floor.

It wasn't Russell that she heard. Liza hadn't moved from her spot in front of the window, and she could still see Russell digging. She was afraid to turn around and see who was coming down the hall.

She just stood there, staring at the shovel as it moved down, then up, then over, the dirt flying through the air to land atop the heap of soil already there.

She stood still somehow, the breaths she took growing more and more shallow, until they barely filled her lungs. Eventually there just wasn't enough air, and she grew dizzy from the lack of oxygen.

The hall light clicked on.

Liza jumped and clamped a hand over her mouth to stop her scream from escaping. She felt eyes on her back, felt a tremor work its way down her spine, through her entire body and linger there.

"Liza?"

"Deke?"

She whirled around as she said his name. The blood drained from her face, and her legs turned to jelly. She sagged against the sink and took a deep breath.

"What's wrong?" he asked, cautiously, walking into the kitchen.

"Nothing." She lied because she wasn't sure what she'd seen, and because she wasn't sure it would matter to anyone that she had seen it. Besides, after the episode with the knife, he was definitely the last person she'd confide in.

"Try again, Liza." He moved steadily closer until he was right in front of her. He reached out. With his hand on her right wrist, he lifted that hand, watching it tremble beneath his narrowed gaze. "You don't stand in the dark, trembling, because nothing is wrong."

"I was just finishing the dishes." She shook her hand free and stepped to the side; for some reason, she felt it important that he not see what she'd seen through the kitchen window. "It was nothing. I thought I heard a noise, but it was only you."

He was still too close, and he was staring down at her intently. He didn't believe her.

Liza wondered how much he knew about Russell, if he knew anything about the hole her brother-in-law was digging, and if so, what he planned to put in it.

"What—?" Deke stopped as the flashlight's beam caught his eye. "Is that Russell?"

As he looked down at her, she held her breath and tried to gauge his reaction. It seemed to be not so much anger as worry.

"Yes," she said.

"Son of a bitch. It was there all the time."

There? What was there? She never got a chance to ask. The next thing she knew, Deke's face was coming down to meet hers.

"The light," he said when his lips were a mere breath away from hers.

"What?" More confused than before, and more than a little scared, she pulled back, but not enough.

It wasn't a kiss he took so much as a slow, sensuous taste of her, his soft lips closing over her upper lip, then drawing it inside his mouth and stroking it once, ever so lightly, with his tongue.

"I turned on the light in the hall," Deke elaborated in a husky voice, then returned for another too-brief taste, this time of her lower lip. "He can see us now—because of the light."

Then he gave up explaining and just kissed her over and over again. Liza was lost. She couldn't make sense of anything that had happened tonight, or what Deke had been trying to tell her only a moment before. She told herself that he'd scared her to death earlier, with the knife, and that there was no telling what he was up to now, or how he might hurt her.

But as the kiss went on it got harder and harder to remember that.

She could recall quite easily now how earlier, as she'd puzzled over his rough caresses, she'd decided that if he wanted to Deke would know exactly how to please a woman he held in his arms.

She was right. He knew just what to do.

His touch was gentle yet firm. He pulled her to him, then positioned her so that her back was resting against the sink and he was resting against her front.

He held her by her arms, trapped her there with his body, held her motionless, his lips moving slowly over hers.

Resist, Liza told herself. Remember the knife at your throat. But, Lord, he made it hard to do that now that he was kissing her so expertly, so sensuously, so timelessly, as if they had nothing else to do but neck in the kitchen.

It made no sense—that much got through the hazy fog clouding her brain—but then, nothing else that had happened today made sense, either.

His lips on hers—that seemed to make sense. That felt right. His big, strong arms around her—they felt wonderful now, they sheltered her. He could threaten, but he could apparently also shelter, depending on how he chose to treat her.

And for just a moment she imagined that she was safe and secure, here in his arms, despite the world gone mad around her. For just a moment, she begged silently, for a long moment, to feel this way....

Then his lips were gone, and she would have protested, but it was all right, because he was kissing his way across her jawline to her right ear. He teased the lobe. He took it into his warm mouth. She felt his breath tremble over her ear before his tongue teased at the shell.

She made a noise—half laugh, half moan—then gasped as he nudged her legs apart and settled himself more intimately against her. He wanted her, too. She could feel how much he wanted her.

His mouth moved on to her neck. Oh, Lord, what was he doing to her neck? It was a barely-there touch, a soft kiss, a light touch of his tongue, then, lower, a little nibble of her collarbone.

She shivered and shook, pleasure surrounding her. Instinctively she pressed her lower body closer to his and felt the answering pressure of his body as he, too, tried to get closer.

Then he used his nose to tip her chin back so that he could kiss his way down her throat. She felt his hands on her hips, lifting her closer to the hard, throbbing length of him.

"Oh!" She couldn't stand it. His nose was nuzzling the hollow between her breasts now, and a second later his lips were there, teasing her, touching only the beginnings of her breasts, leaving the centers tight and yearning.

"Please." With her chin, Liza urged his head down, and at the same time arched back over the sink and twisted her breast up to his mouth. She wanted his touch so bad that she didn't care if she had to beg for it.

It was worth it. She had known it would be. Her breasts were full to the point of bursting, flushed with heat, swelling higher and tighter as his mouth teased them, one after the other, through her clothes.

She wanted it to go on and on. She waited, hoping it would never end, surprised when it did. She thought at first that he was simply finding some other way to please her, but that wasn't it.

The hands that held her hips close to his were suddenly gone. So was the support of the sink against her back. Deke pulled her upright, but his hands didn't linger long enough to steady her.

She was fighting for air—and, unless she was mistaken, so was he.

"*Damn.* I touch you, and it drives every other thought right out of my head."

He sounded angry about it, as if it were a complaint, not a compliment.

Wanting some more distance between them, Liza pushed against his chest. She didn't get an arm's length away. He caught her, his grip on her elbows hard and strong.

"Don't turn around." He whispered it, urgently. "He's still watching, and I don't want him to think we were here watching him."

Watching?

Someone was watching?

Russell. Russell was watching.

She closed her eyes tight against the revelation.

Deke had certainly driven every rational thought from her head, but she clearly hadn't had that effect on him.

Because the whole time she'd been simply enjoying his touch, he'd been trying the easiest way he knew to convince Russell that neither of them had been paying any attention to him or his hole in the backyard.

A knife one minute, a kiss the next. Obviously it didn't matter much to him what he used to achieve his purpose—whatever it was.

"Walk with me to the door, and don't look back," Deke said. It wasn't a request. It was a command—and, still in a daze, she obeyed automatically.

They walked close together, his arm around her back, her side pulled close to his. At first she was too numb to resist when he kissed her once more, lightly. But then she thought of how humiliating it was—she'd all but begged him to put his mouth on her. It was all she could do not to pull away from him as they continued to the doorway.

He clicked the light off. The blessed darkness settled in around them, and she jerked away from his side as if she'd been burned.

"Go to your room and stay there. Don't turn on any of the lights."

Anger, at herself and at him, left her in a reckless mood long enough to resist. "Like hell I will. I want to know what in the world you all are up to?"

"What am I up to?" he shot back at her. "I'm trying to save someone's ass. Someone I care about a lot, and I wish you'd get out of the way and let me."

Deke froze then. He'd opened his mouth without thinking, and told her something he hadn't intended to.

And that made him furious. Not at the fact that he'd actually revealed anything important or dangerous—she would never be able to make head or tail of that comment—but at the fact that he'd lost control, that he'd spoken without thinking, that she had a way of making him lose control.

He'd lost his head completely in the kitchen with her. It hadn't been necessary to kiss her like that, yet he'd jumped at the chance. Oh, it might have worked. Russell might have thought they'd been necking in the kitchen instead of spying on him while he dug up his backyard.

But it was the magnitude of his desire to kiss her, to lose himself in her, that disturbed him. Kissing her wouldn't have been so bad if he hadn't wanted it so badly, if he hadn't enjoyed it so much that it pushed every rational thought out of his head.

She made him lose control, and he couldn't afford to do that.

The way he saw it, his biggest asset in this whole setup was his ability to think his way through whatever came along, and what was he doing now? Tangling with a woman who turned his brains to mush.

"Liza, for the last time, get out of here before it's too late." He was angry, yet at the same time he was pleading with her, pleading as much for her as he was for himself. "You don't even realize the kind of trouble you're up against."

"Maybe I don't. But whatever I'm up against, Jilly's up against, too. And I can't leave Jilly. I can't let him take her on this trip with just Ellen to take care of her."

Deke gripped her arms then and pulled her forward until they were nearly nose to nose.

"You can't take care of her, either," he whispered, shaking her just a little. "Listen to me, damn it. You can't protect her, and you can't protect yourself. Not where we're going. Not from Russell."

She looked at him, and he didn't need the light to see her indigo eyes, big and round, partly hidden behind the long, straight strands of hair that always seemed to fall over her left eye. She didn't believe him. Urgency burned within him. He had to make her believe.

"He's dangerous, Liza."

"More dangerous than you?"

He couldn't help but smile a little then, because the woman had a way of cutting right to the heart of the matter.

"Yes, he is."

"How does he feel about knives?"

He smiled for real then, because she was so unlike any woman he'd encountered in a long time. There was no pretense to her, no vanity, no coy act of little-girl helplessness. He allowed himself just a moment to admire that, and her straightforward manner, while at the same time acknowledging that he could do without her questions or her challenge.

"Damn, you just don't know when to quit, do you?"

"Oh, I know exactly how to do that," she said, the catch in her voice surprising him. "Quitting and running is about all I've ever done, but I'm not going to do that now. I made a promise to myself that no one was going to hurt Jilly, and I'm going to keep it."

"Fine," he said, releasing her and throwing up his hands. He told himself that that was it, he was washing his hands of her. "Just don't think I'm going to look out for you on this trip. Don't think I can protect you, because I can't. I'll be doing good to cover my own ass."

"Fine," she threw right back, trying to keep her voice down. "You cover yours, and I'll cover mine."

He had to bite his tongue to keep from telling her how he'd dreamed of covering her own little bottom. And that made him mad all over again, because he had no business thinking that, and no time for such distractions. Damn her, anyway—her and this misguided, ill-conceived urge to protect her.

Walk away, he told himself, you have things to do. He was pretty sure he knew what Russell was up to in the backyard, but he needed to be sure. He needed to just turn and walk away from her. She wasn't his concern. She couldn't be.

"Fine," he repeated. "Just fine."

So why was walking away from her one of the hardest things he'd ever done?

Chapter 7

Russell wasn't burying anything.

It was a while before Liza figured that out, and she had a really bad moment when he pulled a big, long box out of the ground.

Lord, was he digging somebody *up?* she wondered. But why would he go to the trouble of burying somebody and then digging them up again?

She was upstairs on her knees beside her bedroom window, cautiously looking out, her eyes nearly at the level of the windowsill. From this angle, even if he did look up and there was enough light, all he'd see was the very top of her head. And with any luck at all, from the angle he'd have looking up *into* the second-floor window, he'd see nothing.

Not that it made her feel a whole lot better, because she could see more than she cared to see. The box looked bad. It was big enough for a person, if the legs were all crumpled up—or broken. A man who'd killed someone wouldn't think anything of breaking his legs to get them into a box.

She turned her back to the window and sank down to the floor.

Huddled in the corner against the bed, she went about convincing herself that seeing whatever was in that box couldn't be any worse than the images her imagination was conjuring up.

Just a peek. She could do that. Sure she could. Slowly, so slowly, she turned back toward the window, then winced when she saw that he'd opened the lid and was now looking inside.

And then he pulled something out.

Something small enough to hold in his hand.

The flashlight beam flipped one hundred and eighty degrees until it was shining down at his other hand, at what was in it.

Oh, Lord, what was in his other hand?

From this distance, she couldn't tell, but then he moved the flashlight, apparently tucking it between his chin and his shoulder so that he could hold the other thing in both hands. He was flipping through it like someone with a stack of money—

Money?

She was stunned. She couldn't do anything except stare at Russell as he fingered the money like a man worshiping at the altar.

He buried money in the ground?

Liza laughed out loud. She tried to stifle the sound with her hand, but the laughter rang out.

He buried money in the ground!

It was so ridiculous. She'd been waiting for him to toss a body in there and fill the hole back in with dirt, but all Nick Russell was doing was going to the bank!

This must be his vault, because it was full. He pulled bundles and bundles of it from the big box until he had a stack there on the ground beside him.

Thinking back on it now, Liza knew she should have wondered more than once about the way he used cash for almost everything. He paid her in cash. He gave her cash to buy clothes and toys for Jilly, and to take to the grocery store twice a week. She'd been with Ellen before when Ellen had bought money orders to pay the phone bill or the electric bill.

Now that she thought about it, Liza couldn't remember Russell ever making a trip to the bank. He hadn't worked since she'd come to live there, and yet he always had plenty of money for whatever he wanted to buy.

Ellen claimed they'd sold a very successful business in Mobile before moving here, but Liza couldn't imagine Russell running a wildly successful business. It also didn't explain why Ellen was so frightened of him. Did successful businessmen inspire fear?

And there was so much money there, so much that it wasn't funny anymore.

Why did a man bury his money in the backyard?

It was certainly more than a mere distrust of banks.

Russell went back to the shed and returned with a bag of some sort and a wheelbarrow. He stuffed the bag full of money and then hauled it down the dock to the boat.

He repeated the trip three times while Liza sat there in a stupor.

So much money in that hole in the ground.

No man had any business keeping that much cash around. No *honest* man would take the risk.

Liza had no trouble believing Nick Russell was a dishonest man, but it seemed now that he must be something much worse. As she sat there, frozen into place, Liza let her imagination run wild, thinking of all the reasons Russell might have all that cash that he was loading onto the boat.

He could have robbed a bank.

Maybe he was blackmailing someone.

This could be the ransom money from a kidnapping.

He could be a hired killer who'd just hit a big target.

She could believe he'd do any of those things, but Deke?

Deke? She'd never understand Deke. Just when she thought he couldn't surprise her anymore, he did. He left her scared one minute, aroused the next.

The breath stuck in her lungs, her chest burned, and she fought back the memory of the way he'd held her in his arms a few minutes before. What was he doing here? Why was he helping Russell? To save someone else, he'd said. Who? How?

Liza couldn't let herself think of the possibilities, but whatever the reason, Russell had a lot of money she instinctively knew he shouldn't have, money he was taking on the trip. And in less than twenty-four hours, Liza, Jilly, Ellen and Deke would be on that boat with Russell and his money.

Oh, *no,* she decided right then. *She* wouldn't be on that boat. She couldn't be on that boat. Deke had been right that day at the back of the house, when he'd told her she didn't want to make the trip. She should have listened to him sooner. If she had, she wouldn't be in the spot she was in now, mere hours before they were due to sail.

In a daze, she started searching the room for her battered duffel bag, the one that had seen her in and out of a dozen states in the past seven years.

She had to get away, run away, and this time she wasn't going to feel guilty about it. This was danger, pure and simple.

Finally she found the duffel bag and stuffed it with the first clothes she could lay her hands on, which turned out to be the ones she'd set aside this morning to take on the boat trip. She stuffed in all the rest of her clothes that would fit.

And then she remembered. Jilly.

Liza sank down on the bed and gave herself permission to panic for a minute as she thought about Jilly. *She couldn't leave Jilly.*

There was no telling what Russell was really up to. Liza couldn't leave Jilly to face it alone. She'd promised herself, and Ellen.

Dimly she sat there, remembering the exact conversation when she'd done so. At the time the conversation she'd been having with Ellen hadn't made a lot of sense—but it did now. Ellen had made Liza solemnly vow she would take care of Jilly first and not worry about her sister. Ellen seemed to think she was past the point of help.

So, Liza thought, she would have to take Jilly with her. Right or wrong, that was the way it would have to be. So what if she hadn't made any plans—like where they would go and how she would take care of the little girl.

She didn't know, but as soon as she went to Jilly's room and saw her sleeping so peacefully Liza knew she'd made the right decision.

It wasn't really kidnapping, she reassured herself as she smoothed down the blond curls. Not if it was what Jilly's mother wanted, right? Of course, it would seem like kidnapping to Nick Russell.

But with all that money buried in the ground, Russell was bound to be a criminal himself, so it wasn't likely he'd go calling the police on her.

He didn't really love Jilly, anyway. He didn't even pretend to unless someone was around. Ellen did love her—she must—but she just wasn't strong enough to clean herself up and be the mother Jilly deserved.

Liza had laid out Jilly's clothes for the trip that morning, so packing for the little girl wasn't difficult. Liza zipped the small case shut, then crept down the stairs and left it just outside the front door.

There was no sign of Nick Russell, so she returned to her own room for her bags, planning to leave them by the front door.

Now it was time to make a plan. Russell had been insistent that they leave on the boat tomorrow evening. No, Liza thought as she looked at the clock, *this* evening. It was already well after midnight.

When he discovered they were gone, Russell would probably look for her and Jilly, but she didn't think he'd delay the trip. He had some reason to be there, wherever "there" was, on time. Russell had made it clear in the past few days that he had a schedule, and that they were going to keep to it. Which meant that he wouldn't have time to look for long.

All she had to do was get far enough away that he couldn't find them in twelve hours or so. Twelve hours. She tried to calm herself even as she thought about it.

She didn't want to take any chances of getting caught. She wanted to get as far as she could in those few hours, and for that she'd need money.

Liza actually smiled when she wondered whether there was any left in the backyard. She had saved some of the money Russell had paid her, but not that much. And she wouldn't be able to get to it until the bank opened, hours from now. She didn't want to be that close to Nick Russell come morning.

Where could she get money?

Deke. Of course. He had money, lots of it. Liza had been headed for town the day before yesterday to get some groceries. She'd gone down to the boat to ask Russell for some money. He hadn't had his wallet with him, but Deke had had his. He'd loaned Russell a hundred dollars to give to Liza. She remembered watching him separate five twenties from a thick stack topped by at least one one-hundred-dollar bill.

And he was using the guest room at the end of the hall.

Deke hadn't gone to sleep yet; his nerves had gotten the better of him. He was wondering about all the things that could possibly go wrong, and how he could handle them.

He was still awake when he heard the sounds—his door opening softly, the swoosh, then the click, of the door closing again, footsteps moving lightly across the carpet. Then his own heartbeat drowned out any other clues his sense of hearing might have offered him.

He was sprawled across the double bed, lying on his stomach with an arm above his head, an arm that shielded most of the room from his view.

He couldn't see a face, or much of the person's body. But he saw the shoes, a pair of cheap, worse-for-wear cotton sneakers—*Liza's* shoes—and he had to fight to keep the breath from rushing out of his lungs in a long, loud sigh of relief.

Curiosity about what had brought her here, what she intended to do, kept him lying still on the bed, waiting to see what her next move would be.

She took her time about it. Finally she walked over to the bed and leaned over it, leaning across his body.

Hell of a time for it, but suddenly he wondered if he could trust her. He could, couldn't he? His heart wasn't beating so slowly anymore, the answer to that question hanging in the air. Then he heard her fumbling with the pair of jeans he'd left hanging over the headboard.

Damn, couldn't he trust anyone?

"Oh, hell," he muttered, flipping over onto his back. He knocked her off balance as he did, then barely managed to get hold of her.

She struggled—whether out of guilt or out of fear, he didn't know. But he ended up having to wrestle her down onto the bed, pinning her there with his body.

Startled, Liza caught her breath, and was just opening her mouth to scream when he clamped his hand over her mouth.

They stared through the murky darkness at each other for a long moment while her breathing slowed. It gave him time to wonder just how it was that he kept finding himself much too close to this woman, and why it became harder and harder, each time he got this close, to let her go. Nerves, he told himself. His were shot.

Or maybe he'd just gone too long without a woman. He'd never been one to take a woman casually, purely for entertainment, or as a diversion, but maybe that was what he needed right now.

"Damn." He muttered it under his breath as he stared down into her big, dark eyes, knowing instinctively that there would be nothing casual, nothing easily taken or easily forgotten, between them.

"Damn." This time he said it out loud. He took his hand

away from her mouth. "Are we going to make a habit of this?"

It was only yesterday that he'd pinned her to the cabin floor on the boat after she'd snuck up on him.

"No— I . . ." She lost whatever she'd been about to say when she put her hands up to push him away and found her palms on his bare chest.

Then he saw the cash. She'd been after his money. There was a whole wad of it lying on the bed. "You rotten little thief."

"No."

She could deny it all she wanted, but Deke didn't see any other explanation. Stealing from him. He stifled a bitter laugh. He didn't really know anything about her, after all. The only question was—why?

Drugs was the first explanation that came to him, and it wasn't just because of Charlie and Russell either. A drug habit ate up a lot of money, and junkies did the stupidest things to get it.

No, he admitted as he grew angrier by the minute, he didn't really know anything about her.

Well, he was going to find out, he thought, but before he could, the door opened up behind them, light flooding the room. Nick Russell, smiling like a kid in a candy store, walked into the room and stared at them as they lay there sprawled on the bed together.

Chapter 8

"Well," Russell began with a smirk, his eyes taking in the details of their intimate entanglement. Then he saw the wad of money beside them and continued slyly, "She's making you pay for it, huh?"

Deke rolled off Liza, sitting on the edge of the bed, his face impassive.

"So tell me," Russell said with a sneer, scanning the denominations on the bills thrown on the bed, "she really worth it?"

Liza almost choked. She scrambled around Deke to get off the bed, then shouldered her way past Russell and fled from the room.

Deke was baffled by the whole night. He couldn't begin to explain what was going on, so he just stood up, grabbed his pants and stepped into them.

"Nothing to be ashamed of, boy," Russell—the great philosopher—offered. "A man always ends up paying for a woman, one way or another. Some are just more honest about it than others."

At that precise moment, Deke realized just how much he despised Nick Russell.

Concentrating on maintaining his indifferent facade, when all he really wanted to do was smash that dirty smirk right off Russell's face, Deke zipped and buttoned his pants, then forced himself to meet Russell's eyes.

"Did you come here in the middle of the night just to offer me those words of wisdom? Or was there something else?"

"The boat," Russell said, and left him to wonder about the rest.

"What about the boat?" Deke asked tersely. He didn't even want to think about what could have gone wrong to send Russell up here in the middle of the night.

"It's ready?" Russell asked, suddenly all business.

"It's ready."

"So we could leave right now if we needed to?"

Deke didn't like the turn the conversation was taking at all. The boat was as ready as it would ever be, and Russell damn well knew it. He'd asked before they'd left the dinner table.

He weighed his words carefully. "Wouldn't be any picnic getting out into the channel in the dark with the tide out."

"At sunup? High tide's at six, right? We could get out then?"

"No reason why we couldn't." Deke gritted his teeth as he said the words. He was in trouble, he could be damned sure of it, if Nick Russell knew the stage of the tide. The man didn't know the port side of a boat from starboard.

"Good," Russell said. "Let's get on out. I've been watching that twenty-four hour weather channel, and I'm not sure we'll get out if we wait until later. There's a storm moving in, and I'd like to be gone before it gets here."

Deke wanted to scream at Russell that *he* wasn't ready.

He knew that the reservations he had about making the trip wouldn't go away in the fifteen hours or so he had left between now and the original hour they'd planned to sail.

But he wanted those fifteen hours, anyway.

Mostly he wanted to get Liza and Jilly out of the way. He hadn't been able to do that by himself yet, but he'd still had hopes of making it happen.

He stared at Russell and wondered just how smart the crook was, wondered whether he suspected anything and whether this plan to leave sooner than they'd expected was simply his way of showing Deke who was boss. Or maybe he was just watching, waiting to see how much Deke would protest any change of plans along the way, plans that would make it impossible for him to notify anyone of those changes.

With a sinking feeling deep in his gut, Deke decided he couldn't afford to protest at all. Russell already suspected something was going on with Liza—he didn't honestly think Russell believed that she'd been in here selling herself to him. He latched on to one thought. Agents were already watching the house; surely they wouldn't miss a fifty-eight-foot sailboat floating down the channel.

"So, I'll see you at the boat in about three hours." Russell grinned as he walked out the door. "That'll leave you plenty of time to get your money's worth out of that girl."

Deke fought the urge to slam the bedroom door behind Russell. Instead he closed it softly, rested against the door and stared out the window into the black night.

His money's worth? He'd have settled for some answers. Was she just an innocent woman caught up in something she didn't understand? The thought made him pause in the midst of pulling out his duffel bag and checking to see that he'd packed everything he would need.

Just how innocent could she be? What could she possibly need with his money? Drugs had been the first possibility to pop into his head. And the thought of seeing Liza half out of her mind in some chemical haze made him furious.

He was on his feet and halfway down the hall before he even realized what he was doing. He was going to find out exactly why she'd come to his room and picked his pocket.

* * *

Deke found her sitting by the window on the floor, leaning against the sill and staring out over the quiet water. She tensed at the sound of the door opening and closing behind him, but she didn't turn around.

"Russell's decided he wants to leave as soon as the sun comes up."

Deke eyed her narrowly—noting the tightness in the ramrod-straight line of her back and the anxious sound of her fast, shallow breathing.

She didn't look away from the window, and the dark curtain of her hair shielded her face from his view.

Right at that moment, he wanted very much to see her face, to see the emotions he knew she'd never be able to hide in those big, expressive eyes of hers.

He knew that he should admit, at least to himself, that she was becoming an obsession with him. Even now, when she was defying him, he had a hard time holding on to his anger. She continually surprised him with her spunk, her sass, her zest for life.

And the things she made him feel? *No.* He wasn't ready to think about any of that. None of it made sense, anyway, and the last thing he needed in his life right now was something else that made no sense.

"You need to pack your bag." His voice sounded harsh as it broke the silence.

"It's packed," she said, softly, wearily.

He hadn't taken his eyes off her since he'd come into the room, but if he had, he would have seen the nearly empty closet and the two open drawers. No sign of her bags, but he could tell from the shape of the room that she'd packed quickly.

"Where's your stuff?"

"Downstairs by the side door. Jilly's things are ready, too."

"Oh—" Deke half groaned the swear words that followed. He knew at once what had happened. *She'd been trying to leave.* "Damn it," he muttered, again and again.

She'd been leaving. He'd finally convinced her—or maybe it had been Russell and his buried money. Whatever—it didn't matter now. She'd been almost gone, and Russell had caught her.

For what seemed the thousandth time, Deke wondered how much she knew about the whole deal, how much Ellen knew about the way her husband made his money. Ellen Russell couldn't know everything. Surely, if she knew what was ahead, she wouldn't subject her child to such danger. And if Ellen didn't know, she couldn't have told Liza.

Still, Liza was no fool. From her window here, she would have had an unobstructed view of Russell parading back and forth from his hole in the ground to the boat, his wheelbarrow full of money.

No honest man would travel with that much cash on him, and she had to have reached that conclusion.

God, why hadn't she realized the danger earlier and gotten away? For that matter, why hadn't he worked harder to get her out of here? And what was he going to do with her on this godforsaken trip?

Would he be able to trust her? His heart told him yes, but his head told him that he couldn't afford to trust anyone.

He wanted to trust her, and more than that, he wanted to protect her, but he had to be realistic. It was entirely possible that he wouldn't be able to. A million things could go wrong.

His emotions in a turmoil, he couldn't stop himself from getting a little closer to her, close enough that he could have reached out his hand and touched her hair or her shoulder as she sat there by the window.

Go, he told himself. Just leave her alone. Yet still he lingered.

"It's too late to run, Liza."

"I know." The words trembled with fear, and his heart turned over in his chest.

Deke remained there in her room when he knew he should leave. He wanted to warn her, but of what? Would she even believe him if he told her what was going to happen? Probably not. She was probably scared to death of him now, after that little episode with the knife and the way he'd grabbed her in the kitchen.

He wanted to promise to take care of her, to keep her safe, but he didn't believe in making promises he might not be able to keep.

And he wanted to tell her that he wasn't what he seemed. That if she needed to turn to someone on this trip, she could turn to him. That she could trust him more than she could trust Nick Russell.

But why would she believe him about that, either?

He cursed and tried to walk away from her, but found he couldn't—not without at least trying to warn her.

She finally turned to face him then, and he sank down to his knees beside her on the carpeted floor and studied the torrent of emotions running through her eyes.

It was obvious she wasn't sure whether she should believe him, and he didn't blame her for that.

He had to admire her courage. He could tell she was scared to death, but she wasn't cowering away from it or trying to deny it. Instead, she was preparing herself to face it, to walk onto that boat and deal with whatever lay ahead of her.

"Liza..." Shaking his head in wonder at her, he suddenly wished that he could touch her, just once, the way he needed to touch her. Not in anger, not in frustration, not to try to convince her he was something he was not. But just because he wanted to—because he wanted so much to touch her.

In another place, at another time, nothing could have stopped him from pulling her close and kissing her over and over again. And he wouldn't have stopped at that.

But this wasn't the time or the place, and he had no right to touch her like that.

His hand, unconsciously reaching for her, dropped to his side, and she swayed toward him just a fraction, then caught herself, checking the movement.

She was on shaky ground here, and she needed to tread lightly. She wondered just what Deke knew about Russell's plans—whether he was Russell's partner in crime or merely another paid employee like herself. But mostly, she wondered if she dared trust him.

"What's going to happen out there?" She turned back toward the window as she asked.

"I'm not sure."

That brought her head back around instantly.

"I'm not, Liza. I know what I expect to happen, what I *hope* will happen, but Russell may have other plans."

"Dangerous plans." It was more a statement than a question.

"Yes," he said quietly.

Seconds ticked by without a response. It seemed to take forever, seemed that he'd waited an eternity there beside her. In the silence, he cursed inwardly, feeling powerless. He wanted to promise her that nothing bad was going to happen, that it was in his power to keep her safe and that he would do so. He wanted to say to hell with the government's damned plans and his brother's problems, to get her away from here to some place where she would truly be safe. But he couldn't.

Finally she whispered, "I'm so frightened."

Jaw tightening, wanting to do so much more, he settled for letting his hand ease its way through the thick strands of her straight, dark hair.

"So am I, Liza." He whispered the words back, and there was relief in being able to be honest about that one simple thing. Instinctively he knew that there was no danger in admitting his own fears to her. Besides, he didn't want her to have any illusions about how dangerous the situation actually was.

Then, even though a good two feet still separated them, he pulled back, away from her. Damn it, he had to, before he said something he'd regret later. Getting up quietly, he left her room without saying another word.

Chapter 9

A few hours later, hours that he'd wanted to hold on to, hours that had, instead, rushed past like a stream of sand falling through his fingertips, they set sail.

He'd forgotten how much he hated sailing, he thought as he checked the instruments one last time and settled in behind the wheel for the journey from the sound down to the Intracoastal Waterway.

The channel in the sound was deep in parts, but treacherously shallow in others, so he needed to pay attention to what he was doing.

He'd grown up on these waters, but that was a long time ago, he thought. The sediments on the bottom had a way of shifting from left to right, or curving where they had once been straight, stranding an unsuspecting sailor for hours while the tide swept out and back in again.

It hadn't mattered so much growing up, because he'd never gotten the chance to sail a big, expensive boat like this. He'd spent a lot of summers helping out on chartered fishing boats, and a few on shrimpers. He'd taken the hot, sweaty, smelly jobs because he had once truly enjoyed being on the water.

"It's so peaceful here," Liza said. "How can that be?"

She'd stuck close to him ever since they'd sailed. He didn't understand exactly why, but he was glad, because he wasn't inclined to take his eyes off her. He had an irrational urge, a yearning that strengthened with each mile they put between themselves and the dock, to pull her within the shelter of his arms and not let her go until they returned.

Of course, even if he could pull her close and keep her there, it wouldn't mean that she'd be safe. But he bet it would make him feel better.

It was going to be a damn long trip, he decided.

"Peaceful for the moment," he said as he scanned the horizon, looking through the lights and shadows that dotted the opposite shore and wondering which ones the government agents were hiding behind.

He hadn't been able to warn anyone about the change in the departure time. It had seemed too big a risk to take. And he'd already been warned that the safest contact, once the trip began, was no contact. There shouldn't be any need. After all, the authorities knew where they were going, when they planned to pull into each port and when they would leave. There was a tracking device on the boat, and the Coast Guard would be monitoring radio transmissions.

Anything Deke needed to tell them, he could say when he returned—he hoped.

Still, he'd been warned that, even with them watching, if trouble struck he had to consider himself on his own. They might not be able to get to him fast enough to save his neck.

"It's beautiful, too," she said slowly, apparently surprised at her ability to find any peace or beauty in the midst of such uncertainty. "You must miss it so much when you can't get out on the water."

"No. In fact, I hate it," he said. He could trace the beginnings of the fix he was in right now to another trip on another sailboat.

He'd been twenty-four, headed for his final year of law school. He should have stayed where he was—bartending at night and working construction during the day—instead of taking that time off. He remembered making that decision, telling himself he deserved a break after the rigorous years of struggling to get himself through college and then law school.

Tommy Merriwether, Thomas's son, had been preparing to spend the last six weeks before the fall semester began transporting his father's boat back from the Caribbean to Virginia, and he'd needed help.

The pay had been almost nonexistent, but then, so had the work involved, especially to someone like Deke, who had, at the time, still loved the water, and had longed to be on it after so much time spent landlocked.

So he'd gone sailing, instead of working and then spending a few weeks at home before classes started.

Now he looked over his shoulder and down into the cabin, saw no sign of Russell or Ellen, heard no evidence that Jilly had awakened yet, and chafed at the lack of privacy available on a sailboat, even a big one like this.

"Come here." He pulled Liza over to stand behind the wheel, then encircled her with his arms. It was such a relief—one he didn't question, didn't even try to explain, to have her there within his arms, if only for a moment. "Take hold of the wheel."

He needed to teach her how to sail, he rationalized. Everyone would have to take a turn keeping watch. One person couldn't do it all by himself. It wasn't as if he were doing this just as an excuse to have her close. Besides, if they were this close, they could talk without worrying about Russell overhearing them.

"Pull the wheel back and forth a little bit to get the feel of it," Deke told her while he checked the depth meter and watched the water for channel markers. "See how much the boat shifts in the water as you turn the wheel?"

"Yes."

"Between the high-tech radar and the autopilot this boat practically drives itself." He showed her the dials and switches for both. "Once we get out into open water, all it needs is the coordinates of our destination, and the boat will take us there. It's only in tight spots like this that she needs some help."

They stood there for a long moment, the sun rising in the east, dolphins frolicking in the water off the stern.

Liza gave up and relaxed in his arms. She'd never understand this man—never figure out how he could frighten her one moment and make her feel so safe the next. She did feel safe—safe in his arms, here with the sun making a sparkling trail on the water. It was truly a beautiful spot.

"How could you hate this?" she asked curiously, standing on the tips of her toes to see over the bow to the darkened shoreline beyond.

"Easy. I was on a boat like this, learning to handle it, when my brother turned into a junkie," he said, and immediately wished he hadn't. Damn. What was it about her that made him lose sight of the fact that he had a cover to play out, that he couldn't afford to let details slip out from his real life?

He sighed inwardly, his thoughts turning to Charlie. Once he'd been convinced that he could have stopped all Charlie's problems then, before they'd ever gotten so serious. He would have known—wouldn't he?—if he'd been home where he belonged. Surely he would have spotted the signs when his fourteen-year-old brother started taking drugs.

"No," he said out loud, deciding that there was really no harm in telling her. Besides, somehow, he needed to tell her. "I'm not sure when he started, because I just wasn't around. The first time he got in trouble with the law over drugs, I was on a boat like this, learning to sail."

"So, it's the boat's fault."

He just stared at her for a moment, and she laughed.

"Don't you see? That makes about as much sense as blaming yourself for his problems. Surely you realize that? What about your brother's responsibility to take care of himself? What about your parents?"

"My father left home not long after Charlie was born, and my mother had her hands full just keeping a roof over our heads," he explained flatly.

He'd always looked after Charlie. He remembered one night when it had been storming and the electricity had gone out. It had been late, and his mother had still been at work—Charlie couldn't have been more than five or six at the time. He'd been scared to death of the lightning, the thunder and the way the big trees swayed back and forth in the howling wind.

Deke had held Charlie close, and they'd watched the storm together. And he'd promised to be there for his brother, always, no matter what.

He'd forgotten that promise over the years. And when Charlie had really needed him, he'd been off joyriding through the islands on a sailboat much like this one.

"He was just a kid," Deke said, his resolve stronger than ever to put everything right.

"And you weren't?" she shot back at him.

"I was twenty-four years old."

And even when he'd found out there was some problem, he hadn't taken it as seriously as he should have. He'd missed the signs, somehow, maybe because he'd wanted so badly to believe that his little brother could never have a serious drug problem and that he could never be so casual about breaking the law and getting caught.

Deke had dismissed Charlie's infractions as larks, the acts of a kid doing a little experimenting, maybe just trying to prove himself to a rough older crowd of kids he had no business hanging out with.

He'd rushed home for a week, at the most, sat Charlie down and made him promise to change his ways. But, worst of all, he'd whitewashed the problem even to Charlie, had offered excuses for his brother's behavior—his youth, his poor choice of friends—had even taken a good bit of the blame himself for not being there to watch over Charlie.

And then he'd left. His final year of law school had been starting, and he'd rushed off to North Carolina, hardly looking back.

He looked back now; he'd had plenty of time to do so. And he was determined to follow through with this crazy plan and buy his brother a second chance.

Liza shivered, despite the heat, as she stood in the tiny kitchen—no, the galley. She'd never get used to this boat talk.

She was struggling to make dinner, a creamy seafood stew, while the milk and vegetables were still fresh. They wouldn't keep for long on the boat; the generator that ran the refrigerator also ran the air conditioner, but not both at the same time. It was a tough choice to make, Liza thought, sweating and swaying with the boat as she struggled to cook in unfamiliar territory. She shivered when she felt a disconcerting pair of eyes on her back.

Nick Russell's eyes.

They'd been following her closely ever since she'd emerged from her room early this morning and had loaded her things onto the boat. He was nervous. He'd paced most of the day and had stared at the passing shoreline as they swept down the Intracoastal Waterway and then out into the ocean near Jacksonville, Florida.

Now, with Ellen trying her best to keep Jilly occupied in the cabin she shared with Nick, and Deke on watch, Russell finally had his chance to get her alone. She'd been expecting it all day. So why hadn't she figured out what she was going to tell him?

"Not so hard to stick close to him, is it?" Russell had a nasty grin on his face as he spoke.

Well, if she was going to tell him anything, the truth—at least a little of it—was the safest way to go. That way she wouldn't have to remember all of her lies and keep them straight.

"He's not so hard on the eyes," she said, and braced herself for more questions.

Russell threw back his head and laughed, then looked around the cabin as if he were worried about being overheard.

"So? What have you got?"

"I'm not sure." She braced for his anger. "What am I looking for?"

"I'll be the judge of that."

Liza shrank back against the cabinets. She couldn't help it.

She wanted, desperately, to get away from Nick Russell.

Liza hadn't wanted to leave the shelter of Deke's arms this morning as they'd stood on the deck and sailed away. Why? She had no answer for her own question. All she could do was listen to those little messages coming from deep inside her, down in the core of her being, the instincts she'd learned to trust when she had nothing else to guide her that told her she could trust in him.

"He hasn't told me much." She waited, but Russell waited, too, and she had to continue. "He says he's afraid of you."

Russell smiled—with his eyes alone.

Encouraged, Liza went on. "He—he didn't want me and Jilly to go on the trip."

That didn't make Russell happy.

"He thought we'd be a lot of trouble. That we'd be in the way."

"Well, he doesn't make the plans on this little job," Russell said. "*I* do. Don't you forget that. He works for me, and so do you."

"Of course," Liza said.

"You just do as I say and don't ask a lot of questions, and you'll be fine, you hear?" He stopped, watched her closely for a moment, then said, "Well? That's it? That's all you've gotten out of him? I'd have thought from the looks of things in his bedroom last night you'd know the man pretty well by now.''

Liza just stood there. She didn't want to argue with the man, and why should she? She didn't care what he thought of her. She shrugged her shoulders. ''We haven't had that much time—I mean, there hasn't been that much time for me to spend with him.''

''Well, you'll just have to find some time, now won't you? And I'll try to be more careful myself. I'd hate to interrupt the two of you again, especially since you seem so eager to get to know the man intimately.''

He was laughing crudely as he climbed the ladder that led to the deck, and Liza stood shakily against the counter and tried to pull herself together.

Let him think what he wanted. Let him think she was going to spy for him. It made more sense than openly defying him, and it would buy her time—at least a little—to figure out what she was going to do.

Turning back to the stew, she puzzled over her own tangled emotions.

She'd been afraid, more than she'd ever been in her life, as the boat had finally set sail. And she'd found herself drawn to Deke from the minute the boat had sailed. It was as if, the moment there was no more solid ground beneath her feet, the moment she realized that she was instantly, irrevocably in danger, she'd turned instinctively to him.

She'd wanted to ask him about the look in his eyes when he'd come to her room early in the morning to tell her they were leaving, to tell her it was too late to run.

And it occurred to her now, as she replayed those quiet moments in her bedroom, that his actions simply did not make sense. Neither did the manner in which he'd treated her.

Unless all he'd wanted—that time he'd kissed her beside the house, and later, when he'd threatened her with the knife—was to warn her away from this place and this trip? Farfetched as it seemed, instinct told her she was right.

He still frightened her, in more ways than one, but there was no denying that he intrigued her, as well. Somehow the fear was fading, and the curiosity about his true intentions was growing. It was that look in his eyes that had started this. The look in his eyes when he'd realized that she'd meant to run away early this morning but had been caught before she made it.

He was sorry that she hadn't made it. That was what she'd seen in his eyes—regret.

What if all he'd been trying to do was get her out of this mess, away from this place? What if he would have helped her get away?

And what about now, now that they were under way? Was it too late to ask for his help? Then again, could he do anything to help her now, even if he was willing?

It wasn't as if she were looking for someone to take care of her. Liza made it a practice to take care of herself. But she didn't know what she was facing here. She didn't know what might happen before the trip was over, and it would be smart to know, now, what sort of reception she'd get from him if she found herself in a situation that she couldn't handle alone and asked for his help.

Liza didn't believe in beating around the bush. She'd found that if she wanted to know something, the easiest way to find out was to ask.

So, she thought, resigning herself to the task before her, she'd just ask him.

Chapter 10

"Your brother. He's the one you're trying to protect, isn't he?"

Deke paused long enough to look down into the coffee mug Liza had just handed him.

They were standing on the deck, and the boat suddenly rocked beneath them. Deke was braced for it, but Liza wasn't. She fell back against him, and he caught her in his arms, managing to rescue her and save his coffee, as well.

"Easy. It takes a while to get used to the motion," he said, even as he welcomed the time it took to right both her and the drinks. He needed to figure out what he was going to say to her, although he could have done without the way his arms went so readily around her and the reluctance with which they set her free again.

It was almost sunrise, and he'd had the watch since midnight. Liza was taking over the six-to-noon shift—her first—and for now they were the only ones awake.

Deke downed the coffee in three gulps, then frowned at the empty cup when he remembered that he'd planned to go to sleep after turning over the helm to Liza.

"It's all right," she reassured him, reading him more easily than he would have liked. "It's decaf."

"Thanks."

Deke set the cup down, lifted the top of one of the bench seats and removed a bright orange life vest. "You will wear this whenever you're on the watch. Understand?"

"Yes, but I know how to swim."

"You know how to manage a survival swim, alone, for hours, in that ocean, if you get yourself thrown overboard and either we can't get back to you quick enough or we can't find you?"

She shook her head back and forth and put on the life vest without further argument.

Deke unhooked the safety belt from his waist then, fastened it matter-of-factly around her narrow waist and tried to ignore the brush of his hands against her side and her stomach.

"You don't ever let yourself be alone on this deck unless you're wearing that vest. And you don't leave this space—" he pointed out the pitlike seating area behind the steering column "—without this safety line attached. All right?"

"All right."

"There's enough line to let you get from the bow to the stern, but if you start to topple over the side, it'll catch you."

"Okay," she said quickly, big eyes solemnly trained on him.

He took the small silver whistle hanging from a rope around his neck and put it around hers. "And you keep this right here. If you get into trouble, all you have to do is whistle."

"In case the safety line doesn't catch me or the life vest won't hold me up in the water?"

"Right. Trouble comes up fast out here, and you can't be too careful."

"On any boat? Or on this trip in particular?" Liza watched his every move.

He halted in the midst of putting his own life vest away, finished the task and then turned to face her. "On any boat—but, yeah, on this one in particular."

She closed her eyes and prayed that she wasn't making a big mistake in confronting him, prayed that her instincts were right about him. "It is about your brother, isn't it? That's why you're doing this?"

"Leave it alone, Liza."

Deke didn't want to confess his troubles to her, not any more than he'd already done on deck yesterday morning.

Liza pressed on. She needed to know where he stood. And it was better to find out now, when for the moment she was relatively safe, than later, in the midst of whatever kind of trouble lay ahead. "I've been thinking a lot about that bit with the knife on the boat two days ago."

Deke fiddled with a few gauges on the boat, messing up the settings and then fixing them again. Why couldn't the woman just leave it alone?

"It didn't make any sense to me. You haven't been exactly friendly, yet you haven't been threatening, either. I figure if you really wanted to hurt me you've had more than enough opportunity already."

"Is there some point to this?" he asked, his back to her, seemingly enthralled by the controls he'd been looking at for hours. "Because I've been up all night, and I'm ready for some sleep."

"I don't think you meant to hurt me at all."

"Oh." He tried to sound immensely uninterested.

"I think you were just trying to scare me, to keep me from making this trip because you know what's going on. You've already told me it's going to be dangerous."

Deke smiled then, even as he was cursing under his breath, because she was so unlike any woman he'd encountered in a long time. She didn't give up. She didn't back down, and she refused to be afraid of him. Why couldn't she just be afraid of him? Why couldn't she stay away?

"I think you must have actually been trying to do me a favor, to keep me out of a dangerous situation, and that tells me that you're not the big bad guy you're pretending to be."

He was grim and determined as he turned around to face her again. Maybe he couldn't scare her, but he couldn't have her thinking he was her damn knight in shining armor, either.

"Look," he said intensely, "you don't even know how bad I can be. I'm not sure I know myself, but I have a feeling I will before this is over."

She refused to back down. Her eyes stared into his, challenging him. She stood nearly toe-to-toe with him on the deck, braced against the sway of the boat as it rose and fell on the gentle waves, silently waiting.

"Damn stubborn, interfering woman. Look, I have a job to do, and I'm going to do it. You just stay out of my way, stay the hell out of Russell's, and you might come out of this all right."

"Fair enough," she said shortly.

It wasn't enough to satisfy him. "And that doesn't mean that if all hell breaks loose you can come running to me and I'll make it all better, because I can't. I don't even know if I can save myself."

"Fine."

He wanted to strangle her right then and there, and he couldn't for the life of him understand whether it just didn't show in his face or whether she simply refused to accept it.

Deke cursed again and somehow found himself asking aloud, "Why couldn't you just be afraid of me?"

There—he'd as much as admitted it. Liza had to fight to keep from smiling. She was right. He had been trying to scare her away from this trip, which meant that in his own way, he must have been trying to help her.

All of a sudden, it didn't seem so bad that he was probably the sexiest man she'd ever come across. And it made it easier to live with the way he had of setting off little butterflies in her stomach with just a look from those dark eyes of his.

"I was afraid, a little, sometimes. Russell frightens me more."

Deke laughed bitterly. "Good. You damn well should be scared of him. He scares the hell out of me."

"Then why are you here?" She wanted to know more now, so much more about him. "Why are you working for him?"

"I don't have a choice." He watched her as he said the words, and knew she didn't believe him.

"Everybody has choices," she said bitterly, and he wondered at the choices she'd been forced to make.

"All right. I have choices," he admitted. "I just don't like any of them."

"Neither do I—my own, I mean."

She put her hand on his arm, her touch light and undemanding, and he wondered how long it had been since anyone had sought to comfort him with a mere touch. Too long. Yet it hadn't been so long that he didn't recognize it for what it was, and it made him puzzle over her even more.

"I appreciate what you were trying to do, Deke. The warning, I mean—that day by the house and then on the boat with the knife—even if I do think your methods were a bit extreme."

God, she was teasing him now, he realized. He had to get away from this woman.

"Wait." She caught him with that hand again when he would have left, then looked down into the cabin to be sure no one was near.

Liza took a deep breath and considered whether to tell him the rest. It was a risk. She couldn't be sure what he would do with the information. But she wanted him to know, wanted to confide in him and, somehow, believed he would help her in this. "I want you to understand that I have a job to do, too, and I'm going to do it. I made a promise, to my sister, and I'm going to keep it."

Sister? Deke was perfectly still as the possibilities dawned on him, as did the complications each one would bring. "Jilly's your sister?"

"No, she's my niece. Ellen's my sister... and I promised her I'd take care of Jilly."

He should have known that, Deke thought. He should have been able to find that out, and he hadn't. And he had a sinking feeling deep in his gut that she was telling him the truth.

"You can't even be sure that you can take care of yourself out here," he protested, "much less take care of someone else."

"Maybe I can't," Liza admitted. "But I'm all she's got right now, and I'm going to protect her as best I can."

"Why?" It was none of his business. *She* was none of his business, and he still wanted—*needed*—to know what had driven her to do what she was doing.

"Ellen wasn't always like this," Liza explained softly. "When I was Jilly's age, she was the only person I could count on. If I hadn't had her to stand up for me, to stand between me and my mother and her string of husbands, I don't know what would have happened to me."

"Liza..." he protested wearily.

"I *owe her,* Deke. She's my sister, and she needs my help. You can't tell me you don't understand that."

"No, I can't, but it doesn't change anything. You can't protect her any more than you can protect yourself."

He turned to go, to try to find some place to think this through, to make it work even under these circumstances.

"Wait," she said. "You can't tell Nick Russell."

"Tell him what?"

She seemed genuinely frightened now. "That I'm Ellen's sister."

"He doesn't know?" This was getting worse, Deke realized.

"I don't think so."

"How could he not know?"

"There's no reason he would. Neither one of us has told him, and it's not like Ellen ever brought him home to meet the family when they got married."

"Still," Deke protested, "she must have talked about you, told him your name, described you?"

"Ellen couldn't have described me if she'd wanted to." The hurt was there for anyone to hear. "She ran away from home a long time ago, and she never looked back. Until this summer, I hadn't seen her in fifteen years."

Fifteen years? And she'd never looked back? It hit a little too close to home to Deke to see the pain in her face as she talked about losing her sister. He'd been away from his home for thirteen years himself, and he wondered if Charlie had felt as deserted by his big brother as Liza obviously felt about the way her sister had left home.

Fifteen years, he thought grimly, and shook his head.

"And you still—" Love her? he wanted to ask. Care about her? Still think she cares about you? "You're still willing to take a risk like this to help her?"

"She's my sister, and she needs me," Liza repeated simply. "Of course I want to help her."

How could he argue with that? Deke wondered. He couldn't, not given the position he'd put himself in.

She'd been right; she'd been able to tell by the look in his eyes. And it hadn't been as hard as she'd thought it would be to stand up to him.

Liza smiled as she sat on the deck and watched glorious shades of lavender and pink sweep across the horizon just before the sun rose.

It had been something of a risk, to confront him like that, but she figured that whatever Deke and Russell were planning, it did involve real danger. And a woman in danger needed to know who she could trust and who she couldn't.

Well, she thought, trust was probably too strong a word, but she did need to know who she could turn to for help if she needed it. There'd been no question of confronting him with her suspicions, or, when it came right down to it, of revealing her true situation.

Her choices, if she needed help, were slim. Ellen was useless. Russell was pure evil, if she could judge from her own gut reactions to him—and from the honest fear Ellen seemed to have for her husband.

That left no one but Deke.

She'd been up half the night, trying to recall every moment she'd ever spent with him, and once she'd done that it hadn't been hard to figure out that the episode with the knife was the only thing that didn't fit.

Liza had studied people long enough to know that people always gave themselves away, not in the rare outbursts of temper or anger that stuck in someone's mind, but in the way they carried themselves through their everyday lives.

So she'd zeroed in on the knife incident, and the kiss he'd given her that day in the backyard. Neither one of them had made any sense to her before, until she'd thought of what he might do if he wanted to scare her, to get her out of a dangerous situation. And last night she'd completed the puzzle. Because getting her out of a dangerous situation made sense only if, in some way, he was trying to help her.

Oh, yes, he'd claimed he was no knight in shining armor. But she didn't need one. She just needed someone who would be more likely to help her than hurt her, and, as much as he'd protested, Liza was betting he'd come down on her side if she truly needed him.

Now she could only hope that she wouldn't need his help—or anyone else's.

Chapter 11

Shortly after sunrise on their third day out, a bleary-eyed Deke was exhausted. Trapped somewhere between sleep and waking, he lay in bed—her borrowed bed—still warm from her body, still smelling lightly of spring flowers, of her.

He groaned, rolled onto his back and put his forearm over his eyes.

There was a bunk, a three-sided box cut into the side of the boat with a curtain hanging over the side for privacy out in the main cabin where he'd intended to sleep. But there was always someone rustling around in the cabin, and Jilly was there now. They were trying to keep Jilly in there as much as possible, in fact, because she scared them all to death on deck. A boat was no place for an active three-year-old who had no fear of falling over the side.

Anyway, after going without sleep for the better part of two days, he'd abandoned the bunk and decided to take Liza up on her offer to let him share her and Jilly's bed.

Liza wasn't using it when he needed it, so what was the big deal, anyway?

Her warmth, he thought—that was the big deal. Her warmth lingered long after she'd left to take over the watch; that, and her scent.

And the problem was, the longer he lay there, the more he wanted to be in her bed, with her right there beside him, and he had no business wanting that. Even now, exhausted and barely able to keep his eyes open, he was lying awake thinking about her when he should have been getting what little sleep his schedule allowed.

There was a rhythm to living on a sailboat, and they had all fallen into it. Someone was always on watch and someone else sleeping. All day someone was watching Jilly and someone else was probably cooking a meal.

He had the watch from noon to 6:00 p.m. Ellen took over from 6:00 to midnight, then Deke again until sunrise. Liza had the final leg, from 6:00 a.m. until noon. Originally Russell had had a turn, but he had this annoying habit of abandoning his post. The man was nervous, and when he was nervous, he had to move, preferably to pace. Deke couldn't stand to watch Russell stroll around the boat on his watch.

On a quiet night, with no boat traffic in sight, high visibility across the water and the wind low, Deke could understand someone taking a break—ten or fifteen minutes to grab a sandwich or something to drink. Between the radar, the depth gauge and the autopilot, the boat really did practically sail itself. Still, sailors were cautious people. Most of them believed, like Deke, that there was no substitute for a real brain and a set of human eyes and ears.

It was bad enough to have to depend on Ellen for a shift. But Russell was even worse, because they just couldn't get him to stay up there in front of the controls. Deke was uneasy with Ellen there, but he comforted himself with the fact that she *did* stay there, and even if she ran into trouble, all she had to do was yell or blow the little whistle he put around her neck every evening when he turned the boat over to her. Deke could be there within seconds if she called.

All of which went to prove that there was a lot of work to be done, especially with Jilly to watch. There shouldn't be a lot of time for him to spend thinking about a woman, much less fantasizing about her.

They were in close quarters, and there was no avoiding anyone on the boat, even if he wanted to do so. But he found himself watching for her, watching over her, waiting for her and the few moments they managed to share each day.

He found himself waiting for her all night on the watch. She always showed up a few minutes early, bringing him a cup of hot coffee and a smile that would help him get through his day.

He blustered and barked at her—tried his best, anyway—but she just kept coming back for more, stayed as friendly as she had been before, and kept telling him things he didn't want to know about her.

He'd never have admitted it to her, but these quiet, peaceful moments they spent together had come to be his favorite part of the day.

For a while he could forget what was ahead of him and simply be a man enjoying the company of an enticing woman.

And entice him she did, although he couldn't have said why.

She was small-boned, slimmer than she needed to be, slighter. He'd tried to look at her objectively, as nothing more than a stranger looking over a stranger. Admittedly, she wasn't the kind of woman who would turn a lot of men's heads, but there was something about her, a vulnerability that made a man want to protect her from all harm, mixed with a spunkiness that was both exasperating and exhilarating.

Deke didn't see how she'd survived. From what she'd told him, her mother was a weak, selfish woman who'd spent her whole life running from one man to another, trying to find someone who could take care of her in the manner to which she wanted to become accustomed.

And the older and more worn down her mother had become, the worse the men she'd attracted had become.

Ellen—an Ellen he couldn't imagine by looking at the woman *she'd* become—had shielded Liza from the worst of it, but then Ellen had abandoned her, maybe for the same reason Liza had left herself.

She hadn't told him exactly why she'd run away from home as a teenager, but he had a strong suspicion that one of her mother's "husbands" had decided Liza was a lot more appealing than her mother.

The amazing thing was what she'd done since then. She'd attended classes at three colleges and if she'd actually been enrolled all that time she'd nearly have a degree in liberal arts, at least. Of course, she hadn't had the money to go officially all that time.

It turned out that the first place she'd run to was the University of Michigan, where a high school friend of hers was attending college. Luckily for Liza, the girls' roommate had moved out of the dorm and shacked up with a guy. Liza had had a room for free that year.

She'd gotten work where she could find it at night and had sat in on classes during the day, either by just slipping into the back row and keeping her mouth shut or later, once she'd found out she could for free, auditing the classes until she came up with the money to enroll.

It amazed him, but she'd gotten away with it for years, either finding other friends with half-empty dorm rooms or piling into cheap apartments with a half-dozen other college students, working and going to school. It was a shame she hadn't actually been enrolled the whole time. She was obviously smart and wanted to learn, while half the students Deke remembered from undergraduate school had simply been trying to put off growing up for as long as they could by staying in school and letting their parents foot the bill.

Deke admired Liza—her determination, her spirit, her smile. Trouble was, he found himself admiring her body as much as her brain.

He punched the pillow once, then again, and willed himself to sleep.

Deke woke up with a female sprawled over his chest. Unfortunately, it was a three-foot-tall three-year-old female, and she was upset.

"Jilly?"

She was crying in her sleep, and he sat her up on his belly and tried to wake her. He glanced at his watch, saw that it was almost 10:00 a.m., and wondered what she was still doing here. Jilly usually woke up by eight, and, after he convinced her that he had no intention of playing with her at that hour, she usually ran out into the main cabin to find her mother.

"Hey?" he said as she continued to cry through sleepy, half-closed eyes, "What's the trouble?"

"Oooh . . .'pit up."

"What?" Deke said, afraid he already knew, but hoping she meant something else. She looked a little green to him, and he was afraid he "smelled" trouble.

Then he found the problem. The child had been sick. He tried to get her off him, and when he sat her down on the bunk beside him he plopped her right down in it.

She squealed. He cursed and lifted her back up, and in his scramble to get off the bed he'd got the mess all over himself, as well.

Finally they were both standing by the bed. The mess was everywhere. On the bed, on his shirt, in her hair, on her pajamas.

"I 'pit up!" She stuck her lip out and wailed. "I need Wiza!"

"Hell, so do I."

He didn't know where to begin to deal with a mess like this, or a female the size of this one. Of course, he thought, he didn't know how to deal with any female these days, so it should come as no surprise.

Jilly just stood there looking up at him, like he was supposed to fix everything and make it all better—like he could, even if he wanted to.

"Oh, hell!" He stripped off his own soiled shirt first and was grateful that he managed that without getting any of the stinky stuff on the rest of him.

Then he bent down so that he was at eye level with Jilly, wondering how he could get her out of her soiled pajamas without getting "spit-up" all over her in the process.

"Oooh," she moaned.

" 'Oooh' is right. You stay here while I get a wash cloth so I can clean you up, okay?"

She smiled a little then, her eyes big and round and tear-filled, her lower lip trembling. Something—he couldn't place it exactly—something about her brought back a memory of him taking care of Charlie when he'd been about her age and sick with the chicken pox.

Charlie had been so little, so helpless, so dependent on Deke. And back then there hadn't been any kind of trouble Charlie found that Deke wasn't able to handle.

He grabbed a towel off the closet shelf, wrapped Jilly up in it, sat down on the cabin floor and held her close, because he sensed that she needed that right now more than she needed to be cleaned up. She cried a little more, sputtered, hiccuped and then quieted.

He just held her close and found himself missing those times with Charlie, missing the simplicity of the trials they'd faced, missing the way Charlie had looked up to him, believed in him, depended upon him.

He'd missed a lot of years with his brother, years he couldn't get back, and he'd made a lot of mistakes. It made him even more determined to put things to rights, to follow through with his plans, but it also made him vow that the little girl in his arms would come through this unharmed. He would see to that.

"You all right now?" he said when she started to squirm free.

"Need to 'pit up s'more."

That lower lip came out again, and the color fled her face. Deke moved quickly. He pulled the towel free and spread it on the floor, and with his help, Jilly managed to get the worst of the mess on the towel this time.

She was so pitiful when she looked up at him that time and held out her arms. He pulled the mostly clean blanket off the bed, wrapped her up in it and pulled her close again.

"Oh, hell!" he said after a moment, as the smell came on stronger than before.

"No! No! No!" Jilly scolded, pulling away. "You're not s'pposed to say that. It's a bad, bad word."

"Well, I'm a bad, bad man."

Female laughter greeted his words, but it wasn't Jilly's. Liza was standing in the doorway.

"No, Deke MacCauley." She smiled. "What you are is a fraud."

Her eyes held his for a long moment, and he swallowed hard, reminding himself sternly, even as he bristled against the idea, that he had to keep his distance from her, as much for his sake as for hers.

"Wiza, I 'pit up," Jilly announced.

The little girl frowned, tearing up again and saving Deke from having to answer Liza.

"Oh, sweetie! What's the matter?" Liza pulled her close, blanket and all. "What's wrong?"

"Tummy hurts."

"Still?" Liza cooed.

Jilly considered for a moment, then shook her head. "No."

"It's better now?" Liza went to stroke the little girl's hair, but found spit-up there, as well.

In spite of the chill that had come over him when Liza had called him a fraud, Deke couldn't help smiling at the face she made now. Hiding his smile, he turned his back to her while he rummaged around in the head, gathering up a couple of wet washcloths, some soap, and another clean towel.

"Where do we start?" he asked, once he'd collected everything.

Liza held up the hand she'd been using to stroke Jilly's hair. Deke hesitated—he'd been trying to keep his distance from her, and touching her was not going to be easy.

She was sitting on the bed, holding Jilly on her lap. Carefully, mentally preparing himself for contact with the warm, soft woman he'd been fantasizing about for too many long and hard nights, he sat down beside her on the bed. He took her hand in one of his, and slowly—too slowly he feared—he wiped off her hand.

Both of the females smiled at him then, and he frowned for all he was worth.

"You are a fraud," Liza repeated, certainty ringing in her voice. "I'm more certain of it than ever."

Why? Of all the women he could have found himself trapped with on this boat, why did it have to be her? Why couldn't she be scared of him? Why couldn't she be more cautious? Less inclined to speak her mind? Less stubborn? Less willful? Less desirable?

"Who's driving this boat?" he asked sharply.

"No one," she said, still smiling at him. "Do you want to drive, or do you want to clean?"

"Drive, definitely."

And with that he escaped—for the moment.

She came looking for him that night, soon after Ellen went to bed and Deke came up on deck for his shift.

"So..." She settled into the cushions behind him. "Tell me again what a bad, bad man you are."

Here it comes, Deke thought. The interrogation. He had been expecting it, so he should have been prepared. But even if he wasn't, he told himself, she was just a woman. It wasn't like she could make him tell her anything.

She could guess, she could suppose, but that was all it would be—her own suppositions. He wouldn't confirm anything.

"Liza, just leave it alone, okay?" He stayed at the wheel, his back to her, and hoped it didn't sound as much like a plea as his ears told him it did. "All I did was try to help a sick kid."

"You treat her better than her own father does, and she knows that, too. Kids' intuition is even better than adults', and that child is crazy about you."

Jilly did have this annoying habit of following him around lately, and if she was any kind of an example, females must learn to flirt in the cradle. But what the hell was he supposed to do about that? Growl at her, too? It sure hadn't gotten him anywhere with Liza.

"She's better?" He was hoping to change the subject.

"Not much. She's sleeping, thank goodness. But as soon as she wakes up and I try to get some liquids down her she throws it right back up."

"Is it serious?"

"Probably just a bug. I think it's been going around at home. We'll see how she is tomorrow. As long as we can keep some liquids down her by then, we shouldn't have to worry."

"And if we can't?"

"Well, the biggest problem is dehydration. Kids can go without food for days, but not without liquids. We'll have to get her to a doctor if we can't do that. Is that possible?"

"I think so. Once we reach Jamaica, we shouldn't have any trouble finding a doctor. We should make port around noon."

"Good."

She stood, and he sensed the movement. He felt the tension in him begin to ease. She was going below. She'd be out of reach, and he'd be much happier.

But she didn't go. She paused directly behind him, and then he felt her hands at either side of his waist. Deke bit back a curse and held himself rigid beneath her touch.

Her hands were soft, gentle, undemanding, and yet the feel of them scared him to death.

He didn't do anything to encourage her—he made sure of that. But he wasn't able to bring himself to discourage her either, and when he didn't show any resistance, she moved closer. Liza wrapped her hands around his waist and leaned into him, her front pressed to his back, her head resting against his shoulder.

This was where she wanted to be. She grew more certain of it every day. She wanted to be close enough to feel the heat of his body, to feel his chest expand with every breath he took.

She needed to be close enough to figure out exactly what he was up to, how deep into trouble he was and whether she could help him get out. Because there was something about him—something that couldn't be explained in words. It could only be felt. He made her feel—alive and hopeful, strong and sexy, desperate to be a little closer and determined to find a way to make it work between them.

Deke felt her sigh, felt every breath she took, felt the fine trembling she set off deep inside him and wondered how long it would be before she felt it, too.

"Would it be so awful to be my friend? Just friends? Everybody needs a friend now and then."

"I don't," he said tersely, and gripped the wheel in a punishing hold, because it wasn't at all what he wanted to be holding. "I need a little time, a little luck, and a clear head. That's all, and I can make it."

Still, she didn't move, and it was torture to have her this close and not touch her, as well.

Deke turned, expecting that by doing so he would make her back off. But the move didn't bring any distance between them. She didn't drop her arms, and he found himself even closer than before, where he both wanted and didn't want to be.

Through the muted lights of the control panel and in the darkness that lay beyond them, he stared down at her.

Her chin came up just a fraction, bringing her lips even closer to his, *too* close to his.

"That's all you need?" She hesitated before she said it, enough that he knew she wasn't asking carelessly, knew she was aware of exactly how he would take the question.

He swore out loud then. His hands gripped her upper arms, not allowing her to move any closer, but not pushing her away, either. "We can't be 'just friends.' That's not what this is about."

"I don't understand just what this *is* about, but I'm not running away from it."

"If you were smart, you would, and if I were a better man, I'd make sure that you did," he said angrily. But then his eyes wandered to her mouth, those full, lush—

He felt his lips moving down closer to hers before he could think about it, felt the pull, stronger than any wind he'd ever encountered on the seas.

She sighed softly as he erased the distance between them and brought her body to rest fully against his.

The wind was blowing softly, and it had chilled her skin. He warmed her. It had blown her hair up around her face, but he caught it in his hand and smoothed it back behind her ears. Once he'd settled her against him, once he could feel every dip and sway of her body, once he was so aroused there was no mistaking it, he brought his lips down to hers.

She was expecting him to kiss her. He knew by the way her lips parted ever so slightly, by the way they rose, a fraction of an inch, up to meet his. But her eyes were closed, and he didn't like that. He wanted to see those indigo eyes of hers, because they would tell him things that she wouldn't.

Deke fought back his own impatience, let go of his own reluctance, and kissed her lazily but thoroughly. Then he drew back and waited.

Finally she opened her eyes. He smiled—he couldn't help himself—at the desire there in the smoky, steamy depths. A desire she made no effort to hide from him, one that invited him to come to her, to give and to take, to show her the way it could be between them.

His body ached for her, had for so long that he couldn't remember when he hadn't been fighting the feeling, and even as he told himself to be careful, he could feel his desire roaring out of control.

If she'd been anyone else, if they'd been in any other situation, he wouldn't have hesitated for an instant to make her his.

But she wasn't anybody else. He wasn't free to do as he wished, and dishonesty had never sat well with him within the confines of an intimate relationship. He'd been nothing but dishonest with her; how could he possibly entangle her life with his, even if only for the moment? Worse than that, he'd subjected her to a danger she didn't even know existed.

No, he couldn't take her. But, by God, he couldn't let her go yet, either.

He lifted his head and scanned the horizon. It was an absolutely clear night, and he could see for a few miles, at least. Nothing ahead of them. Nothing behind them. Nothing showing on the radar screen. He had a few minutes. Surely he could take a few minutes with her.

"Come here." He whispered it urgently, even as he propelled her backward, then down against the cushions in the seating area at the back of the boat. He followed her down, covering her body with his, and she smiled up at him, scrambling his senses.

Her mouth opened eagerly beneath his. Her hands clutched him to her, even as her body arched. Deke kissed her again and again and again—he had more than enough doubts about his self-control, and kissing seemed the safest option open to him. But he hadn't counted on how intoxicating the sweet taste of her mouth would be, nor how eagerly her body would undulate against his.

He kissed her once more, long and slow, desire seeping through his body like a potent, addictive drug. His hands were up under her T-shirt, and then his lips were there, too, stroking back and forth across her breasts, one after the other, then back again.

She writhed and moaned beneath him. Her body silently begged him for more, and somehow he found his hands stripping away her shorts, then her cotton panties, and cupping her bare bottom in his hands.

He stroked her then, intimately, stoking the fires until they burned higher and higher, feeling her body rising off the soft cushions and moving sensuously against his hand.

"Oh, please," she begged, and he wondered if she even knew what she was begging for. "Please."

"Just let go, Liza," he coaxed, his voice rough. "Let go and follow me."

Trust me, he meant, though he didn't use the words. He'd never before asked for her trust, but he needed it now, trust in the most intimate sense. Strange, he realized, to ask her to trust him in this way and this way alone.

And trust him she did. She gave herself up to the feeling, to his touch, his kiss, his nearness. Deke felt her body tense, go still beneath his, then melt, limp and lifeless, back into the cushions.

He watched her eyes. They'd opened—in surprise? Yes . . . He couldn't help but smile as he recognized her surprise at the little bit of simple pleasure he'd shown her.

She deserved more, much more, from a man, and he desperately wanted to be the man to show her how much more pleasure could exist between a man and a woman.

But he couldn't be that man. He knew that, even as he continued to stroke her, slowly now, softly, gently easing her back down to reality. He kissed her some more, kissed her eyes closed, kissed her soft cheek, her warm lips, and wished he could kiss her straight through until morning, morning after morning.

"Why?" she asked, between his soft, soothing kisses. "Why did you stop?"

He could make himself let her go, make himself get to his feet and brace himself against the quiet pitch and roll of the boat. He could get the words out, but he couldn't keep the longing out of his voice. "Because I had no business starting this in the first place."

"You . . . didn't want to stop?"

Deke had turned his back to her to give her time to sort out her clothes, but at her question he turned to face her again. With her clothes rumpled, her face flushed and her eyes as big as the moon, she stood there, as determined as he'd ever seen her. He should have expected that, and he decided that the best way to counter it was to be perfectly honest but tell her as little as possible.

"Would that be enough, Liza?" He stood rigid before her, afraid to touch her, because he might not get away this time. "Could it be enough, if I admitted that I wanted you at least as much as you wanted me? If I told you I haven't gotten a decent night's sleep since I got on this boat, because I keep turning over onto my belly in that bed and burying my nose in the pillow, because it still carries your scent, because usually the bed's still warm and I know the warmth came from you?

"If I admitted to all that, would it be enough?" He whispered it, and the sound barely carried above the soft hissing of the wind and the waves.

She looked at him, the questions hanging there between them, unasked but still there.

"Could you just let it go at that, Liza? Because there's nothing else I can tell you, and I don't want to lie to you."

He thought she'd protest for sure. Instead, she just stood there, hurt and confused. "For now," she whispered. "I'll . . . For now."

He barely heard her response as she slipped past him, went below and left him to a long night of aching loneliness.

Chapter 12

Three days later midnight had come and gone, and Liza figured she'd waited long enough for Deke to come to her. If she waited for him, she might well wait forever.

She set off after him in a cab. The villa Russell had rented for the time they were in port sat on a hillside overlooking the secluded harbor where they'd docked the boat. Over the years, its occupants had beaten a path down the hill to the beach below. She usually took the path to the beach, but not tonight.

It had rained off and on since they'd arrived in Jamaica three days before, and the last time she'd tried the path it had been slippery and muddy. That wouldn't do for what she had in mind now.

It had been a trying three days.

Russell, if possible, had grown more tense with each passing hour. He'd prowled around the house, snapping and snarling at anyone who got in his way.

Ellen had hidden in her bedroom, when she wasn't helping Liza with Jilly. The two women had run themselves ragged trying to keep Jilly out of the rain and out of Russell's way.

But at night, once Jilly was asleep, Liza could only think of Deke. He kept to himself by staying on the boat. The man was avoiding her, but she wasn't going to let him get away with it any longer.

Liza settled herself into the cab, arranging the billowy white skirt of her dress around her and tugging, a little self-consciously, at the low bodice of the strapless gown she wore. She took a deep breath. She wasn't sure what made her more nervous—the night she'd planned, or the cab ride. Jamaicans had to be the most reckless drivers she'd encountered thus far in her life. A mere cab ride was a test of courage here.

Oh, well, she thought. If she could stand the ride, then she could certainly follow through on the rest of her scheme.

Liza was planning to seduce the man. Then she was planning to pry out of him, one way or another, just what he and Nick Russell were really doing on this trip.

And then they'd deal with it. Liza was certain they could. He wasn't a terrible person. She was sure of that. Evil had a presence in people, a presence that could rarely be hidden for long, and she'd never sensed it in him.

Whatever kind of mess he was in, he could surely get out of it, especially since they hadn't yet done whatever they'd set out to do.

She knew that by the growing tension in both Russell and Deke. But she also sensed that they were going to make their move soon, and she intended to make hers first.

She wanted to knock down every barrier between them, and then she wanted to be his. She wanted to belong to him and have him belong to her in the most intimate way possible. Let him try to keep his distance then!

Seduction, confession, and then solutions. It was a good plan—if only she could follow through with it. She knew there were solutions to all their problems. Together they would find them. Liza had made her way through every bit

of trouble life had ever thrown at her, and this would be no
different. It had to be no different, because she wasn't interested in simply having an affair with Deke. She was
thinking more and more that what she wanted was...
forever.

The first step was the seduction.

She could do that. It wasn't as if she'd never seduced a
man before—of course, her only other subject had been an
eighteen-year-old, and it didn't take a lot to seduce a teenager.

But all in all, it had been a highly successful move on her
part. At seventeen, soon after she'd run away from home,
Liza had decided to face the biggest fear she'd carried with
her when she'd left.

She'd watched her mother make a fool of herself over
more men than she could count. It seemed her mother
needed a man in much the same way she needed food on the
table and a roof over her head. Men were a necessity to her
emotional well-being.

Liza had been openly critical of her mother's life-style,
until the day her mother had started firing back. Her best
ammunition had been the warning that Liza would find
men just as necessary as she had, that once Liza knew the
pleasures a man could bring her she'd never be without one
in her life again.

The thought had scared Liza to death, and at seventeen
she'd decided she'd worried enough about it. She'd set out
to seduce the first attractive boy she could find.

Kenny Roberts, a college freshman majoring in engi-
neering, hadn't put up much of a fight. And sleeping with
him hadn't made much of an impression on Liza.

Oh, it hadn't been terrible, but it hadn't been particularly memorable, either. Nothing she was compelled to experience again and again. Nothing to cause her to make a
fool of herself. Nothing that would rule her life as it had her
mother's.

But Kenny Roberts had been a mere boy.

Deke MacCauley was a man, and obviously an experienced one. A man who set her nerve endings to tingling, one who at times frightened her, but who also excited her, frustrated her, confused her and even, she suspected, protected her, although he'd never have admitted to the last.

He left her breathless and longing for more.

"Oh, Lord!" What was she getting herself into? She nearly tripped over her own high-heeled sandals as she got out of the cab, then paid the driver and made her way down the private dock to the boat.

Liza wondered how Deke would react to her appearance tonight. He'd pointedly ignored her for the three days they'd spent in Jamaica, but she wasn't going to put up with that treatment any longer.

He wanted her. She could feel it—that unmistakable tug of desire that relentlessly pulled her ever closer to him, was drawing him to her, too.

Yet he resisted—surely because of whatever he was hiding from her. Whatever the problem was, it was keeping him from coming to her, and she'd had enough of that. *She* was going to find *him*.

She stepped onto the gently rocking boat, then paused to rid herself of her sandals. Then she heard the voice. Not Deke's. Russell's.

"Damn," she whispered, turning to leave. She'd been sure Deke would be alone on the boat. He'd spent the last two nights here, when she knew Russell had been at the villa.

Liza was putting her sandals back on and wondering how she'd get back to the villa when Russell's voice got louder.

"I told you, I'm going to take care of everything," he practically shouted. "We got into the country without any trouble from customs, didn't we? We'll slip out and get back in again the same way."

Customs? Liza wasn't sure what the usual procedure was, but she hadn't seen any customs officials when they'd docked here. Russell had simply taken their passports to the customs office to be stamped to show they'd entered the country.

"I hope so." That was Deke's voice she heard now. "Getting caught with a few hundred thousand dollars on board is one thing. Getting nailed with a few hundred pounds of Colombia's finest is another."

Colombia's finest? Liza stopped cold. It couldn't be. Surely they weren't talking about what she thought they were talking about. Deke wouldn't do that.

"We're not going to get nailed with anything," Russell said. "We're going to sail on down there, nice and easy, give them the money, load up our coke and make our way back home."

Liza couldn't help it. She gasped. Then she jumped up, one shoe on, one shoe off. The second one clattered across the deck—the sound seeming unnaturally loud in the otherwise quiet night.

"What the hell?"

Russell growled as he ran up the steps to the deck with a look on his face that frightened her as much as the gun in his hand.

He grabbed her by the arm and pulled her roughly to her feet.

"Well," Russell said, leering at her, "what a surprise."

If the punishing grip Russell had on her arm and the gun he had shoved against her shoulder weren't enough to scare her to death, the look on Deke's face was. He was obviously furious, though she could have sworn fear had flashed in his eyes when he'd raced up behind Russell.

Why would he worry? Liza wondered bitterly. Surely Deke MacCauley, drug smuggler, wouldn't worry about a little gun. Besides, he had a gun himself.

"I guess you heard enough to know where we're going tomorrow," Russell snarled.

"Fishing," Liza snapped. "Isn't that what you said? Deep-sea—"

She gasped as he twisted her arm a little tighter and brought her face down closer to his.

NO RISK, NO OBLIGATION TO BUY…NOW OR EVER!

GUARANTEED

PLAY "ROLL A DOUBLE" AND GET AS MANY AS FIVE GIFTS!

HERE'S HOW TO PLAY:

1. Peel off label from front cover. Place it in space provided at right. With a coin, carefully scratch off the silver dice. This makes you eligible to receive two or more free books, and possibly another gift, depending on what is revealed beneath the scratch-off area.

2. You'll receive brand-new Silhouette Intimate Moments® novels. When you return this card, we'll rush you the books and gift you qualify for ABSOLUTELY FREE!

3. Then, if we don't hear from you, every month we'll send you 6 additional novels to read and enjoy months before they are available in stores. You can return them and owe nothing, but if you decide to keep them, you'll pay only $2.71* each plus 25¢ delivery and applicable sales tax, if any*. That's the complete price, and—compared to cover prices of $3.39 each in stores—quite a bargain!

4. When you subscribe to the Silhouette Reader Service™, you'll also get our newsletter, as well as additional free gifts from time to time.

5. You must be completely satisfied. You may cancel at any time simply by sending us a note or a shipping statement marked "cancel" or by returning any shipment to us at our expense.

*This lovely heart-shaped box is richly
detailed with cut-glass decorations, perfect
for holding a precious memento or
keepsake—and it's yours absolutely free
when you accept our no-risk offer.*

"ROLL A DOUBLE!"

PLACE LABEL HERE

SCRATCH HERE

**SEE CLAIM CHART
BELOW**

245 CIS AH7E
(U-SIL-IM-03/93)

YES! I have placed my label from the front cover into the space
provided above and scratched off the silver dice. Please rush me
the free books and gift that I am entitled to. I understand that I am
under no obligation to purchase any books, as explained on the
opposite page.

NAME _____

ADDRESS _____ APT. _____

CITY _____ STATE _____ ZIP CODE _____

CLAIM CHART

	4 FREE BOOKS PLUS FREE HEART-SHAPED CURIO BOX	
	3 FREE BOOKS	
	2 FREE BOOKS	CLAIM NO.37-829

SILHOUETTE "NO RISK" GUARANTEE

- You're not required to buy a single book—ever!
- You must be completely satisfied or you may cancel at any time simply by sending us a note or shipping statement marked "cancel" or by returning any shipment to us at our cost. Either way, you will receive no more books; you'll have no obligation to buy.
- The free books and gift you claimed on this "Roll A Double" offer remain yours to keep no matter what you decide.

If offer card is missing, please write to: Silhouette Reader Service, 3010 Walden Ave., P.O. Box 1867, Buffalo, NY 14269-1867

"You got a smart mouth on you, girl," Russell said menacingly. "And I'm not sure I can risk having you running that mouth when you shouldn't, especially now that you know where we're really headed."

He unsnapped the safety catch on his gun. It clicked, the sound as loud as her shoe clattering to the deck a moment before.

Liza was starting to sweat in the balmy tropical night.

"Easy, Russell." Deke stepped up to her other side and took hold of her right arm. "Fire that gun and we're going to attract a lot of unwanted attention."

Russell hesitated, too long to suit Liza. Finally he lowered the gun.

Liza felt her knees buckle beneath her. Russell let go of her altogether, but Deke held on tighter. He was all that was keeping her on her feet.

Plastered against his side, she paused for a moment to figure out whether she felt any safer than when Russell had her. She couldn't say.

A drug smuggler. She shook her head and tried to make the words sink in. *Deke—a drug smuggler. How could she have been so wrong about him?*

"What the hell are we going to do with her?" said an obviously agitated Russell.

"I can handle her," Deke said easily.

"'Handle me'?" Liza let anger get the best of her as she snapped back at him.

"Shut up, Liza." He was nearly cutting off her breath, his hold on her was so tight now.

"She's gonna talk," Russell said. "And we can't let her."

"She won't say a word." Deke's calm, cool voice almost had her convinced. "What can she say? That we planned the whole deal and she had nothing to do with it? Nobody would buy that. She's been with us every step of the way— or at least it shouldn't be too hard to convince the authorities of that. She can't take us down without getting herself into trouble, as well."

Russell paused to reason it out. He didn't seem convinced.

"Besides," Deke added, "surely you've noticed—the woman's crazy about me. We've made some plans for when this is over. We're going to take my share of the money and run."

He grinned down at her as he made his claim, but it was no loving look that he gave her. Deke was daring her to contradict his story.

"Can't say I haven't noticed her mooning over you," Russell said.

Liza gritted her teeth and kept quiet. She'd tell Deke exactly what she thought of him later, hopefully when they were alone. For now, she'd play along with him. At least he didn't have a gun pointed at her. Besides, gun or no gun, she'd still rather take her chances with him than with Russell.

"I can handle her," Deke repeated.

Russell still hesitated.

A car horn sounded in the distance, one long beep, then two short ones. There was a cab waiting at the road near the dock.

"We expecting company?" Deke said.

"My friend from customs," Russell said. "We need to nail down our deal."

Still he hesitated. Liza realized that she and Deke both were holding their breath, waiting to see what Russell did.

"Go ahead," Deke said. "You take care of customs. I'll take care of her. I'll meet you back here by dawn, and we'll be on our way."

Russell looked from the waiting cab to Liza and then back again. Finally he nodded and turned to go.

He was halfway down the dock before they both exhaled shakily. Deke's hold on her eased only a fraction.

"Do me a favor," he said, in that harsh voice she'd come to expect from him. "Don't do anything else that's stupid until his cab pulls away."

"Me?" He allowed her to turn to face him. "You're telling *me* not to do anything stupid? You smuggle drugs for a living and you're telling me not to do anything stupid?"

"I don't smuggle drugs for a living," he snapped.

"Oh? This is some sideline? What's your day job, Deke? Bank robber? Kidnapper? Hit man?"

Deke laughed out loud. He couldn't help it. God, the woman had nerve. And she could turn him inside out faster than anyone he'd ever met. She'd taken him from stark terror to admiration in seconds flat. He'd nearly died when Russell had the gun on her, and now here he was admiring her spunk and her sass.

And he had no idea what he was going to do about it.

Seeing Russell holding a loaded gun on her had been his worst nightmare come true. And in those seconds, as he'd waited for Russell to lower the gun, he'd been forced to admit that she'd come to mean much more to him than just some woman he both desired and admired.

Not that either emotion could have any bearing on the present situation. His protective instincts toward her couldn't get any stronger than they'd already been, but he had no time for any other emotions. He had a job to finish, and he had a duty to protect her as best he could. There was no room for anything else.

Besides, she was sure to hate him, anyway, now that she knew what he and Russell were doing. And he couldn't, even if he wanted to, tell her the real truth. It would endanger her that much more.

Russell's cab pulled away, and Deke finally let go of Liza. She stood there on the deck with her arms wrapped around herself and her hands running up and down her arms.

"Cold?"

She shook her head. "More like stunned."

Deke didn't know what to tell her now, but he had to tell her something. He had to tell her enough to keep her from going to the authorities—the wrong ones. The Jamaican authorities knew what was happening, but only the most senior officials. If Liza went running to some underlings and they made a move without checking with the right officials first, it could mess up the whole operation.

"Come on down below. It's warmer there, and I've got some coffee on. We can talk there."

She told him no again, silently, with just a shake of her head.

"How about a sweater, then?"

Now it was her turn to laugh; at first she laughed quietly, but then it got louder, less in control. Shock was setting in, and he didn't like the sound of it at all.

"What are you afraid of? That I might get a chill or something? A minute ago your partner in crime had his gun stuck in my shoulder—and now you're worried about me getting too *cold?*"

Her voice was strained from the start. It trembled, then broke on the last word.

Trouble was coming.

"Liza?"

She yanked off her one shoe, hurled it into the water, then kicked the other one off the deck and into the water, as well. Then she turned and hurried away in her bare feet.

"Liza, wait." Deke hesitated. He couldn't run after her, because he had to secure the boat. "Liza?"

She was running by then. Down the dock, over to the beach and then down beside the waves, her white dress shining in the moonlight.

Deke gave himself a split second to curse his fate. Then he scrambled to lock up the boat and chase after her.

Chapter 13

The faster Liza ran, the more frightened she became.

She ran down the beach, racing through the uncertain footing of the wet sand. There was a path about a half mile down the beach that led up the hillside to the villa. She found it and headed up, but not before she heard his footsteps behind her.

All of a sudden, he frightened her—really frightened her. He was chasing after her, down this deserted beach, and after what had just happened, it was painfully obvious that she didn't really know anything about him or what he might be capable of doing. She wanted to put as much distance between them as she could, and then...then she might well have a nervous breakdown.

Cocaine, she thought. Smuggling. Guns. Money. Danger. Criminals.

How could the man she'd come to know be nothing more than a drug-smuggling criminal?

She gasped as she lost her footing on the slippery path and came down hard, one knee connecting with something—a fallen tree limb, maybe an exposed root. She couldn't tell in the dim light.

But as she paused there, straining to get enough air into her lungs and waiting for the sharp pain in her knee to ease, she could hear him behind her.

"Liza?"

He was closer than she'd thought. Liza scrambled desperately to her feet and ran on through the night.

Cocaine. How could he have gotten mixed up in cocaine smuggling? Why would he? He was a smart man. Surely he could have done anything he wanted to with his life. How could he choose to be a smuggler?

"Liza?"

He was even closer now. She'd probably be able to see him if she took the time to look back over her shoulder. She wasn't going to be able to outrun him. The path was too steep and slick. She was too tired, and he was too strong.

She kept running, anyway.

Deke caught her on the path about a half mile below the villa. He caught the skirt of her dress and held on tight.

Liza came down hard. Her feet slid out from under her, and with him tugging on her clothes from behind she landed on her stomach on the muddy ground.

He must have thought she'd give up easily, because he let go, and she half crawled, half walked, a few more steps.

"Damn it, Liza. Give it up," he growled, his hands closing around her ankles.

She kicked him, and, judging by the outraged sound he made, he hadn't expected the move. She must have managed to hurt him with the kick, because he let her go again. Stoically she began crawling again.

"For God's sake, woman, just be still," Deke shouted, exasperation tingeing his voice. He caught her by the dress again, but this time he immediately reached for her right arm, which he used to roll her over onto her back.

He pinned her down with his body, straddling hers as he sat on top of her and held her arms above her head.

The man was angrier than she'd ever seen him. His eyes blazed, his jaw was rigid, his hold was uncompromising.

"What do you want from me?" She didn't care for the soft, unsteady quality of the words, but it was the best she could do at the moment. The shock was wearing thin, and that was the only thing keeping the pain at bay.

For a second, there was nothing but the sound of the ocean roaring below and of both of them gasping for breath as he stared down at her.

Defiant to the last, determined not to let him see how much he'd hurt her, she stared right back. Finally he let go of her arms, shifted his weight off her and onto his knees, then waited.

"Well?" she challenged. Deke didn't know whether to be relieved or dismayed. She was at least as mad as she was scared.

He cursed, low and hard, scrambled to his feet, then picked her up—mud and all—and slung her over his shoulder before she could protest.

"I'll make a list," he said, and started up the hill.

It was after 2:00 a.m. when he carried her into the villa. She'd given up protesting by the time they got there. He didn't put her down until they were in the private bathroom of the bedroom she was using.

"What are you going to do to me?" she asked hotly as he searched the walk-in closet that was part of the spacious bathroom.

"Either clean you up or drown you. I'll let you make the choice."

She did need cleaning up. The mirror clearly reflected that. Her dress was more brown than white now, and the mud clung to her arms, her shoulders, even her face and hair.

It was curious—the way she felt, almost as if she was watching the events unfold rather than being a part of them. She barely recognized herself as she stood there now, so different from the excited, hopeful woman who'd been here before. She couldn't begin to understand what had happened.

"Here. This should cover you." Deke came out with two white terry-cloth bathrobes. He started to hand her one, but decided against it when he saw how dirty her outstretched hand was. He threw them both on the vanity instead.

"Right," he said, pulling his soiled shirt over his head and reaching for the snap of his cutoffs. "One way or another, I'm going to take a shower. You can get in here with me, or you can sit on the other side of this door and convince me that the whole time I'm in there you haven't moved a muscle."

Liza didn't say a word, but she was careful to keep her eyes on his once she heard the cutoffs drop to the floor.

"Look, Liza. Russell and I are going to be gone for three days." He stepped into the shower and pulled the door closed. "If you want to, you'll have time to call every cop in the Caribbean and tell them what we're up to—if you still want to. I just don't want you to call anybody until I've had a chance to explain."

"Explain?" She choked and sputtered on the word.

The sound of water pounding against tile drowned out the word. Then the shower door opened, and Deke stuck his head out.

"Come over here, sit down and talk to me so I know you haven't taken off."

"Bastard," she muttered just loud enough for him to hear.

Deke just laughed.

She couldn't believe he was laughing. It made her mad all over again. "You honestly think there's anything you can say to convince me to sit by and watch you two go through with this?"

"Maybe."

"Well, you're wrong."

"Maybe."

"You bastard," she repeated, this time with even more feeling. How could he have done this to her? Lied to her this way?

"I'm not going to deny that."

She turned to look at him then, but quickly turned her head away again. She could see more of him than she cared to through the shower door.

Instead she sank to the floor and sat with her back to the shower door, her elbow propped on the toilet seat. Then she pulled her knees up to her chest and wrapped her arms around her legs.

Colombia. Drug cartels. Cocaine. This had to be a nightmare. Things had to be different by morning, when she woke up—this couldn't be real.

The cold drilled into her very being. It went past the protective cocoon of shock, past the disbelief and denial. She felt dizzy, then sick, as if she'd eaten something rotten and her stomach was taking note of it.

A drug smuggler?

She'd tried searching her bruised heart to figure out exactly what she felt for him—but she just couldn't do it. She couldn't begin to comprehend the way in which he'd betrayed her.

She was seething—the anger burning slowly and steadily inside her, but she still couldn't believe it. She also had no idea what to do now.

Deke was out of the shower in no time. She kept her mouth shut, and her eyes glued to the floor. All she saw were his feet and a pair of tightly muscled legs dripping water onto the tiles.

How long would it take, she wondered, before any of this seemed real?

"Liza?"

Lost in thought, she wasn't even sure what he'd said. "Yes?"

"Shower-time."

A shower? Yes. That sounded good. She could close the door—close him out—and be by herself. Maybe she could begin to make sense of it all then.

She stepped into the shower, methodically took off her clothes and threw them out on the floor, turning on the water.

Not paying enough attention to what she was doing, she managed to turn the shower on full blast with ice-cold water.

Shivering and crying under the cold spray, she felt as if everything had come crashing down upon her. Oh, Lord! She was awake. It was real. And he was nothing but a crook.

She sank down to the tile floor, leaned against the side wall and let the tears fall. They mingled with the cold water running over her. More miserable and confused than she'd ever been in her life, probably still in shock, she could do nothing but sit there, shivering and sobbing.

"Liza?"

For a second Deke thought she'd somehow escaped, while he'd taken the clothes he'd rinsed out and put them in the dryer. Then he looked closer and noticed her sitting on the tile floor in the shower.

And the sight of her there, cold and miserable, with tears running freely down her face, left him with no doubt that there actually was something left of his heart.

Why did it hurt him so much to know that he'd hurt her, that he would do nothing but hurt her even now?

He turned off the water, grabbed a towel and then her.

"God, Liza, it's freezing in here."

Try as he might, he couldn't help but notice how soft, how supple, how smooth, her skin was, and how much of it was there for his hungry eyes to see. He rubbed her briskly with the big towel, keeping his eyes level with hers, then, heaving an inward sigh of relief, wrapped her up in the terry-cloth robe.

She looked as miserable as he felt, and there was nothing he could do about that.

"I'm sorry, Liza. God, I'm sorry."

Her eyes flashed angrily at him for just a moment before she deliberately looked away from him.

"I believed in you." She made it an accusation. "I knew Russell was a rat. I knew with that much money the two of you must be doing something illegal—but this?"

"I don't make my living smuggling drugs, Liza. I've never done anything like this before, and I never will again."

She wanted to believe him, he could see that in her eyes. But why would she? Hell, he barely believed it himself.

"I'm just—" He searched for words, praying he could find the right ones. "I'm stuck, Liza. I'm backed up against a wall, and there's nothing else I can do."

He raised his hands then, not in anger, not in any implied threat, but in a plea for understanding, one that came from deep within him. He placed a hand on each of her arms, just above the elbows, and his thumbs felt the slight ridges of the muscles there. His fingers curled around to rest in the soft, soft, tender flesh on the underside of her arms.

Deke rubbed his fingers up and down, hoping that her acceptance of his touch meant that he had a chance.

"How can you be stuck here?" she challenged. "What kind of a hold does Nick Russell have over you?"

Deke looked her straight in the eye, no pretense between them now, no games. "Not on me. My little brother. He's in trouble, Liza. I'm trying to save my brother's life. And I'm doing the only thing I can to save him."

She was silent for a long moment, and for that moment he thought it just might be that easy, but then she started asking questions.

"How can you—?"

"Don't, Liza. I can't give you any answers," he said, sincerely wishing that he could. He knew it wouldn't be fair to her. The less she knew, the better—for her own safety.

"That's it? That's the explanation that's supposed to keep me quiet while you two go off and do your big drug deal?"

Deke released her, leaned back against the vanity and crossed his arms, nodding his head. "Look, Liza, you have no idea how dangerous Nick Russell and his friends are. If you turn him in, he'll make sure you pay for it." The expression on her face remained angrily stubborn.

"Then there's Ellen to think about, and Jilly." He might be more successful with this argument. "Ellen's gone along with Russell's deals for years, and she's living off the proceeds. The authorities are going to nail her, as well as him. Then what's going to happen to Jilly?"

"What's going to happen to her if she goes on any more drug-buying trips with her parents?" she snapped back. "Lord, I can't believe you knew all along what was going to happen on this trip. You knew how dangerous it was going to be, and you let Russell bring her along."

"If you'll recall, I didn't want either of you on this trip, and I tried to stop you from coming along."

"Well, you should have—"

"Yeah, I could have what? I don't know what else I could have done, but I wish to God I'd thought of something ages before it ever got to this point."

"Are you scared?"

"Hell, yes, I'm scared. I'd have to be crazy *not* to be scared."

"But . . ." She took a deep breath and closed her eyes. Then she stared up at the ceiling. "This is too much. It's just too much. It's crazy."

She walked into the bedroom, paced back and forth between the door and the window. "It's just crazy," she repeated.

She was near the breaking point, Deke thought, and she was right. This was crazy.

"I know it is, but I can't do anything about that now. I've come too far. There's nothing to do but play it through and hope it works out."

And then more tears started to fall. Big, slow-moving tears that pooled in her eyes and then spilled over onto her cheeks.

She sank slowly down to the floor and let them come.

No one could have stopped him from sitting down on the floor behind her then, pulling her back to him so that her back rested against his chest, and wrapping both his arms around her.

She didn't fight him. She came willingly into his arms. He hadn't been so happy in months as he was the moment he felt her resistance melt away, felt her body lean into his, felt the fine trembling that had shaken her ease after a long moment sheltered in his arms.

He held on tight, drawing comfort from her as he offered it in return.

"Liza, I have a job to do, and I'm going to do it. But if you'll let me, if you can find it in your heart to trust me just a little, I'm also going to do everything I can to keep you safe."

As he saw it, that was the only promise he could honestly make.

Chapter 14

They stayed there on the floor, wrapped in each other's arms, for a long time. The night was quiet, the moon merely a sliver of light, and the time passed much too quickly.

He told her a little about Charlie, about when they were little. He told her how he'd wanted so much to take care of his little brother and how hard it was to realize that he'd failed him by not being there when he should have.

The drugs, the wild crowd, the trouble with the law, all could have been avoided if he hadn't been so selfish.

Liza tried, again and again, to talk him out of making the trip. It was crazy. It was dangerous. It was an irrevocable step that, once taken, would change his life forever. She was convinced that they wouldn't get away with it, that if the Colombians didn't get them, someone else would, and then his whole life would be ruined.

Too late, he told her. The decision was made, the players had already been set in motion. He couldn't change things now.

At one point, she dozed off in his arms. He picked her up and carried her to bed.

He had an hour or so before he was supposed to be back at the boat. He decided he'd have to risk making a phone call to his contact. There was no way to avoid it. The authorities would have to be warned that Liza knew what they were planning to do and that she might try to turn them in to the Jamaican police. He made the call, got his clothes out of the drier, and dressed. Then he returned to the bedroom.

Later he realized that he should have left when he'd had the chance, should never have gotten that close to her again. It only made it that much harder to leave.

Now he stretched out beside her on the bed and pulled her into his arms. He stroked her hair and stared at the ceiling, wishing he could have just one more day with her. Wishing he could be honest with her about exactly who he was and what he was trying to do. Wishing she'd understand once he did tell her. Hoping he'd make it back and get a chance to explain everything to her.

He at least owed her that.

Liza heard him slip out of bed. So, Deke was going to meet Russell, after all, get on the boat and go through with his crazy deal.

She was still having trouble taking it all in.

But as she waited there, overwhelmed and confused, one emotion kept coming to the surface, an emotion that wouldn't be denied. Fear.

Fear that she was about to do what she'd vowed never to do—make a fool of herself over a man. She found herself wanting to believe in him—when surely no sane woman would—found herself wanting to make excuses for him and, worse yet, making plans for reforming him.

She knew better, she told herself. She'd always been amazed at how otherwise sane women could excuse the most outrageous behavior in their men.

But making a fool of herself wasn't her only fear. Even stronger than that was the fear, the very real possibility, that nothing would work out as he'd planned, that everything would fall apart, that he wouldn't make it back . . . that she would never see him again.

Frantic, outraged at him for putting her in this position, but scared to death for him, she went scrambling for something to wear.

She found him in the garage, startling him. She drank in the sight of him, the loose, easy way he had of standing, the way his too-long dark hair just couldn't seem to stay in place, the way the T-shirt clung to his chest.

How had he come to mean so much to her?

And why was she so afraid—convinced, almost—that this was her last chance, her very last moment with him?

"So that's it," she said finally, shaking with a combination of anger and fear. "You're just going to turn your back and leave."

Deke flipped the switch to the automatic garage-door opener and stared at it as if he'd never seen a garage door in motion before.

He didn't want to turn and look at her. He didn't want to see what this whole damn mess had done to her, what *he'd* done to her.

He had sensed that she was starting to care for him. He'd had no business allowing that to happen, but he had.

Of course, it wasn't as if he'd had a choice, Deke fumed. He couldn't deny that there was something between them— something so powerful that it had caught him by surprise, had captured him before he'd had a chance to shore up his defenses.

Now he wondered how he'd ever find the strength over the next week or two to resist her.

"Fine," she said. The anger fueled her impatience, and she didn't bother waiting for him to respond. "I guess there's nothing I can say to stop you."

Frustration and guilt eating at him, he suddenly turned and grabbed her, caught her against the side of Russell's rented car and pinned her there with his body, his chest against her back, his hands free to roam up and down the arms she held so rigidly to her side.

He watched as she stared down through the darkness and into the interior of the car as if it fascinated her. Now that he'd let himself see just how much she was hurting for him and for all the moments they might never have to be together, he could feel his heart aching. He hurt for her now more than he'd ever thought it possible to hurt.

"This isn't easy for me, Liza."

Bitter silence was her only response, and he found he liked that even less than the angry words she'd hurled at him earlier.

"Liza..." These days he could pack a mountain of longing into just her name.

His arms encircled her shoulders, and he gave her a squeeze. He noted that he was almost tall enough to rest his chin on the top of her head. She was a tiny little thing, although he seldom thought of her that way.

"If I had to do it all over again, I would never have allowed you to get so caught up in this," he whispered as he pushed his nose into her soft, straight hair and inhaled deeply. He wanted to carry the warmth and the smell of her with him when he went.

"What do you think this is about?" she asked bitterly.
"It's not about me. It's about you. I'm worried about you. Scared to death for you and what might happen out there on the boat."

"Well, don't be. Worry about yourself. Take care of yourself and Jilly first. Promise me. That has to be your first priority. No matter what happens to me or what Russell does. *Promise me, Liza,*" he demanded, urgency in his voice.

"Why?" Anger, the strength of which left her trembling in his arms, shot through the word. "Because you're the only one allowed to worry about anyone else? Because the all-powerful Deke MacCauley is the only one who gets to worry about other people, the only one responsible for righting everyone else's wrongs, whether it's his pitiful, stupid brother's or mine?''

"No—''

"Yes, of course. Excuse me. How silly of me to forget. It's your fault that Charlie's a cokehead. I mean, you only raised him from the time he was a baby. He was your responsibility, and you botched it. God forbid you'd try to have your own life at the expense of his.''

"Please, Liza.'' He ignored her words, conscious only of the clock. He wished he never had to let her go. "We don't have much time.''

"And then there's me. Somehow it's all your fault that I'm here, that my sister asked for help and I came, because I wanted to protect my niece. And your fault that I stayed— that I wouldn't listen to you and go away. Did I get it all?''

"Stop, Liza. Please.'' He squeezed her closer and wished—oh, how he wished—that he'd never been crazy enough to agree to this whole thing, that he'd fought harder to get what he needed on Russell without ever having to make this trip.

"No, I won't stop. *I* brought myself here. *I* decided to come along on this trip, but somehow you think it's your fault, because being Deke MacCauley is right up there with God when it comes to responsibility.''

"All right,'' he whispered into her right ear, then kissed it delicately. "All right. I'm sorry, baby.''

"I don't want you to be sorry,'' she said as she leaned her forehead against the car window and the first sob escaped. "I just want you safe.''

He held her up for a moment when the strength went out of her; she'd used all she had to fight back the tears. She would have pulled out of his arms if he'd been willing to let her go.

"I'm going to do everything I can to get back to you, Liza.''

He kissed her temple, then her cheekbone, her chin, and finally buried his lips in the sensitive hollow between her neck and her shoulder.

Liza shivered in his arms. The trembling shook her whole body, and set off an answering quiver in his.

What he wouldn't give for just a few more days with her, a few more hours, whatever he could get, now that there was no time left.

She leaned her head back against his shoulder then, and the long curve of her neck, as it blended into her shoulder, presented a temptation he couldn't resist.

A moment. Surely he could take a moment for himself, for her, for what they both wanted so desperately.

She gasped when he settled his mouth over the sensitive cord of her neck. First his lips made a path from just beneath her chin to her collarbone. Then his tongue followed it, and finally his teeth, taking little bites of her along the way.

He couldn't stop the unmistakable way his body responded to hers, couldn't keep from pressing his lower body to hers. He fit right there, the hardness of his body in between the soft curve of her hips. He thrust against her once, twice, felt her answer the sensual movement with one of her own.

She was wearing this snug little blue cotton thing, something she must sleep in, he thought, because he'd seen it before, draped across her bed on the boat.

Something short.

Something that fitted just tight enough to show off every curve she had.

Something with enough of a V neck that he could see a little more than the beginning curve of her breasts.

Something that had been driving him crazy since even before he'd seen it on her body.

It wasn't at all slinky or lacy or sheer, but a woman wouldn't get any sleep in an outfit like this. Neither would the man lucky enough to be in bed beside her.

He'd wondered, too, just what she wore under it, and now he found out.

Nothing. He groaned as he lifted the ends up and cupped the bare flesh, that warm, soft flesh on either side of her bottom.

There was a desperation taking hold of him now, a desperate wish to hold back time, to hold on to her and never let her go.

He continued to rock back and forth against her body, and he used his hands to guide her in a sensual rhythm that left him gritting his teeth in an effort to find some self-control.

Liza lifted her arm up behind her to pull his head down to her neck, and the movement brought her breast up a little higher. Her nipple stood erect against the thin cotton nightshirt. Cut wide on the arms, he noted feverishly, and wide enough so he could see the sides of her breasts coming free of the material.

He wanted to taste that tender flesh, wanted to feel her writhe with pleasure in his arms when he did so. Holding her like this, feeling the way that he did, he wondered if he'd ever be able to let her go.

Her flesh was warm and firm beneath his hands, and, still moving against her sensuously, he let his fingers roam as far as he could reach down the outside of her thighs, then slowly up the front.

He meant to stop before he ever got to that spot at the juncture of her thighs. But it beckoned him.

Deke had known just how she'd feel, had known the sweet heat and the dewy softness of her from a thousand dreams he'd had about touching her this way. About thrusting into her body and losing himself in her, in a pleasure like none he'd ever known.

He couldn't help himself. One hand, then the other, skimmed across the soft curls, and when she opened her thighs—oh, so slightly—and arched against his hand, he was lost.

Pushing up her nightshirt, he wrapped one hand around her middle and held her up when she would have fallen. The other hand slid down into those curls, down into those soft folds of flesh. It was just the way he'd imagined it, only better. She was just as warm, just as wet, just as ready for him, as he'd fantasized she would be.

"Please." Close to the edge, she begged him for release. "Please."

He stroked her, tenderly, slowly, murmuring words of encouragement in her ears, then slipped one finger inside her and stroked some more. He brought her close, would have taken her all the way, but she stopped him.

Somehow, he couldn't figure how, with him pressed so tightly against her back and the car against her front, she turned to face him.

"With me," she said, then pulled off his T-shirt, took a second to rub her hands against his chest, and, before he could stop her, started working on the snap and the zipper to his cutoffs.

"This time," she elaborated with a smile, as the catches came free and the denim dropped to the ground, along with his briefs, "I want you with me."

"Liza." He wanted her desperately, more than he'd ever wanted anyone before, than he'd ever believed possible, but he held back, nearly shaking from the force of his desire. He knew it wouldn't be fair to her, to take her this way when he had nothing more to offer her than the flash and the heat of the next few moments. He gritted his teeth again. He owed it to her to offer her the chance to back away.

"Liza, we're in the damn garage, with the garage doors open. Hell, I think the sun's going to come up any—"

Breathing in sharply, he somehow found the strength to stay upright when she took him into her hands and stroked him.

"We're at the only house at the end of a dead-end road on a private estate. No one's going to drive by. And we don't have any time to waste," she whispered.

He felt as if every nerve ending in his body converged on the hard flesh she cupped in her hands. It didn't seem possible, but he grew even more rigid under her gentle caress.

"I can't promise you anything." He bit out the words, fighting for control. Hell, who was he kidding? He didn't have a prayer's hope of self-control for very much longer.

"I'm not asking for anything except right now, right here, with you."

And with that, he gave in to the longing that he could no longer deny.

Deke lifted her onto the fender of the car, nudged her legs apart and settled himself between her thighs. She pushed up her nightshirt and eased back on her elbows, half reclining against the hood of the car, smiling at him.

Moving back slightly, he stepped out of his cutoffs and briefs, then fitted his body to hers once again and watched her in the dim predawn haze as she waited for the final action that would bring them closer than ever before.

How had he ever hoped he could resist making her his? How had he waited this long?

Placing his hands on her bottom, he cupped her hips and, with a quick, hard movement, sank into the tight, damp heat of her. It seemed to take forever to get inside her, an eternity in which he just went down, deeper and deeper, inch by excruciating inch.

"Oh, Deke!"

"Dixon. My name is Dixon." If he was going to make love to the woman, she damn well deserved to know his real name.

"Dixon." It sounded so good coming from her. "Don't stop."

His hands on her hips pulled her tightly against him, fused her body with his, but in some dim recess of his mind he knew that he'd never be close enough.

He took a minute to lean over her body, to press her soft breasts to his chest, to take her mouth beneath his, his tongue thrusting slowly and easily in and out of her mouth, echoing the other, more erotic movements he made between her thighs.

They were both gasping for breath, when he straightened and began thrusting in earnest.

With each move he knew that he wanted more, so much more. Mostly he wanted time to make love to her the way she deserved, unhurriedly, languidly, with no end in sight to their time together. He wanted the right to tell her the truth about everything. Then he wanted another chance to get to know her all over again, with no one's neck on the line, no danger and no worries, about her safety or his own.

But he had none of that, nothing but this moment with his body rocking against hers, with her trembling beneath him, her hips bucking against his as her excitement built to a frenzy.

He watched her there beneath him even as she watched him, her indigo eyes so bright, her lips slightly parted, as she uttered little whimpering cries. Her hands reached for him, stroking quickly down his belly, then around his hips, trying to pull him closer.

He found it incredibly erotic, the way her whole body suddenly tensed, hung there, suspended, a fraction of an inch off the hood of the car, as she strained frantically to get closer to him. He paused for just a moment while the powerful tremors shook her, while she cried out his name and then went boneless beneath him.

And then he, too, was lost.

Settling into a fast, hard rhythm as old as time, for one glorious moment he felt the world and all his worries fall away. He was above it all with her, in a place where no one else could reach them, where they existed only for each other's pleasure, for the joy to be found in joining together body and soul.

The trembling ceased, finally. He found himself leaning over her, resting his upper body heavily against hers, her body cradling his, and kissing her over and over again.

Wild passion wound down, giving way to a curious languor that he knew would ease in time and leave, in its place, nothing but reality.

He clung to the mindlessness that reined in the wake of their journey and fought like the devil against the harsh world that was creeping in.

He kissed her once more—for the last time, he told himself. Then kissed her again, slowly, tenderly. Her arms held him tight when he would have pulled away.

"Don't you dare regret this," she whispered softly into his ear.

"All right." The words were no more than the touch of his lips against her forehead. "I won't."

"I won't." She watched him closely as she continued, "But I know you well enough to be certain that you will, regardless of what you just told me."

He would have protested then, but she touched her finger to his lips and held back his words.

"Don't beat yourself up because every now and then you let yourself be part of the human race. Is it so awful to be imperfect, Dixon?"

He retreated at the sound of his real name. Bittersweet on her lips, it was a reminder of all he'd tried to forget.

He straightened, separated his body from hers, and she instantly felt the slight chill that clung to the early-morning air. That quickly, Dixon, her lover, was gone.

The smuggler, Deke, the man with the job to do, was back.

As she had known he would, he already regretted it.

"I am far from perfect," he said as he picked up her nightshirt off the floor and turned it right side out. Offering her a hand, he pulled her into a sitting position, then pulled the nightshirt over her head, all the while trying to avoid looking at her until she was covered.

She'd been studying his face, trying to see past the front he'd put up, to the emotions behind it.

Oh, Dixon, she thought, you're so hard on yourself.

He was trying to cover her, but she hadn't been paying attention to what he was doing. As a result, by the time she realized what was happening, she was nearly stuck inside her own clothes, because she hadn't pushed her arms through the armholes.

They struggled together, one pulling one way and one pulling another, until the deed was finally done.

It seemed immensely important to him that she was clothed, and then that he was, too, before he turned back to face her.

"No, Dixon, you're not perfect. Like I said before, your biggest flaw, as I see it, is the way you seem to think you're responsible for everyone else's problems."

She was still sitting on the car, and without further ceremony, she pulled him back into her embrace.

"I'm sorry. I had no right. I shouldn't have done that." He stood rigid within her arms.

"You shouldn't have let me tear off my clothes, tear off yours, and ravage you like that?"

That nearly got him to smile. "I could have . . . I should have . . ."

"It was what I wanted—where I wanted to be."

He seemed at a loss at that, and as she snuggled against his warmth, Liza hoped that at least a little of what she'd said had gotten through to him.

She closed her eyes and tried to imprint upon her memory this wonderful sensation of being safe within his arms, of the way it felt to have his hard, masculine chest beneath her cheek, his heart beating heavily.

"I have to go."

She panicked for the time it took her to draw two hasty breaths. She'd wanted desperately, blindly, to have these few moments with him, to bind him to her in a way that couldn't be denied.

Had she been hoping, in her subconscious, that the bond might carry over into a few other areas? That he might explain to her in detail what was going to happen? Why he felt it had to happen? How he'd gotten caught up in all of this?

More important, had she thought the bond of their lovemaking would be enough to hold him to her?

Well, if she had been foolish enough to even think that, she'd been mistaken.

And she wasn't sure she could stand to see him go, knowing what might very well happen to him while he was away.

It had been years since anyone had been this important to her. Years when she'd known that it was safer that way—that losing someone couldn't hurt that much if she made sure no one was that important to her in the first place. Years since she'd faced the fact that she always lost the important people in her life.

He backed away, and already she was lost without the warmth and the strength of him.

"I don't believe in making promises I'm not sure I can keep," he said, "so I won't—I can't. Damn it, Liza, there's nothing I can say to you right now."

"Say you'll come back to me."

"Liza—"

"Just say it," she demanded hoarsely. "Say it as if you believe it, if only because *I* need to believe it."

She was shivering—whether from cold or from fear, she couldn't have said. But suddenly she was bone-weary, deep in her heart.

He ran his warm hands up and down her arms, then used one hand to lift her chin so that he could see her eyes.

"I'll come back to you."

Her eyes, suddenly filled with tears, held his for a moment, then dropped as she fought against allowing those tears to fall.

"I have to," he said, sounding more confident of it this time. "We're not done yet, Liza."

No, she thought angrily, they weren't. They deserved so much more than they'd had already.

She slid off the fender of the car, blinked back her tears, and stood there like a stone as he turned and left.

Never had she been more aware of the preciousness of time, of the need to take advantage of every moment of life—so that at times like this, as she watched and waited to catch one last glimpse of him before he turned out of the driveway, then out of sight, she could do so with no regrets.

They had so little time and had wasted so much of it already. And for now she could only wonder whether their time together might just have run out.

Chapter 15

Was it worth it?

Deke swore when he finally let himself consider an answer as he stood on the deck of the boat, steering it away from the island, leaving Liza behind.

Was she right? Was he, once again, wrong? She'd asked him, in her rage earlier this morning, whether saving his brother's life was worth risking his own this way.

Maybe he hadn't put it to himself in those terms. Maybe he hadn't fully understood the danger, or admitted that danger to himself, before. But the question remained. Why *should* he be taking the risk?

Hell of a time for doubts, he thought, now that he was on his way to Colombia to help Nick Russell buy his precious cocaine.

But where did his brother's responsibility end and his start?

Charlie was old enough to know better than to get mixed up with the likes of Nick Russell, yet he'd done it just the same. Maybe Deke *had* made it too easy on him in the past by bailing him out the other time he got caught with cocaine, but that didn't make Deke accountable for his brother's knack for doing stupid things.

This was it, he promised himself. This was the last time he was going to bail Charlie out. If, in the future, Charlie got himself into trouble, he could get himself out or take the consequences. Deke would be there to support him in any way he could, but he wouldn't make all of Charlie's troubles go away anymore.

He couldn't, and Charlie had no reason to expect him to.

Too bad it had taken him so long to realize it, so long that, from what he could see, there was no way out of the job he'd committed himself to doing.

He considered, briefly, his chances of backing out now, and decided that the chances of doing it successfully were slim to none.

As he saw it, trying to quit at this stage would only put everyone on the trip in more danger. Oh, he might be able to slip away himself, but he wouldn't be able to get Liza, Jilly and Ellen safely out of Nick Russell's way. The risk was too great.

No, he would have to play it through, he thought grimly, looking over his shoulder and back toward the island, to the villa sitting on the hillside, hungry for another glimpse of the woman he was leaving behind.

It was crazy, he knew, to think what he was thinking at this point in time, when his life was in such a shambles. But he couldn't fight the feeling any longer.

He was almost certain he was in love with her.

He looked back over his shoulder to the house yet again, wondering where she was, what she was doing, whether she would be waiting there, safe and sound, when he returned.

When he returned.

He wouldn't even think of any other possibility.

He had to come back. He'd never had as much of a reason for living as he did right now. He'd never felt this strongly about a woman, never wanted one so badly that his knees nearly gave way when he thought of being together with her again the way they'd been earlier this morning.

Deke didn't have to close his eyes to remember. All it took was looking down into the bluer-than-blue water, its color so pure, so bold, that it perfectly matched her eyes.

He'd felt her eyes on him as he pleasured her. He'd gazed down into those eyes of hers and watched as they took on that smoky, dazed look of pure passion.

But it wasn't just physical desire that drew him to her. She was high-spirited, determined, gutsy, and incredibly vulnerable at times. A contradiction, to be sure, but a combination of attributes that he was finding more and more irresistible.

Deke had hated to leave her, but he knew she would be safer on the island than she would have been on the boat with him and Russell.

Still, it had been so hard to leave her there, had been hell to fight this need he'd developed to pull her to his side and never let her stray more than an arm's length away.

And it was hard—so damn hard—to fight the panic, to stop himself from thinking that he might never see her again.

Liza couldn't figure out who had made her madder—herself or Deke.

She wasn't a dumb woman. She wasn't!

But the fact that he was a damned drug smuggler stared her in the face.

She still couldn't believe it. Oh, she'd known he and Russell were involved in something dangerous, probably something illegal, but this was downright stupid, dangerously stupid.

Obviously she'd been kidding herself about him. Somehow, as she'd been falling for him over the past few weeks, as he'd stood beside her and watched over her along the way, she'd convinced herself that there was something different about him.

Or maybe she was just kidding herself about what he felt for her—period. Maybe she was a little naive, but she'd believed that he cared for her—more than that, actually—

and that when it came right down to it she'd be able to make him see reason, especially after the passion they'd shared. She'd thought she could convince him that the danger was too great, the risk too strong.

She'd actually believed that she could talk him out of participating in whatever Nick Russell was planning to do.

Liza laughed dryly at her own foolish thoughts. She'd believed that he'd change for her, that she could somehow reform him.

How many foolish women had said that about their men?

She didn't need to look far to see what kind of mess a woman could get herself into by hooking up with the wrong man. Her own sister showed her that every day.

And yet here she sat, on the patio of the villa, which looked out over the Caribbean Sea, hoping to catch a glimpse of the familiar red-and-white sails returning. She was hoping, more than anything in the world, that he'd make it back in one piece, and wondering if she could knock some sense into him once he arrived.

It was early for her to be up, and too early for him and Russell to be back, and yet here she sat on a lounge chair, wrapped up in a blanket and trying to stay warm in air that wasn't that cold to begin with.

The chill she was fighting wasn't in the morning breeze. It was inside her, deep in her bones, and it had been there ever since he'd left yesterday morning.

And she was afraid it would remain long after he returned, because she had no intention of allowing herself to become involved with a drug smuggler, no matter how irresistible she found him.

She would resist him, she told herself. She'd find a way.

And if she couldn't, she might just have to save him from himself. She certainly couldn't sit idly by and watch him continue like this with his life. It was too risky. He was bound to run into trouble sooner or later, and if he was lucky, his version of trouble would be the police.

She didn't even want to consider what would happen to him if he ran into trouble from the other side.

And for that reason—she couldn't fool herself into thinking it was her own sense of right and wrong—she had to consider turning him in.

Oh, Lord— What was she going to do?

She couldn't begin to figure it out right this minute, because for now there was only one thing on her mind. She was praying, as she hadn't in years, that he would come back to her safely.

Liza sat there until the sun came up, then went inside to wait for Jilly to wake up. She found Ellen in the kitchen making coffee.

"Morning," she said.

"Morning," Ellen said quietly, without turning around.

They'd grown more and more uneasy around each other as the trip had progressed, until it had gotten to the point where they had little to do with one another, and barely exchanged more than a few words each day.

Liza tried not to judge people, because she didn't care for being judged herself, but she was finding it increasingly difficult to excuse her sister's behavior. It had been bad enough before, when she'd sensed that Russell wasn't a good father to Jilly. But now that she knew the extent of Russell's evilness . . . The way Liza saw it, Ellen could ruin her own life if she chose to, but she had no right to subject her child to this kind of danger.

The sound of a coffee cup clattering against the countertop startled them both. Ellen had dropped the cup, and had scalded her hand with the coffee in the process. Yet when Liza turned around she was just standing there staring at her injured hand.

Liza pulled her over to the sink so that she could run cold water over it, and while she held her sister's hand under the water, she realized that it was no accident that Ellen had dropped the coffee.

Her hand was trembling violently. Her whole body was trembling.

"Oh, Lord, Ellen. What did you take this time?"

"Nothing." She laughed weakly when she said it. "That's the problem."

Liza found a dish towel. She sopped up the mess with one hand and held the injured hand under the faucet with the other.

"*Right*." She didn't even try to hide her anger. "'Nothing' did this to you? Are you always this jittery?"

Turning the tap, Liza motioned for Ellen to stay put while she got another dish towel out of the drawer, and put some ice cubes in it.

"Here. Take this—if you need it." She handed the ice pack to Ellen without looking at her. "Can you even feel the burn, Ellen?"

Liza turned to the cupboard, got a cup, and busied herself pouring her own coffee.

She was simply too angry to deal with Ellen right now. She needed cream, half a spoonful of sugar, a rush of caffeine. The task took on the utmost importance as she struggled to ignore her sister.

Slamming the refrigerator door closed once she'd returned the cream, she shoved the silverware drawer closed after she found a spoon, sloshing coffee over the rim of the cup as she stirred furiously.

"Do you hate me so much, Liza?"

Liza paused in the midst of taking a sip—and probably saved herself from scalding her tongue. How could she answer that? Did she even know exactly what she felt for her sister?

"I'm disappointed in you, Ellen." She put the cup down, gently now. "I'm not sure I know what else I think of you."

"I wouldn't blame you if you did—hate me, I mean. I hate myself most of the time, whether I'm sober or not."

Liza just looked at her and wondered how the sister she remembered, the one who had been so strong, so protective of her, could have turned into the pitiful woman before her.

It made her sad and angry at the same time.

"I am sober now, though."

"Oh, Lord, Ellen, don't—"

"I am. I threw all the pills away before we set sail."

"Ellen . . ." Liza took her sister's shaking hands in her own and held them up between them. "Look at you. You're shaking so hard, you can't even hold a cup of coffee."

"It's withdrawal."

Liza looked incredulous. She'd seen her sister high enough times to know how it looked. This was no different from the behavior she'd seen before.

"It is," Ellen insisted. "Valium is funny that way. It takes a while to get it out of your bloodstream, and there's a kick to it that doesn't hit you until about two weeks after you quit."

Liza had never heard of such a thing, but then she didn't know a lot of Valium addicts.

"It's all right," Ellen said. "You don't have to believe me. I probably wouldn't believe me either if I was in your shoes. And it doesn't matter that much, anyway. I know it's much too late . . . for us. . . . I mean, I know what you must think of me."

How could Ellen know, Liza wondered, when she wasn't sure herself? Questions flitted through her mind, distracting her. Why? Why had Ellen left her all those years ago? Why had her sister never come back for her? And how had Ellen ever ended up like this?

"I need a favor, Liza.

"Not for me. I wouldn't ask for me," Ellen said quickly. "For Jilly."

Liza sipped her cooling coffee and took her time about responding. She was so angry, so disappointed, and she wasn't sure she could contain the two emotions. Then again, she didn't see any point in trying.

"If you're so damn concerned about your daughter, why in the world would you let your husband expose her to this kind of danger?"

"I didn't know," Ellen sobbed. "I didn't know what he was going to do."

"Oh, Lord, Ellen. How could you not know? You're his wife. And it's not the first time he's done this, is it?"

"He promised," Ellen said, wrapping her arms around her waist and holding on tight. "He promised that if I stayed with him he wouldn't do it again."

"And has the man ever made a promise to you that he's kept?"

They fell silent then, except for the sounds of Ellen's sniffling and sobbing.

"Mommy? You crying?"

Neither of them had noticed Jilly padding down the hallway in her nightgown and her bare feet. She looked worried as she hovered there, up against Liza's legs, clutching her worn blanky.

"No," Ellen said shakily, wiping her tears away quickly and pasting on a smile.

Liza picked up the little girl, still warm from her sleep, light blond curls tumbling in ten different directions.

"Don't lie to her, Ellen. She's smart enough to know what tears look like."

Then she hugged her niece and gave her rapid-fire kisses on her cheek.

"Hey, don't take all my kisses," Jilly scolded. She was convinced that she had only a certain number of kisses available on any given day, and she rationed them carefully.

"All right. I'll give them back." Liza got to kiss her five more times then. "Now, give your Mommy a good-morning hug and a kiss."

Jilly was more cautious around her mother. Clinging to Liza, she hung back for a moment, then went into her mother's arms.

"Mommy? You okay?"

Liza jumped in when it became clear that Ellen didn't know how to respond. "She was just a little upset a minute ago, Jilly. You know how you get upset sometimes and need to cry? Moms get upset sometimes, too."

Children were incredibly adept at reading adult's emotions, she'd found. And emotional upsets often took on an added importance to children when it was obvious that an adult was trying to lie to them and say everything was all right.

"Why don't you give her a kiss and make it all better," Liza suggested.

Jilly complied. "All bedder?" She had trouble with "t" sounds.

"Much better," Liza reassured her, quickly answering for Ellen, who looked like she was about to start crying again. "Now, why don't we go get dressed? Then we can see about some breakfast."

Jilly was eager to come back into Liza's arms.

"I want ice cream."

"Forget it," Liza said with a laugh as they walked down the hall to the bathroom. "Not for breakfast."

"Dinner?"

"Maybe."

Ellen just stood there and watched them as they went, the expression on her face one of profound sadness. She should have been the one laughing and playing with her daughter like that. And she should have been the one to see that Jilly was safe from whatever Russell was doing. Bitter tears filled her eyes. Was she always destined to fail her daughter?

"What can I do to help Jilly?" Liza said that afternoon as she and Ellen watched the little girl water the flowers next to the patio with her little plastic watering can.

Ellen had been quieter than usual after their argument that morning, and Liza felt guilty for having been so hard on her.

"You know I'll do anything I can for her."

"Take her away," Ellen said quietly.

"All right. But where? And what would your husband do if I did disappear with her?"

"I'm not sure what he'd do," Ellen admitted. "But I know where you can take her. Nick has a sister named Mary Ann. She, uh...she's been more of a mother to Jilly than I ever was. Jilly had been living with them off and on up until Nick moved us here, because I just couldn't handle her myself, and I didn't want her near Nick."

"And she's—" How could she put this, Liza wondered as she watched Jilly drench the same few flowers over and over again with water from the little plastic pool they'd filled for her to play in. "This woman...she's not like Nick."

"Not at all. She's wonderful," Ellen said.

Liza could believe that someone else had played an important part in raising Jilly before this. She'd often puzzled over how much self-confidence the little girl had, and over the ease with which she responded to discipline—when there was someone around to discipline her.

And yet, it had been clear from the outset that neither her mother nor her father had ever paid Jilly much attention or known how to manage her. Liza had assumed that there'd been some other nanny that she'd responded well to, but apparently the woman had been more than that to Jilly.

"You think Jilly would be happy there?"

"Jilly loves her, and her little girl, Bitsy."

Liza had heard Jilly talk about the mischievous Bitsy. She would pretend that they were together playing, and if there was trouble—a spilled glass of juice or a crayon mark on the wall—Jilly would sometimes blame Bitsy. Liza had assumed that Bitsy was nothing more than an imaginary friend of Jilly's.

"We used to live not far from them in New Orleans," Ellen continued. "I wanted Jilly to stay there when we moved to Georgia, because I thought she'd be better off. But Nick insisted on taking her with us— I think because he liked the image it gave him, like he was some ordinary family man.

"Well, anyway, I ... thought of taking her there myself, just leaving him, but I knew he would have come after us."

Ellen waited for Liza to challenge her on the idea that she could work up the courage to steal away with Jilly herself, but Liza remained silent.

"And he would have known just where to look for us," she said. "Besides, I didn't want to make trouble for Mary Ann."

"What about now?" Liza asked.

"Mary Ann just moved a few months ago to New Mexico, somewhere in the middle of nowhere, she says. They were careful about moving. She's gotten to be frightened of Nick, too. He did something—I'm not sure what—before we left New Orleans, and she doesn't want to have anything to do with him anymore."

"She doesn't think Nick could find them now?"

"Well, at least not easily," Ellen said. "She's willing to take Jilly and raise her like she was her own, and she's a good mother. A better mother than I could ever hope to be.

"Look. I know you think I'm a lousy mother, and I can't argue with that." Ellen was crying softly as she said it. "But I do want what's best for Jilly. I want her to be safe and happy, and I know I'm not the best person to give her that. I love her enough to give her up so that she can have all those things."

Liza loved Jilly, too, but she'd been doing some thinking of her own. About how well she could raise the child herself. She could give her all the love she needed, and— She stopped. She'd been on her own long enough to know that it would be difficult to support them both.

Liza had never had a job that allowed her to do much more than get by. The jobs she'd had hadn't provided enough money to pay for day care, and they'd almost never supplied health insurance.

And she couldn't give Jilly a ready-made family.

She loved Jilly, too, enough to ache at the thought of losing her, but she wanted her to have the best of everything in life.

"You think that's the best thing for her?" Liza almost choked on the words, because she was already anticipating Ellen's answer.

"Yes, I do."

Fighting back her own tears as she watched the little girl splash in the shallow water of the pool, Liza nodded. "And what about you? What are you going to do?"

"I meant what I said earlier about the pills. I haven't taken anything in fifteen days. I want...I want a clear memory of the last few weeks I have with Jilly."

Liza wasn't aware that she was crying until she felt the tears running down her cheeks.

Ellen laughed sadly. "I threw the pills into the water, because I knew if I had them anywhere around I probably wouldn't be able to resist."

"Oh, Ellen..."

Ellen held up her hand to silence her sister. "Don't. Just don't. I can't explain how I've done this to myself, but— *I've* done it. I spent years blaming everyone but me, but that's not right. It's my life, and this is what I've done with it. I'm...just going to have to live with that."

"You don't have to live like this," Liza insisted. "You don't have to have anything to do with Nick Russell."

"I don't know how to get away from him," Ellen said wearily. "He has this hold on me—I can't explain it, but I can't break it, either. I'm not that strong. I'm just praying I'm strong enough to get Jilly away. That's the most important thing to me now. If I can do that, then...maybe... I don't know. Maybe if I know she's safe, I can think about doing something for myself.

"So," Ellen said tentatively, "you'll take her there for me."

"Yes," Liza promised.

"As soon as we get back to the States? I...I just want to know she's safe."

Liza promised again, but her insides tightened in a knot—what Ellen was asking was illegal. But then, the thought of what her little niece would be exposed to if she wasn't taken away stiffened her spine. She would do as Ellen asked. *If* they made it back.

Chapter 16

It shouldn't be this hard to keep his mind on his job, Deke warned himself as he turned his face into the wind and let the cool spray of the surf rain back upon him.

The little speedboat swept through the choppy water and through the twilight—unnoticed, he hoped, by the watchful eyes of Jamaican customs—carrying him and his partner in crime, Nick Russell, toward the shoreline.

Toward Liza.

That was how he saw it. Not as one step closer to finishing this crazy job, but one step closer to this woman he cared deeply about.

What a way to go, he thought. If one didn't drive him insane, the other was sure to do so.

The actual drug purchase had gone more smoothly than he could have imagined. They'd simply cruised down to Colombia, dropped anchor off this little village at the edge of a thick jungle, and in plain sight of the villagers, had exchanged bundles of money for sacks of cocaine.

The actual deal had taken all of twenty minutes to complete. They'd hardly exchanged a word with the Colombi-

ans who'd unloaded the merchandise from a little speedboat and taken the money in exchange.

He still couldn't believe it had been that easy to carry off
the actual exchange. He'd barely had a chance to work up
a nervous sweat.

But he had one now. They'd been waiting just outside
Jamaican waters for a day now, waiting for Russell's customs buddy to get to work, where he was supposed to be,
so that he could clear them through customs without the
hassle of the inspection that usually accompanied entry into
the country by boat.

They'd gotten into Colombia with no trouble, but now,
when they had a boatful of cocaine and needed the man the
most, he was nowhere to be found.

So they were waiting. Meanwhile, Deke worried and
wondered—not about getting past customs, strangely
enough, but about Liza. He wondered what she was doing
and how he could stay away from her now that he'd tasted
the heaven only she could bring to him.

He braced himself as the boat slowed, then bumped up
against the dock at a busy midisland marina. Tired of
waiting, they'd already agreed upon their plan. Russell's
friend obviously wasn't working with the boats entering
into the country. They were betting that someone had gotten sick, and he was filling in at the customs office. If he
was there, and they could bring him their passports, he
could stamp them right in the office.

Instead of bringing their own boat in, they were simply
going to get Liza, Jilly and Ellen out of the country.

They'd entered the country legally with the help of Russell's friend, but as far as their passports showed, they'd
never left to make the trip to Colombia. They'd simply
gone fishing. Now, before they left, they just needed exit
stamps from Jamaica, or whoever saw their passports
would become suspicious.

It wasn't a bad plan, except that heading for the customs office meant leaving the boat unguarded. Russell
didn't trust Deke to stay alone with the boat, and his cus-

toms friend wouldn't trust Deke enough to illegally stamp the passports for him.

If was so ridiculous it was funny. A crook worried about someone else stealing his ill-gotten gains. Deke wasn't worried. He had no doubt a dozen or so FBI agents were watching the boat to make sure no one else skipped town with Russell's haul. They would make sure the drugs stayed there undisturbed, because they wanted to collar Nick Russell and his whole distribution network in the States. How many crooks had their drugs so well protected?

He and Russell had finally agreed that Russell would go get the passports stamped while Deke got Ellen, Jilly and Liza. Then they'd slip out of the country by taking the speedboat to the Loralei, which was anchored a short distance away.

He checked his watch and Russell checked his as they settled on a time to gather back at the dock for the trip back to the boat. Then Deke flagged down a taxi, gave the driver the address of the villa and sagged back against the seat.

Almost there. Almost close enough to take her into his arms and reassure himself that she was safe. If he could just get close enough to touch her, he'd be all right.

It was daunting to realize that, after dealing with his brother's addiction, handling a smuggler like Nick Russell and pulling off a deal with a Colombian drug lord, he couldn't handle one small woman.

He'd been warring with himself ever since he'd turned his back on her and left, and up until now, he'd believed he'd made at least some peace with himself. There hadn't been any alternatives. He'd *had* to leave her.

But, once again, he'd been wrong.

It was an admission that didn't come easily to him, a condition that he loathed and had difficulty accepting. He simply hated to be wrong.

He was a careful man, he told himself.

He was a cautious one, he'd argued with himself. A methodical, rational man who normally had no problem maintaining his self-control.

She'd stripped all that away from him, as easily as she'd ripped off his clothes.

He couldn't stop himself from smiling at the memory of that morning, the one he couldn't force out of his head.

Almost there.

In the time he'd been gone, he'd worried more about her than he had about himself, even though he'd reassured himself, over and over, with the knowledge that there was no danger to her. He'd left her safe. The same government agencies that were watching him and Russell on the boat would also be watching Liza.

She was safe. She had to be.

So, where was she?

He'd said the words casually when he'd slipped into the villa that night, shortly after midnight.

Ellen hadn't been able to give him an answer. She'd been asleep in a chair in front of the television, with Jilly tucked in beside her, and when he'd woken her up, she'd had no idea where Liza could be.

Now, nearly an hour later, he was repeating the question over and over, each time more anxiously than before.

He'd packed his belongings, Nick Russell's and Liza's while Ellen packed her things and Jilly's. He'd loaded the suitcases in the car, sent Ellen and Jilly back into the house to get some sleep, and now he stood there in the garage, next to that damned car, and asked himself again—where in the hell was she?

Frustrated, he ran his hand through his hair. Early that morning, he'd pleaded with her to trust him, to wait right here for him, to lie low, to make no waves, to simply have faith that he would make it back and that he would get her out of this mess.

He'd had no right to ask for her trust, but he had.

He'd had no right to touch her, either, but he had. He had no right to want her like that again, yet he did. Grimly, even as his mind tried to come up with places she could be, he acknowledged that "wanting" her was exactly the problem. It was at the core of the war he'd been fighting with himself. He couldn't touch her again.

A sexual relationship, to him, wasn't something to be entered into lightly, hastily or carelessly. Deke was past the days when a casual sexual encounter held any appeal for him.

As far as he was concerned, sex was best when it came as part of a relationship, one that could be sustained for some period of time, one with some hope of progressing into permanency, one that involved respect, caring, compatibility, and a basic honesty.

He faced the truth. He cared for Liza, deeply. There were times when he even believed that he was in love with her. And he respected her in more ways than he could count, but he had nothing to offer her in terms of a relationship. None of the things he knew were important, especially honesty and the hope for a future, were his to give.

He cursed inwardly. He'd violated his own rules with her. He'd certainly been hasty and careless in the way he'd taken her. He'd allowed his own physical needs to blind him to what he knew in his head—that he wasn't being fair to her.

His thoughts came to an abrupt halt when he banged a fist against the car. Damn it, where was she?

With each passing moment, it seemed more and more urgent that he know, more and more obvious that he'd been kidding himself when he tried to make himself believe that he could put those moments they'd spent together out of his mind.

So, where was she? He was ready to shout it out and let it echo across the hills. Where was this woman who'd so thoroughly turned him inside out, and why did it seem as if he could survive anything, if only he could have her with him again?

Something had gone wrong.

Liza was sure of it. She'd fought off the panic for the past thirty-six hours, but it was growing. It was expanding inside her chest until she felt she was ready to burst from the pressure of trying to hold it in.

He should be back by now, and he wasn't.

He should never have gone, but he had, and she hadn't been able to stop him.

She shouldn't have cared, but she did, and she didn't know how she'd ever be able to stop—whether he was hers to care about or not.

Care? She mused over the word—it was easier to try to analyze her feelings for the man than to let herself imagine what might have happened to him.

She more than cared for him, more than wanted him, more than needed him.

Oh, Lord. She looked up at the crescent moon, to the stars and beyond, searching for an answer. They should have been back a day and a half ago. What could have gone wrong?

She walked for miles on the beach that night, pushing herself to exhaustion in the hope that if she got that tired she'd be able to sleep, instead of lying in bed and adding to her already-long list of terrible things that could possibly have happened.

Liza was about a half mile from the house, walking up the road, when she heard a noise ahead of her. She looked up, and her breath froze in her lungs.

Deke.

He was back, and the sight of him left her so stunned she just stood there and watched the play of muscles in his arms as he loaded a couple of suitcases into the trunk of the car.

"Deke."

She merely breathed the name.

There was no way it could have carried all the way down the road and into the garage to where he was, and yet, somehow, he was turning around, staring through the darkness, calling her name in return.

Deke heard something, a loose stone bouncing across the pavement, perhaps. He turned, then had to marshal all his efforts to remaining upright as emotion swept through him.

Relief, greater than any he'd ever known, flooded through him. It drowned out everything else and left him simply unable to move now that he could see her, safe and sound, standing in the driveway.

And then she was running to him.

When she got close enough, she jumped into his arms, and he crushed her to him as he lowered her to the floor. He bent his head down so that he could bury his face in her hair. Inhaling deeply, he breathed in that scent that was uniquely hers.

And then, for one glorious moment, all the pieces settled into place and his world righted itself.

"Oh, Lord." She laughed a little, sobbed a little, then smiled up at him, pulling away from him just enough that she could look at his face.

Her hands came up to touch him, softly cradling his face. "I didn't think you were coming back to me."

Back to her. That was it, exactly. He'd come back to her, been drawn back to her by a force that was so much stronger than he was.

"I told you I would."

"And doubted it yourself, even as you said it."

She shivered in his arms. He drew her closer, pressed her head to his chest and wondered if she heard his heart racing in time with this wild melody she'd taught it. He wondered if she knew half the strength of his reaction to her.

He opened his mouth to tell her, then paused. No promises, he told himself. He had none to make, none that he could be sure he could keep.

But he could kiss her. Kissing her wasn't making love to her, and that was what he'd agreed he couldn't—wouldn't—do again. He could kiss her, and that would have to be enough.

Like a man facing a banquet but given only a moment to take what would never be enough to satisfy his hunger, he lowered his lips to hers.

And it wasn't enough. She gave him only a moment, her mouth open and eager beneath his.

"Damn." She pulled away to arm's length, but he wouldn't let her go any farther.

"What?"

Her hands continued to push against his chest, in vain. Tears filled her eyes, and she cursed again.

"Liza?"

"It was just so much easier to be mad at you when you weren't close enough to touch."

He dropped his hands, freeing her of his touch, because he understood. It was so much easier to lie to himself about his feelings for her when she was miles away.

It was the danger, he'd rationalized—or the adrenaline, or the fear, or some combination of them all—that had broken down his control and allowed him to lose himself in her that morning before he'd left.

Unfortunately, all those things had multiplied—and so had the longing that overshadowed all else, that sharpened all his senses and intensified his pleasure until it was so great it blinded him, deafened him, left him unable to put two coherent thoughts together.

Which was probably his biggest problem even now. He was simply unable to think straight.

Or, to put it more bluntly, his thinking seemed to be originating at some point south of his belt buckle instead of between his ears.

He'd witnessed the troubles that afflicted more than one man who thought with that particular organ. He knew it was a condition he couldn't allow to continue.

So he'd told himself, in the endless days that he'd been gone, that it was a fluke, a mistake, a wild reaction to the stress under which he'd been operating lately.

That explained perfectly why he'd reacted to her so strongly, to the pleasure she'd brought him, a pleasure like none he'd ever known.

Right here, he realized, and he started to sweat. He was standing right there in the garage, leaning against the very car they'd made use of that night.

What excuse could he use this time for allowing himself to be swept away, for ignoring the promises he'd made to himself and the lecture he'd given himself on what was fair to her and what wasn't?

A man shouldn't be in the business of constantly finding excuses for his behavior, and God knows he'd made enough excuses for himself lately.

Danger. Fear. Stress. He was suffering under them all. But those weren't the only emotions, he thought as he looked down into her face and watched her fight some battle of her own.

"I couldn't stop thinking about you... about us... the way it was before we left."

"Neither could I," she said, wide-eyed and with color flooding her cheeks.

A tingling heat—from the shared memories, or from the longing for more than memories—rose between them. It vibrated in their midst with a power and presence, an energy, all its own.

What was it? he asked himself. What was this hold she had over him? What kind of name could a man put on a longing like this? And how could he hope to resist it.

He was trembling, he realized, from the effort it took to keep his arms by his side, to let her stay where she was. Trembling from the need to find the strength to walk away from this spot, even as he wished with all his being that he could go back in time, instead of having to face the future.

His chest and shoulders eased forward just a fraction. He intended to reach for her. He intended to take her by the arms and pull her to him again, but he never got the chance.

"I can't forget." She said it sadly now, almost desperately, as she held out her hand, ready to push against his chest, if necessary, to keep him at a distance. "And I won't deny that it's what I wanted at the time."

"But..." he said, knowing an objection was coming, knowing he should be glad, but unable to summon up that particular emotion.

"But I promised myself that it won't happen again."

He exhaled, long and slow, and told himself he should be grateful. But that was another emotion he seemed to be lacking at the moment.

The taste of her lips still lingered on his, as he eased those few inches away from her.

He leaned back against the car for support, and stood there staring at her, all the while wanting more than anything to lift her back up onto the fender, push up her dress, pull down her panties, and forget all the reasons he couldn't sink into her.

"I made myself the same promise," he said, grim with determination.

"Then don't look at me like that." She sounded as if she were begging now. "Don't think about what we did, and don't make me think about it."

"Oh, Liza..." He almost touched her face. She flinched, and he pulled his hand back just in time. He jammed the hand down into his pocket instead. "Ask me anything but that. Anything in the world, and I'll give it to you if I can. But don't ask me to stop thinking about it, because I can't."

"Ask you anything?" He watched the hurt in her eyes give way to despair, and then to what he was sure was anger. "I already asked. I asked you not to stick your fool neck on the line in this crazy smuggling deal with my sister's husband."

His eyes dropped to the floor and he remained silent. What could he say?

"But I'll ask you one more thing," she said, her voice low and intense. "Don't make me fall in love with you, Deke. Don't let me ruin my life by chasing after a criminal and trying to convince myself that I'm going to change him."

It was his turn to flinch, and he hurt then, more than he would have believed possible under the force of mere words. What else could she think of him? He hadn't told her differently.

Deke briefly considered telling her the whole truth, but knew it would be an entirely selfish move on his part. She had the most expressive eyes he'd ever seen, and Russell had already noticed what was going on between them, the attraction, as well as the reluctance, the reservations, the uncertainties.

If all that changed, if he told her something that changed it, Russell would notice that, as well. One look at Liza could give it all away.

And she could easily slip up, say something that would blow his cover. That wouldn't just put him in danger. It would endanger her, as well.

He couldn't be that selfish.

"I'll try to stay out of your way," he said, and inwardly laughed bitterly at the idea. Distance would be hard to come by with both of them on the sailboat together for the next week or so.

"You want to know something really funny?"

No, he didn't. He was sure there was no humor in their situation, and damn sure that she'd found none, either.

"I thought you were different. I thought," she said, eyes suspiciously bright, "that when it came right down to it you wouldn't be able to go through with it. I thought I could change you. Isn't that ridiculous?"

"Liza." He waited for her to look him in the eye before he continued. "I've never done anything like this before, and I never will again." He'd said the same words some time ago, but it was worth trying them again. Maybe this time she would believe him.

"Are you sure? You've been gone for days. It's no telling what kind of trouble your little brother has gotten himself into," she taunted.

"My brother's in a drug treatment hospital in the mountains, trying to clean himself up before he gets himself killed."

"Even so," she shot back at him, refusing to let sympathy at the news soften her, "he won't be there forever. How far will you go the next time to save him, Deke?"

"I'm not sure," he said tersely. Silently he congratulated her. She hadn't known him long, but already she knew what buttons to push to get to him.

"Except that you haven't reached that point yet."

"No. I've passed it."

With anger and hurt in her eyes, she challenged him with her gaze.

"I have, but I don't blame you for not believing me."

"Should I? My sister believed Russell when he promised he'd never make another drug run like this, and you can see where believing him has gotten her."

And what was he going to say to that? That he wasn't anything like Nick Russell? She'd laugh at him for sure, and with good reason. She knew what they'd just done.

"I don't want to hurt you, Liza." It was all he could say.

"Then don't. Do me a favor and stay away from me, because I'm not sure I have the strength to stay away from you."

"All right." He'd do it if it killed him. Surely he could do that for her.

"I've fought my whole life to find some respect for myself, to be able to look myself in the mirror and not be ashamed of the woman looking back at me. I've watched more women than I can count make fools of themselves over some man, including my own mother and my sister, Deke. I can't end up like them."

"I understand," he said. "I'm having some trouble looking in the mirror myself these days."

He searched for something, anything that he was free to tell her that might help her to understand him—he wanted so much to be able to make her understand—but there was nothing he could reveal. Raging inwardly against the tangled chain of lies and deceptions that held him back, he turned sharply on his heel and walked out of the garage, leaving her to follow behind him.

Chapter 17

He'd stayed away, Deke thought as he tugged impatiently at the buttons on his shirt, then stripped it off. And it had damn near killed him.

He owed it to her, he knew, and yet now that she was here, standing against the fender of the car, where he'd imagined having her time and time again, he couldn't summon up the strength to resist any longer.

Deke couldn't sleep without dreaming of her. He dreamed he was free from every promise he'd ever made, to his brother and a dozen government agencies. He dreamed that he explained everything to her. She understood. She forgave. She came into his arms, eagerly, without having to be ashamed of herself for wanting him regardless of what she believed him to be.

He couldn't stay awake and not think about her. He'd watched her for two days now as she struggled to stay out of his way on the boat, one that steadily seemed to be shrinking in size. It was impossible for them to avoid one another, and at least twice a day he was tortured by the feel of her as she brushed past him in the narrow confines of the sailboat.

So he had no sleep, and no peace when he was awake. It was no wonder he felt this strange lethargy flooding through his limbs, now, at this moment when she'd given in, when he realized she'd come to him.

He watched in awe as she slipped up onto the car fender, then went to work unbuttoning the man-size shirt she wore. He recognized it as the one she wore so often over her bikini. A shirt that she often left unbuttoned to the point where, just barely, because he was so much taller than she was, he could see the beginning swell of her breasts. A shirt whose hem brushed maddeningly back and forth against her smooth thighs.

There had been times when Deke thought he might have to go to his grave still wanting to take that damn shirt off her, and here she was doing it for him.

She smiled at him as the third button came loose in her hands. He swallowed hard and wished his hands were the ones unbuttoning her shirt. Of course, he was trembling so badly that he knew she could probably get the job done faster than he could.

Besides, he was afraid to move, afraid that if he did she would disappear, as she had in his dreams.

Hard and hurting, he watched as the last button came free, watched as she slid the shirt open from her neck down to her thighs, showing a tantalizing strip, maybe two inches wide, of bare skin, all the way down.

He didn't have to wonder, now, as he had so often in the past, exactly what she was wearing under that shirt. Nothing. Nothing at all.

Deke smiled, trying to calm his heart as it sent the blood thundering through his veins.

This time, he promised himself, it was going to last. He was going to make it last. He had a long list of things he'd wished he'd done to her before, when he'd had the chance, a list that had grown day after day as he'd wondered whether he'd ever get this chance again.

Another chance. He would have shouted for joy, except that he didn't want to attract any attention. After all, they were in the damn garage. Parking his car would never be the same again.

Finally he let himself touch her. He extended his hand, let his fingertips brush down the soft strip of skin exposèd by the open edges of the shirt. So soft. So warm, although she shivered, her skin beaded with pleasure, in the wake of his touch.

His hand stroked on down, over the soft, sensitive skin of her belly, and he watched as her eyes closed, watched her mouth open in a silent gasp, maybe a plea, as he reached the end of his journey, found the tangle of curls at the juncture of her thighs.

He merely skimmed the spot. He couldn't allow himself to linger there—not yet, not when there were so many other places he wanted to explore first.

He had to keep his wits about him, he reminded himself, had to forget, for the moment, how easily he could be inside her once again.

Grabbing her hand, he tugged on it until she slid off the car and stood, still and trusting, before him.

He turned her around so that she stood with her back to him, and then he pulled the shirt down, baring her shoulders so he could fit his mouth to that sensitive spot where neck met shoulder. He skimmed the area with his tongue, and then, after feeling the response quiver through her body, he nibbled at that sensitive skin.

"Dixon."

His name was a breathless plea on her lips—his real name.

His mouth moved on down, sucking, licking, nibbling his way over her right shoulder, across the top of her arm, then diagonally across her back to her spine until she was shaking so hard he wasn't sure how she was still standing.

Finally he let the shirt drop, stood up and encircled her waist with his arms, allowing his hands to feel their way slowly across her stomach, then up, rib by rib, to the delicate underside of her breasts.

He spread his fingers around them, took their weight in his hands and ran his thumbs back and forth along the outside curve of each breast. He groaned. He remembered these curves. He'd spotted one that first morning through the oversized arm holes on the nightshirt she'd worn. He'd meant to taste them then, to tease them and memorize the shape and the feel of them, but he'd gotten sidetracked.

Not tonight, he promised himself as she sagged weakly against him. He caught her and held her in place by sandwiching her lower body between the car and his own body.

Caressing her breasts still, he rocked his hips against her in a gut-tightening rhythm, one that satisfied and frustrated all at the same time. It was wonderful to feel her body cradling his arousal, but frustrating as hell, too, because he still had his pants on, because he wasn't moving like this inside her.

He wanted his skin against hers, and he wanted his mouth on her breasts, now.

"Damn," he muttered. Gently he pushed her down to rest on her stomach against the top of the car, then stepped back to rid himself of his clothes. "Don't fall."

She laughed. "Don't let me."

He took a deep breath and drank in the sight of her, naked as a newborn, in the pale light of the moon, or what little of it made its way into the garage.

The night air bathed his skin. It left him feeling wicked and free.

He decided that she had the nicest bottom he'd ever seen. He'd thought that before, when he'd watched her romp around the boat in a T-shirt and a bikini bottom. But now, with no cloth getting in his way, he could say for sure. It was the nicest one he'd ever seen. And it was just sitting there, waiting for him, once he finally decided exactly what he wanted to do with it. No, he thought with a smile, once he figured out in what order he would touch her, do the things he'd been fantasizing about.

He started with one fingertip. It traced its way up the back of her leg, went behind her knee, and moved in a seemingly purposeless direction along her thigh.

She moaned and squirmed under his touch. He merely smiled and gave the other leg the same treatment. And then, because it was simply too inviting to pass up, he made the same journey with his mouth.

Her legs were firm, her muscles trembling, and she protested weakly, "I can't stand it."

"You can't?" he said innocently, pulling his lips away from a point midway up the back of her right thigh. "Do you want me to stop?"

"Don't you dare."

He continued on, up and around one hip and then onto the other. He nibbled on that fleshy curve, teased her with his hands on her thighs, stroking up and down the back. Then he reached the sensitive skin on her inner thighs.

He wanted to tease her some more by thrusting against the curve of her bare bottom. He wanted to bury himself inside her. He wanted to taste her, and he still hadn't gotten to that delicate outer curve of her breasts.

He cupped a hip in each hand and kneaded the smooth flesh while he considered his options. He'd never get to them all, not in one night. He'd need a week at least to do half the things he wanted to do to her.

"Dixon?"

"I'm thinking," he said, loving the sound of his name on her lips. He turned her over and settled himself between her thighs.

"About what?"

She looked dazed, he realized, and the thought brought him immense satisfaction. He'd wondered if it was the same for her as it was for him, if his power over her was just as strong as hers over him. And the way she looked now told him all he needed to know.

"About how wicked you make me feel."

Her only response was a ragged cry—his name. It had never sounded better to him, he thought, as his lips skimmed up the inside of one thigh. She protested weakly, by trying to push her legs together, but he wouldn't let her.

She didn't know, he thought triumphantly. She hadn't let anyone touch her like this before, and she had no idea how good he was going to make her feel.

Her hands came down to push him away, but stilled at the first touch of his lips. He dropped little kisses along those curls, teased her mercilessly, then set out to drive her mad.

She jerked in surprise, her head coming up off the top of the car, her whole body tensing, as he settled his mouth over the most sensitive spot of all.

"Oh," she moaned raggedly, then collapsed back against the hood of the car.

With his hands, he showed her how to wrap her legs around him. She hugged him to her with those legs and with the hands that settled into his hair and pulled him even closer.

He wanted her mindless with desire, oblivious to everything but the passion they shared, and she was. He wanted her to beg for him, and she did.

He wanted—

A buzzer?

Surely not, he thought as he reached for her again. His hands closed around her waist, grabbing onto—air?

Damn it, where had she gone?

The buzzer? He cursed again, loudly this time, more crudely than before.

"Deke?"

It was Liza, and when he closed his eyes, he could still see her, her body spread out beneath his, ready to receive him. But there was nothing there when he reached out to touch her.

Damn. He could have lain down and cried, right then and there. Dreams didn't get that good. Surely they didn't.

"Deke?"

"What?" He growled it.

"What's wrong?"

He made himself open his eyes, then wished he hadn't.

Aw, hell!

He was on the boat.

And Liza wasn't naked, although she'd obviously just jumped out of bed at the sound of the buzzer. And as if he needed anything else to remind him of what he'd so nearly had, she was wearing that nightshirt he'd torn off her in the garage. Her hair was in disarray, and she had a heavy-lidded look about her that was too close to the look she'd given him a moment ago, when he'd had her on top of the car.

She was driving him crazy.

He was on deck, on watch, sitting out in the open in the cool night air, supposedly watching over the boat as it moved through the sea, and he'd been having X-rated dreams about her.

"Nothing's wrong," he growled as he glanced at the dials and spotted the problem—the depth meter. Quickly looking off to the left of the console, he identified the shadow of one of the cays in the area. They'd obviously skimmed too close to it.

"We're just a little closer to that island than I realized, and I'm about to run this poor boat aground," he said, grim amusement in his voice, as he altered the course slightly to pull the boat in a wider circle around the edge of the small island.

"Sleeping on watch?" She had the nerve to smile as she said it. Oh, yeah, he thought, his gaze fascinated by her lush mouth. She was driving him crazy, and, damn it, she was enjoying it.

"No." He smiled right back, figuring she had it coming. "I had my face buried between your thighs with you begging for me, and I was just about to give you exactly what you and I both wanted so desperately."

She paled instantly. He could see it, even in the dim light shining from the console. She would have turned and fled down the steps to the cabin then, if he'd let her. But he didn't. He couldn't let her go so easily with this frustration eating at him.

He grabbed her by the arms and, because he seemed to be a glutton for punishment, pulled her close enough that he could just barely feel the tips of her breasts brush against his chest.

"What have you done to me?" His voice, low and desperate, pleaded with her to explain it to him. He needed to know, although he doubted he would ever understand.

"What have you done to me?" She sounded as perplexed as he did, and that helped. It wasn't enough, but it helped.

"You've bewitched me." He whispered the words against her lips, and then kissed her mouth, remembering the way she'd tasted in his dream.

Oh, he was a glutton for punishment. He knew it as he kissed her desperately, hungrily, because he realized that at any moment she'd come to her senses and remember that they weren't supposed to be doing this, that she'd asked for his help in staying away from him, and that he'd promised to give it.

He was supposed to stay away. He could touch her like this, but only when she came to him in the night in his dreams.

"Dixon."

Yes, he thought. Dixon. Dixon was her lover. Deke was her liar, her crook, her downfall.

"Dixon?"

He heard the regret, heard the longing, the confusion, in her voice, all the same emotions that were flowing through his heart at that moment.

He stepped back, just an inch or two, but kept his arms around her and leaned his forehead down against hers.

"Someday," he whispered, "this is all going to be behind us. We're going to get out of this mess, and then it's going to be different between us. I promise."

She shook her head sadly, pushed lightly against his chest, and he had no choice but to drop his hands and let her back away. She'd already made it clear that she didn't want to hear any of his promises.

Chapter 18

Had she judged him too harshly? Liza wondered as she watched Deke from the window of the bedroom.

They were in one of the little keys near Key West. It was their last night there, and, as he always did, Deke was heading down the path that connected the villa to the deserted cove where she played with Jilly each day.

He was going swimming again, and she was worried. He was a strong swimmer, but he shouldn't be down there alone at night. No one should.

Liza couldn't help but laugh at that. She'd managed, somehow, to keep herself out of his bed, but she still worried about him swimming alone at night. A telling admission for sure, but she knew that she wouldn't sleep, no matter how hard she tried, until he returned.

In vain she searched her mind for some explanation for his actions. Not an excuse—that wasn't what she sought—not some way a weak man would try to justify his wrongdoing, but an actual explanation for what he'd done. Something she could understand, if not respect. Something she could accept.

After all, people did make mistakes. Lord knows she was far from perfect.

Sighing, she wondered if she could have such strong feelings for an uncommon criminal. He wasn't a common one, of that she could be sure. But still, she argued with herself, he'd done it. He'd gone with Russell. He was captaining a boat full of drugs, guiding it back into the States. And he'd risked everything, his own life, though she would have sworn he wasn't a reckless man.

He was thoughtful, kind, caring, conscientious. He was stronger, smarter and sexier than any man she'd ever known. And she wanted him desperately.

But if she gave in now, forgave him for this, how many other times would there be? How many more promises of changing would never be kept? How many times would he tell her that he was doing it for the last time, only to disappoint her again? How many times would she disappoint herself by believing him and staying with him regardless of what he was?

She wanted to go to him, to grab what little time they had left before they returned, before he put himself in danger again distributing the drugs they'd bought...before she had to live up to her promise to save the both of them by turning him in.

Sometime later, after she'd tidied her room, checked on Jilly and tried to read a little of the island's history in a tourist guide, she realized that he'd been gone a long time.

She fought with herself for another ten minutes, but then couldn't hold out any longer. All she wanted to do was make sure he was safe, she told herself as she made her way down the narrow, sandy path to the cove.

It was a gorgeous night, warm, the breeze gentle, the waves a dull roar coming through a fine mist of fog that hugged the shoreline.

Liza paused at the dune line. Swaying back and forth on tiptoe to get a better view, she scanned the water. She could just see a swimmer's arms stroking steadily through the water, parallel to the shoreline. Deke swept back and forth at a relentless pace that left her breathless just thinking about the energy it required.

He was safe, for now, and for the moment that fat knot of worry that sat heavily in her chest almost constantly these days eased a bit.

Safe. At least he was. She wasn't so sure about herself when a few minutes later, he swam into waist-deep water, stood and then walked out of the surf.

Damn, she thought, frozen to the spot. He *would* swim without a stitch on. She found it impossible to force her eyes away from him.

Tall and lean, with the muscles of his thighs stretching and contracting, he moved easily out of the water, then paused to look toward the villa.

Looking for her? She'd never been able to pick him out through the darkness from her window, but she wondered if he'd ever seen her, if he knew how she waited for him to return each night. She decided he probably did. He always seemed to see much more than he had a right to see when it came to her.

"I'm down here tonight," she called out, compelled to move closer.

The tightening of his jaw was the only indication she saw that she'd surprised him.

He made no move to cover himself. He just stood there, rock-solid and dripping wet, reminding her of a beautiful marble statue she'd seen one day in the aftermath of a rainstorm.

Hard, she thought, yet so touchable, so warm, so gloriously alive. Why did he have to be so damn attractive? she wondered distractedly. Why did he have to be the only man who'd taught her about a desire so strong that a normally sane woman could get drunk on just a taste? About a passion that threatened to push every rational thought out of her head? One that made her, ever-sensible, ever-cautious female that she was, want to forget about all her tomorrows and live only for the moment, with him.

He made it hard for her to breathe, she realized as she
hesitated there. She just stared at him. There'd been no time
that night, when they'd been together in the garage, when
she'd been so desperate for him, for her to really look at
him.

That morning. She winced inwardly. It had been a purely
desperate move, fueled by the fear that she would never see
him again, that she would always regret not having had at
least a few moments with him.

And it wasn't just desire that she felt for him, although
at the moment she found the strength of that attraction
simply staggering.

Give up, she told herself. Give in. Take the moment, with
no thoughts of the future, no promises. There would be
time—too much time, she feared—for regrets, later, when
the trip was over and she was gone.

She couldn't miss him any more than she already did,
couldn't want him any less, now that she'd had just one
hurried moment in time. So where was the harm in being
with him for the two or three days that they had left?

In her passion-clouded mind, she could see none, could
see nothing but him.

He stood there silently, watching her watch him. She
heard him curse low and long, at himself or her—she
couldn't tell.

"Don't look at me like that," he demanded darkly, then
turned and headed back to the waves.

"Like what?" she asked.

"Like you're enjoying the view." He just kept on walking.

"I was." She said it without thinking, more to herself
than to him, but he heard her and whirled around. Her
cheeks flamed when she realized what she'd admitted.

"I was enjoying the view." She said it louder this time,
almost defiantly, and so that there was no mistake about
whether he heard her or about exactly what she meant.

She'd thrown him off balance with that. He looked like he was about to choke, and the thought of unsettling him pleased her immensely. He always seemed so self-assured.

He might have been made of marble then, he grew so still as he stood there in two feet of water. And she felt a moment's panic now that she'd thrown herself at him and he was hesitating.

"You do still . . . want me. Don't you?"

"Liza, I could swim to China and back in the dead of winter and still ache for you."

"Then . . ."

"You told me to stay away, and I promised I would."

And he kept his word. He didn't say it, but then he didn't have to. Maybe he thought she wouldn't believe it, now that she knew what he and Nick Russell had done, but she did.

Despite everything else, there was a sense of honor about him, a deeply held, deeply personal code that he measured himself by under normal circumstances.

She'd watched him as he struggled with it all along the trip. Struggled and lost, but only for the time being. He would get it back. Liza wanted to believe that, and she wondered where she'd be when he did, wondered what it would cost her if she stayed around and waited until that happened.

He would get back his self-respect. That was what her instincts told her about this man. And she trusted her instincts.

What would she regret more—being with him, or being without him? For now, there was no contest. Being without him carried more pain than she'd ever believed.

"And if I told you that . . . I'd changed my mind? A woman is allowed to change her mind, isn't she?"

"Liza." Her name rolled off his tongue, with a thousand questions attached to it. "God knows I don't want to stay away, but I think it's for the best—for you. I don't have any right . . ."

But he still wanted her. She could feel it radiating from him like a force field.

Liza walked toward him and into the lukewarm water, heedless of the way it soaked the bottom edge of her nightshirt, until she was close enough to touch him.

With one finger, she traced the path of a single rivulet of water that ran down his chest, just to the right of the center. She felt him tense, heard the hiss of a harshly drawn breath, felt his chest swell with it, even as she followed that line of moisture as it tangled in the hairs on his chest, dipped and swelled over the finely defined muscles of his stomach. She lost the trail, and her nerve, as it dipped even lower.

"I don't want to talk about rights or wrongs, yours or mine," she said as she gathered up the wet hem of her nightshirt. She kept talking, knowing she had to or he would never accept that, for now at least, her plea that he stay away from her was null and void.

"I don't want you to make promises you can't keep or to apologize for anything you've done or might have to do before this is over."

She watched him, saw the struggle it was for him to stay still, and wondered why he still tried. Apart from a muscle twitching in his jaw, he seemed to have no reaction to the sight of her slowly pulling the wet fabric up over her hips and above her waist. Lord, she was turning into a wicked, wanton woman.

"And I don't want to think about the future. Whatever happens will happen, and I can handle it, whatever it is," she assured him. Her heart called her a liar, but she ignored it. She needed, *he* needed, tonight.

The nightshirt cleared her waist, her breasts, then her head, and she threw it toward the beach, not caring if it made it.

The night air was like a warm, silky caress on her breasts, her back, her stomach.

"I want to swim," she said innocently.

She felt so free now that she was no longer fighting so hard against her own body. Liza didn't intend to wait for him. She expected him to struggle much longer than she had before giving in.

But he surprised her a few minutes later when, as she stood in the surf, she felt his hands on either side of her thighs. Her eyes looked up into his and found a tangled mixture of desire and something else there—dread of losing control, of giving in to something he'd fought so hard to resist?

Still, he pulled, ever so gently, against her legs until her thighs came to rest against the tense muscles of his. Then his hands slid up to her hips, and she lost every bit of air in her lungs as he fitted his lower body to hers and she felt the unmistakable need he was fighting to control.

His hands, so warm and so sure, moved up to her waist, to her shoulders, and soon her breasts were nestled against his wet, warm chest.

He cupped her buttocks then and tilted her head up to his, held her still. He groaned deep in his throat, then began kissing her face, softly, quickly, catching a cheek here, the corner of her lips there, as if he were afraid to let himself do anything more at the moment.

"You make me forget." The words seemed torn from deep inside him. "Everything else but you just flies out of my head, and then everything is you. All that I see, all that I hear, all that I feel, all that I want. You. Just you."

And the admission freed him. It set off a reaction in him, and his mouth fused itself to hers in a hot, wild kiss that left her weak in the knees. He must have felt it, too, because the next thing she knew he'd lowered them both into the water, to kneel in the fine sand along the bottom and sway with the ebb and flow of the tide.

Her breasts barely cleared the surface now. He cupped them in his hands and teased them with his thumb, squeezing them gently all the while. Then he took them into his mouth, first the left, then the right, then back again, as if he couldn't decide which one he wanted more. He was nipping at her, suckling gently, as if starved for the taste of her.

Liza let her head roll back against her shoulder and looked up into the night sky.

This couldn't be wrong, she told herself as she closed her eyes and gave herself up to the glorious feel of his tongue teasing her nipple. Nothing that felt so right could be wrong.

Ever since she'd seen him walk naked out of the water, she'd felt all fluttery inside, as if he'd turned on a thousand shimmering lights inside her body, and she was glowingly alive with the feeling.

Now that he was finally touching her, the lights were bursting inside her, showering her with heat and leaving her weak in their wake.

A wave came along then, surprising them both, nearly topping both their heads, and leaving them both laughing and sputtering when they finally righted themselves.

"Careful," she said, as, still on his knees, he half tugged, half dragged her into shallower water. "I only came down here tonight because I was worried about you swimming alone. I didn't want you to drown yourself."

"Liar," he taunted, capturing her breast once again.

She just laughed, until she couldn't anymore, until the things he was doing to her stole every bit of breath from her body. He was sitting in the water, and he'd pulled her down onto his lap, but she wanted more. She wanted him inside her, filling that achingly empty space.

Her hands clutched at him, frantically now, as the need built to a fever pitch. She leaned back in the water, intending to take him with her.

"No way," he said as he saved her from herself. "You'd drown for sure, and you'd probably take me with you, because I'm not about to let a little water stop me from having you now."

They let the next few waves help carry them a little farther up onto the beach, until Liza was lying on her back at the edge of the surf. Her head was on the sand, but her toes were still in the water.

On his hands and knees now, he paused. His eyes raked hers. His chest rose and fell heavily with each breath he took.

"Witch," he muttered, the sound low and laced with longing. "You've bewitched me."

Liza would have protested that surely it was the other way around, but then his teeth sank gently into one of her toes, then another, then the side of her knee.

She gasped and squirmed beneath his mouth, but she couldn't get free. By then he was lying between her legs, nuzzling the sensitive skin of her inner thighs.

Too much. The sensations, piling one atop another, spilling over, bathing her entire body, were too strong, too intense. He was moving ever closer to that spot, to that ache, to the desperately empty space that she so wanted him to fill.

"Dixon!" His name was a breathless, desperate cry that she couldn't have held back for anything as she felt his lips close over that spot.

A little wave rolled in, pushing the surf a little higher, so that it swirled under the back of her shoulders and behind her head.

Liza suspected it got him, too, because he laughed wickedly and, with a hand under one hip, urged her up a little higher on the beach.

Then he just grinned at her as she lay back in the sand, waiting for him.

"The other night on the boat, I was dreaming of you, and you interrupted me."

His eyes glittering through the darkness of the night, he knelt between her legs.

"I didn't get to finish what I'd started in the dream, but I'm going to. Now."

Her whole body tensed, rose up off the sand and then sank weakly back against it at the touch of his mouth, there, on that spot, that terribly empty spot.

"I can't—" She barely got the words out before a cry of pure pleasure escaped from her lips.

"Yes, you can."

"I can't stand it." She bucked beneath him, but he held her captive, refusing to let her escape his marauding lips, until she wasn't trying to escape any longer, until she lost her fear of the intensity of the passion he'd unleashed.

Now, with her hands on his head, she was clutching him to her, her body undulating under the sweet pressure of his mouth. She was moving with him, urging him on, until the pleasure built inside her, until the ground beneath her fell away and she was floating, weightless, suspended on the edge of the world, with him.

She called his name, clung to him, until the trembling ceased.

"Hmmm?" she said, not sure what he'd said, not surprised that she'd missed it, considering the fact that he was kissing her again. Her belly, this time, with soft little butterfly kisses that tickled and warmed her all at once.

"I said you taste salty and sandy." The words were muttered against her breasts.

She smiled, shifted to accommodate him, as she finally felt his weight settle on top of her, inside her.

Then he kissed her mouth, somehow smiling as he did it.

She laughed—also wickedly, she thought. "You taste of salt and sand and me."

Somehow, much later, they found the strength to get back in the water, rinse off at least some of the sand, and trek back to the villa.

Liza thought at first he was taking her in through the garage entrance, but then Deke stopped beside the rental car. One look at his face told her why.

"Where are we going?" she asked innocently.

"For a ride," he answered, lifting her up onto the fender of the car. "You want to go for a ride?" he asked, his voice seductively low.

"That depends," she said, feeling the need rising inside her once again, "on where we're going to go."

"Don't worry." He stripped off his clothes, then hers. "I know the way. I must have been there a thousand times in my mind."

Chapter 19

Liza woke up, cold and alone, wishing it wasn't so. She was in her little bed in the cabin on the boat. Bravely she pried one eyelid open and found the red glow of the clock. Lord, she hated that clock. Especially right about now.

It was ten to six. Ten minutes until she was supposed to be on deck to take over the watch. She let the eyelid droop down, rolled over and wished she didn't have to move.

She wanted to go back to the Keys, back to that morning, back to a time when she hadn't awakened alone. It hadn't been that long ago—only two and a half days—but the time in between, made up of one day of sailing, then a thirty-six-hour stop in Florida for engine repairs, had been terrible. They'd been together, but they hadn't been able to be *together*.

He had the watch from midnight until six. She took over from then until noon, while he slept for a few hours, then took another stretch from noon to six. Ellen took the last shift, from six till midnight.

So if one of them wasn't sleeping, one was on watch—or Liza was taking care of Jilly.

She wanted to go back to the island, back to that night. They'd come in from the garage and gotten into the shower together. He'd washed the sand, the sea and the scent of their lovemaking off her. Then he'd crawled into bed with her, and reached for her yet again. Sometime before dawn, she'd awakened, tired still, and a little sore, but wrapped up in his arms.

"I wonder," he'd said as he'd dried her off so gently that night after they'd climbed out of the shower, "what it would be like to make love to you on a bed?"

He'd rolled her up in the towel, thrown her over his shoulder and lowered her, none too gently, onto the bed. Then he'd gone back to her door, aiming for the lock.

"I want to be hidden away behind a locked door," he'd said, as the lock clicked into place. "In a place where no one knows us, where no one has any hold over either one of us, where it's just you and me and time. I want so much time."

Someday, she'd wanted to tell him. Someday it would be like that. But she didn't. She couldn't. She'd set the terms of their relationship. She hadn't asked for any promises, and he'd offered none.

Now. That was all she'd bargained for. Here and now, with him, with no claims to his future.

And she was going to make the most of it while she could. There'd be plenty of time for regrets later.

Liza crawled out of her lonely bed, pulled on a sweatshirt and black stretch pants and stumbled into the galley. She was finally getting this boat language down.

It was early still. Everyone else was asleep, and for a few precious moments, she and Deke could be alone. With two mugs of coffee—the real thing for her, decaf for him—she climbed up on deck.

She sensed trouble immediately. "What's wrong?"

He smiled when he saw her, gulped down a mouthful of the coffee, then gave her a quick kiss. "Good morning."

"Good morning. What's wrong?"

He shrugged, sipped some more, then kissed her again, quickly, on the lips.

"What?" she prodded.

"Nothing, Liza, really. The man on the dock, the one we passed just before we left Miami. I think I figured out why I know him. I thought at first...work...some job that I had years ago. But now I think I knew him from home. I think he was a friend of Charlie's."

She waited, not understanding why it mattered.

He couldn't tell her why the thought had made his blood run cold. They'd merely passed each other on a crowded dock, but there had been something about the way the kid looked at him, about the way he turned around and watched him walk away. He'd said something to Nick Russell, seemed to know him—but whether he was a long-standing acquaintance or just someone Russell had met in the day and a half they'd been there, Deke didn't know.

What if the kid had remembered him? Fear, cold as ice, slid down his spine. If he knew Charlie, he could know too much about Deke, like the fact that he'd gone to law school, that he worked as a federal prosecutor.

One of his worries, when he'd agreed to this crazy scheme, was that he was a little too close to the place where he and Charlie had grown up. But he'd relied on the fact that he hadn't been back in a long time, and that Charlie was so much younger than he was. Where he'd grown up, as well, wasn't the kind of place people stayed, not the ones who had any ambition. He and Charlie hadn't shared their friends, and Deke had hardly been back since he'd left thirteen years ago.

But if the kid had been friends with Charlie recently, if he'd been around the few times Deke had come home long enough to bail Charlie out of trouble—then he might know. He might know what Deke did for a living. And what could be more startling than Russell hanging out with a federal prosecutor? Certainly something to remark upon to a friend.

"It was nothing," he told her. He smiled, then kissed the taste of coffee from her lips. "I just hate seeing a face I know and not being able to put a name to it."

They were almost home, he reminded himself as he went below to try to sleep in a bed still warm from Liza's body, a bed that still held the scent of her. He closed his eyes and told himself to be thankful that it was almost over and that soon, very soon, they would both be safe.

And he tried not to wonder, as he always did these days, what he was going to do with her once this whole mess was over. What was he going to do with these feelings he had for her.

Time, Deke thought as he stripped out of his clothes and crawled into the bed. That was what he wanted. Time, with her, with just the two of them, to figure out what they had.

He could get that time to sort out those feelings, he told himself as he rolled over so that his head was buried in the pillow and he was surrounded by her sweet smell.

One thing he knew—the feelings he had for her weren't going to go away. He was sure of it.

He was kissing her, for real this time, and he wasn't sure he could stop. She'd just finished her watch at noon, and he wasn't due to take over until after lunch, which she was fixing.

With Russell on deck, taking a rare turn manning the controls, and Ellen cleaning and dressing Jilly, he and Liza had found a precious few moments to spend together. And he intended to spend them kissing her. He had her pinned up against the galley wall with his mouth locked on hers and his hand up under her shirt, under her bra, holding her breast.

"Damn," he said.

"What now?"

It did crazy things to him when she looked at him that way—a little dazed, a little surprised, satisfied with what they'd started and disappointed that they couldn't finish.

"The shower stopped." He straightened her clothes for her, because it gave him another excuse to touch her. "Ellen and Jilly will be out here soon. Besides, I'm starting to worry about my breakfast."

"That's the risk you take when you start distracting the cook," she said.

She smiled as she turned lazily back to the stove. He just stood there and watched her, aching to touch her. He was in bad shape—bad. He'd had her in his arms not thirty seconds ago, and already his hands were itching to touch her again.

The sound of Ellen and Jilly singing a limerick came from inside the forward cabin, and he latched on to it.

"I didn't hold out much hope for Ellen, but she seems to be doing much better. She seems almost straight."

Liza shrugged. "She's getting there."

"She's even making progress with Jilly. Maybe there's hope for her yet as a mother."

"No. It's not like that." She scooped the omelet she'd been cooking out of the skillet and onto a plate that she'd placed on the counter for him. "Ellen's given up on mothering Jilly. She's just trying to store up some memories for when she's gone."

Deke got a fork, some salt and the plate to take to the long, narrow tabletop that folded down from the wall when it was needed. "Where's Ellen going?"

"She's not." Liza poured him coffee, then poured herself a cup. "I can't explain why, but I don't think she'll ever leave Nick Russell. But she can't risk letting Jilly stay around him either."

"She took a hell of a risk already for a woman who's supposedly so concerned about her daughter. She had to know what he was up to."

"You want to talk about taking risks with other people's lives?" As she asked the question, Liza set his coffee down on the table, none too gently.

Deke suddenly seemed to have lost his appetite. "I tried to warn you away. I would have helped you get out, you and Jilly."

"But you, just as much as Nick and Ellen, have put us both in danger."

He paled at that and put down his fork. He couldn't argue with that. He'd told himself the same thing often enough.

"Look," she said, "I don't want to argue with you about this. I think you must have your reasons for what you're doing. Maybe you'll tell me someday, and maybe I'll understand. But that's just it. I feel the same way about what Ellen's done—I hate it, I'm mad as hell at her—at you both, but I still can't stop myself from . . . Ellen's my sister, and I love her. I . . . I care about you, too."

Did she love him? Was that what she'd meant to say before she caught herself? He went still at the thought. How could she love him?

Deke stood, put his hands on her shoulders, squeezing for a moment. He had to be wrong. She wouldn't let herself love a man who'd done what she believed he'd done. Disappointment mingled with relief at his logic. Then he thought of something else, and his heart froze. Maybe she did love him, despite everything, and she hated herself for it.

He threw his hands up in the air and put his back to her. He hoped to God neither of those two alternatives were anywhere near the truth. Because if she loved him, then what he'd done to her—to them both—could never be forgiven.

Almost home, he told himself as the frustration ate at him. They were almost there. They were going to make it, and then he could tell her. He would explain, and he would make her understand. She *had* to understand.

"Liza, I never would have forgiven myself if anything had happened to you."

"I know that." She put her hand on her neck and rubbed at the tight cords there. "Anyway, Ellen feels the same way about Jilly, and I promised her I'd get Jilly out of here. I'm taking her, and we're leaving as soon as we get back.''

''*How* soon?'' He turned then, and the worry showed in his face.

''The moment we get back, Deke. I figure you and Russell will still have some business to take care of, and we'll just slip away. Ellen has some money she's been saving for Jilly, and she has a place for us to go.''

''You can't go. At least not right away.'' The urgency was clearly evident in his voice. The authorities would be picking up anyone who left that house the first two or three days, since most of them would be part of Nick Russell's drug distribution network. He didn't want the FBI getting its hands on Liza and Jilly. His eyes darkened. If he had to, he intended to lock them inside their rooms until everything was settled.

Deke's biggest fear now was that the FBI would bust into the house like a dozen Rambos with their guns blazing, and that one of them would be hurt.

''It's going to be too dangerous at first, Liza. There're going to be a lot of... people coming and going the first couple of days, and I don't want you to get mixed up with any of them. When we get to the house, just stay put. Stay low. When the time comes, I'll get you both out.''

She looked skeptical, but she wasn't arguing, either. He took that as a good sign. ''Besides, you and I have some things to discuss first.''

Liza stuck her chin up in the air and blinked hard, but not before he saw the way her eyes glistened.

Deke swore. He felt like such a heel. He'd made nothing but wrong moves ever since he'd met her.

''There's so much I want to tell you.'' The moisture was seeping out of the corner of her right eye, and he carefully brushed it away with his thumb. ''Don't leave without giving me a chance to explain.

''Promise me that, at least,'' he urged when she didn't answer.

Silence greeted him, a heavy silence, so great that he picked up the metallic sound of a voice coming over the boat's radio.

The way it was quickly muffled left him feeling vaguely uneasy. He had a sixth sense, an instinct that had, in the past, warned him more than once of bad times ahead. Granted, that feeling of dread *had* been working overtime all the way down to Colombia and all the way back, for no reason, but now it screamed at him. Jumped-up-and-down, beat-him-over-the-head–bellowed at him.

"Liza." He had to work to keep his voice steady. "No matter what happens, remember what I told you about when we dock. Just get to the house and stay there. I'll get you out of there as soon as it's safe."

"MacCauley!" Russell's voice boomed down at them, and Deke started to sweat, even though it wasn't all that hot. "Get up here."

"Promise me, Liza."

She heard everything she needed to hear in the tone he was using and the one Russell had used. She grabbed him as if she were holding on for dear life. *"What's wrong?"*

"I don't know." He held her tight and wondered how he could ever let go. *Almost home,* he told himself. Damn it, they were almost there. "Promise me, Liza."

"MacCauley!" Russell stood at the top of the open hatch, blocking out the sunlight as he yelled down at them. "I said on deck. I got a problem."

So did he, Deke thought as he sought to pull Liza even closer for a last bittersweet moment. Obviously, so did he.

Ellen emerged from the cabin then, with Jilly close behind her. "What's going on?" she said.

"We don't know." Liza turned her head, which had been buried against his chest, so that she could talk to her sister.

"I'm coming." Deke yelled up at Russell, then pulled Liza's face back to his for one long, desperate kiss, not caring that they had an audience. "I don't know what he's up to, but I want you and Jilly and Ellen to stay down here and let me handle it."

"Handle what?"

"I don't know, but don't you dare come up there until I tell you it's okay. Promise me."

She shook her head, pleaded with him. "Don't go!"

"I have to, Liza." He didn't know where he found the strength to pull away from her, but he did. "Promise me you'll stay out of the way. No matter what."

He scrambled up the stairs before she could answer, before she could stop him.

Nick Russell backed up a step for every one Deke took forward until they both stood facing each other on the deck.

"What's the trouble?" Deke said, tensed even more when he realized how nervous Russell was. Nervous men did the stupidest things.

"Somebody's trying to tell us something on the radio, and I can't get the damn thing to work."

"Sounded like it was working fine a minute ago." Rather than turn his back to Russell, Deke casually backed his way to the radio.

"It was—a minute ago."

Deke's eyes had adjusted to the brightness of the sunlight now, and he could see well enough to tell that Russell was sweating. Okay, so they were both sweating. That evened the odds somewhat, didn't it?

He gave the radio only half his attention and watched Russell out of the corner of his eye. "It's dead."

"Oh?"

As if the dirty little SOB didn't already know that. "The wires have been—"

"Cut?" Russell laughed as he held up a knife.

The blade of the knife caught the light just in that instant, momentarily blinding Deke. And in that bit of time, when he couldn't see what was in front of his face, his mind irrationally flashed to Liza. He thought of all he could have told her if he'd only had another day, another hour, another minute.

Then he snapped back to the matter at hand. This time his mind raced with alternatives, weighing his options. He had only two, as far as he could see. He could play "dumb" or he could go ahead and admit it. His eyes narrowed. Just how stupid was Russell? Crazy enough to add attempted murder to the charges against him?

"Cut?" Deke said, deciding that bluffing was worth a try. Hell, Russell might not know anything for sure. "Real smart, Russell. You can't figure out how to make it work, so you destroy it?"

"It was smart. Now you can't call any of your friends." Russell held the knife out in front of him, with the point just out of Deke's reach. He punctuated his words with a slight jab of the blade tip. "I bet you've got a lot of friends out there."

"Pays to have friends," Deke said, and hoped he'd caught Russell without his gun. He'd rather take chances with his knife any day.

"They didn't pay you enough to make up for what I'm going to do to you."

Deke decided he wanted to see Russell sweat a little more. Besides, he knew the best weapons he had were his brain and his ability to use it to throw Russell off balance.

"I wouldn't be too sure," Deke said. "You don't know who's paying me."

Deke grinned as Russell's smile faded. The man wasn't that sure of himself, after all.

"I do," he insisted. "I know what you're trying to do to me. I got a call before I cut the radio. Your brother's old friend, Jim Gardner. Remember? You didn't recognize him on the dock. It took him a while, but he finally recognized you a few hours ago. Gardner used to work with me back a few years ago, when Charlie did, too."

The knife seemed to waver as Russell paused.

"Guess I shouldn't have told you that, Mr. Big-Shot Prosecutor from Virginia. But I figure it doesn't much matter. You're never going to get the chance to tell anybody anything."

Well, hell, Deke thought. If he knew that much, bluffing any longer was pointless. In a strange way, he felt relieved. No more hiding.

Russell would know that the most damning testimony against him would come from Deke. He was furious at himself for having placed himself in this position, but this wasn't something totally unexpected. Any panic he'd felt receded. He was calm; he might even have said deadly calm, if he hadn't been so skittish about using that particular word right now. Eyes narrowing, he knew it was time for business.

"You know, I'd been wondering just how stupid you really are, Russell, but even this far exceeds my expectations. You're sitting here with a boatful of cocaine and at least half a dozen federal agencies watching you, agencies, mind, that have been tailing you since we left Georgia, and you think getting rid of me will save you?" Deke laughed as he watched Russell anxiously scan the horizon for other ships. "You're caught red-handed, Russell, my man. Now, the only question left for you to answer is whether you want to go to prison or whether you want to risk getting the death penalty for killing me."

Russell paled, and Deke pressed on. "What do they have in Georgia? I can't seem to recall. Would you get the chair, or a nice little injection that would let you just drift off to sleep? I despise the injection stuff myself. Seems a little too civilized a way for a murderer to go.

"Of course," he continued, "there are some people who argue that the death penalty is a more humane sentence. At least then, it's over with quickly. Prison, on the other hand, is a hell like you've never dreamed of, and you could live another thirty or forty years in prison."

"I'm not going to prison," Russell boasted nervously.

"Oh, you're going."

"Not if you're not there to testify against me."

Deke just smiled as he prepared to outline the case the government had against Nick Russell, whether they had

Deke to testify or not, and to point out again that killing him would only get him into more trouble with the law. He was beginning to enjoy this.

Russell had advanced to the point where the knife was nearly within Deke's reach. "You'll never be able to testify through a slit throat."

To the left, behind him—too close behind him—Liza screamed. Deke whirled around to face her. "Damn it, Liza, I told you to stay below!"

"Look out, he's—"

Deke never heard the rest of what she said. He realized, too late, that he'd turned his back on Russell and his knife. He twisted back around quickly, and that probably saved him. Russell missed his throat, but caught his upper arm.

The pain, more a white-hot, searing brand, stunned him for a moment, leaving him paralyzed and giving Russell time to raise the knife for another strike.

Deke didn't waste another second. He dropped to the deck and rolled. His right hand went up to his left arm, and he was relieved to find it still hanging there. Ignoring the pain, he used his right leg to trip Russell, smiling coldly, grimly, when he heard the knife clatter along the deck.

Good. Now let the man come and get him without the blade. Deke made it to his feet, bad arm and all, but Russell was faster. He was a little too close once Deke was standing, and Deke backed up a step, then two, then...

The line. Damn it, how many times had he told them that a line should never, ever be left out like that.

He was off balance, falling backward, and Russell's shove was all it took. He was too damn close to the edge, and the next thing he knew, he was really falling.

A damn unsecured line, he mused as he flew through the air. He barely had time to draw a decent breath before the water closed over his head.

He gasped as the salt water bit into the knife wound, and suddenly he was choking on the water he'd taken into his lungs. Then he heard the scream, *Liza.*

Oh, God, he prayed as he kicked hard, aiming for the surface. He blanked out the pain in his arm and in his water-logged lungs.

He couldn't leave her alone with Russell.

Chapter 20

Liza had been so close. Another foot, and she might have been able to grab him, to save him.

She lurched forward, but fell, landing hard and winded on the deck, just in time to see Deke sink under the murky green water, see the reddish tinge the water took on as the blood from his wound spread.

"No!" She screamed it over and over again. "No!"

For a moment she could do no more than lie there against the hard wooden deck, dazed and dizzy. There was simply no strength left in her body, there were no paths of reason open to transport to her pitifully overloaded brain what her ears had just heard and her eyes had just seen.

She'd heard them arguing, and had sneaked up to see if she could find out why Deke had been acting so strangely down in the galley. Then she'd seen the knife, glinting in the glare off the water. Now she'd seen the blood, his blood, and the water mixing with the blood, as he sank beneath the horrible mixture. Numbly she tried to rein in her disjointed thoughts. This couldn't be happening.

"Deke?" she whispered weakly.

Russell was behind her, laughing. Liza heard him now. The sound made her furious, and from the fury came strength. She scrambled to her feet and lunged at him, catching him by surprise and nearly knocking him down.

"You bastard," she screamed as she tried to break free from the hold he'd gained on her arms. "You could have killed him."

Russell didn't look at all concerned. "I can't help it if the man's clumsy, now can I?"

She struggled harder against his hold. "You pushed him. I saw you."

"Now you just calm down, little girl."

Liza was too dazed by what she had seen and heard to pick up on the veiled threat in his words. Finally she shook free of his hold.

"Where do you think you're going?"

She ignored him and scrambled over to the wheel, disengaging the autopilot and scanning the water to see how much room she had to work with. "I'm turning this boat around so we can go back and get him."

Russell just laughed. "Go back and get who?"

He said it so calmly, she knew right away that he was serious, deadly serious. Liza swallowed in the hope of choking down the panic, real panic this time.

She felt it now, felt the danger of the situation settle around her like a cloak of darkness. Surely he didn't mean what she thought he meant. Okay, so they'd gotten into a fight, so Russell had drawn a knife. It didn't mean... Surely that didn't mean...

"You can't just leave him there," she said, trying to sound rational.

"Who?" He pushed her to the side, none too gently, so that he could turn the autopilot back on and take the wheel. His eyes stayed on the channel ahead.

"You know who!" Suddenly she was shaking with fear.

"I didn't see him surface. In fact, I don't think I ever saw him in the water."

She just glared at him, her stomach roiling sickeningly. Nick Russell meant to leave him there to die in the water.

"How could you not see him in the water? You pushed him in, you—ah!"

She cried out in pain as Russell twisted painfully on the arm that she'd used to reach for the wheel.

"Now let's get this straight, Liza." He got right up in her face as he said it. "I didn't see anything. I didn't hear anything, and neither did you. If anybody asks, he was up here on deck all night by himself. He could have fallen overboard anytime in the night. We'd have no way of knowing, no way of finding him.

"And if I got caught for trafficking drugs? Well, I figure I'd just say Deke was using my boat for smuggling, and when I found out, he panicked, that, rather than face me, he decided to take his chances in the water." Russell looked ridiculously pleased with his dim-witted idea.

"Yeah," he said. "My old buddy Deke must have jumped overboard."

The panic was growing stronger now, so powerful that she wasn't sure how long she could fight it. It became more and more overwhelming with every moment that passed and took them farther and farther from Deke.

He had to be all right, she told herself. He would be if she could just get to him. She wasn't sure how badly Russell had wounded him with the knife, but she'd seen the blood on deck, had seen it as it colored the water that had closed over his head. Screaming inside, she told herself he didn't really have to swim, just stay afloat, until she got the boat turned around and went back for him.

One thing at a time, she scolded herself. She had to get back to him first. Then she'd sort through the rest.

Liza made one more grab for the wheel. She and Russell struggled over it for a long moment.

"You can't just leave him there," she yelled, managing to get both her hands on the wheel.

She was feeling hopeful. Maybe he was going to give in, maybe he was finally realizing what he'd done, she thought when he let go of the wheel. She gripped it like a lifeline, but it wasn't enough to keep her standing when his open palm smashed into her face.

The cushions of the bench seat broke the fall for everything except her head, which cracked against the wooden trim. It seemed to rise up to meet her, slamming into her cheekbone and jawbone.

Her whole face throbbed as she slumped against the cushions while the world spun, the gulls sang overhead, and the boat rose and fell on the slight chop in the channel.

Russell's face, his sickening smirk telling her that he wasn't the least bit concerned about his actions, slowly came into focus. He seemed to tower over her, and she cut off another scream, acknowledging that she'd never be strong enough to overpower him.

She couldn't go back for Deke. Oh, Lord, she hadn't even waited there to watch him surface. Surely he'd made it back to the surface? Surely Russell hadn't hurt him that badly.

She lashed out at Russell again in her frustration and anger. "Murderer!"

With a rough hold on her arm, Russell hauled her to her feet, grabbed a handful of her hair and yanked her head up to meet his gaze. He glared at her, eyeball-to-eyeball with her.

"Now that's a mighty strong word to be throwing around, Liza. Murder, as a matter of fact, is a hard thing to prove. You've got to convince a jury that someone planned it, that someone intended for it to happen, and that's damn hard to prove without a body."

"I know what I saw—ah!"

He yanked on her hair, twisted it down so that she had to fall to her knees to keep from toppling over again.

"Now, if you're smart, you'll be real careful when you recall just what you did and didn't see a few minutes ago, because we're still a couple of hours from the dock, and a lot of things can happen in a couple of hours."

A lot of things could happen. He meant it. Why hadn't she seen that before—the violence that this man was capable of?

She stared at him for another long moment while she considered what to do next.

Ellen's voice broke the tense silence. "That's enough, Nick. I'm sure Liza understands your point."

Russell didn't let go of her hair as he pulled her to her feet and pushed her roughly toward the stairs that led below deck. Ellen, who'd been standing on the steps, backed down to make room for them.

There was terror shining out of Ellen's eyes, that and a plea to Liza not to make any more trouble for herself, and one to Russell not to hurt her sister.

"It's all right, Nick. Liza understands."

Russell pushed Liza into the cabin and shoved her onto the bed.

"I'm going to settle for bolting the door for now, but if you give me some reason to worry about what you're doing in here, I'll come back and hog-tie you. Understand?"

Liza didn't answer, so Ellen did for her. "She understands."

"Where's Jilly?" he roared.

"In our cabin," Ellen said.

"Get her."

"Nick?"

"I said get her. That little brat means about as much to her as MacCauley, that lying son of a bitch."

Ellen escaped for the moment, and Russell went right on. "So what kind of story did he tell you, Liza? Did he lie to you, too? Did you think you were puttin' out for some kind of dangerous criminal? Or is that a little too dirty for your tastes?"

Was he a smuggler? Liza could have brought herself to beg Russell for an answer then, if she'd thought there was any hope of getting the truth out of him.

Would she ever know the truth? Ever get a chance to ask Deke himself? Oh, God. She prayed fervently that Deke was alive.

"Well? I bet he didn't tell you he was some kind of hot-shot lawyer who puts people like me behind bars, did he?"

Ellen returned then, with a frightened Jilly clinging to her.

"In the cabin," Russell ordered. "I'm going to need you on deck to sail this damn boat, and Liza needs something to keep her occupied, maybe to make her think twice before she starts spouting off any other foolishness like what she said on deck."

Jilly came eagerly from Ellen's arms to Liza's. She was shaking and sobbing.

"It's all right, Jilly. I'm right here, and everything's going to be fine," Liza soothed automatically.

She hated to think of how much the little girl might have seen or heard of the incident on the deck. She pushed Jilly's head against her neck and tried not to let her hatred of Nick Russell shine through as she watched him, praying that he'd leave soon.

"You'd best just forget about your boyfriend, Liza. Worry about yourself and that girl instead of him. Hell, there's probably nothing left of him by now anyway. If the water didn't get him, the sharks did."

Russell slammed the door then, and Jilly gave a start at the noise. The little girl sniffed, snuggled closer, and Liza held on tight, wishing desperately for the feel of a familiar pair of arms to hold her close and reassure her.

Oh, Lord! She felt the tears running down her throbbing cheek. She hadn't even thought about sharks. Deke had teased her earlier on the trip, when she'd been afraid to get into the water because of sharks. He claimed sharks were always in the water, but that he never worried about them. They usually had plenty to eat without coming to tangle with a human being, he'd joked.

Of course, when he'd plunged into the water then, he hadn't been bleeding from an open wound, the way he had when he'd gone overboard.

Liza felt the fear for him take her breath away, and she squeezed Jilly tight.

"Wiza? You crying?" Jilly's lower lip trembled as she, too, started to cry again.

She couldn't do this, Liza thought, frantically. Not right now. She couldn't handle this. She wasn't strong enough, not for this.

She rested her forehead against the little girl's for a moment, drawing strength from the love she felt for her niece, and told herself she had to pull herself together for Jilly's sake.

"I'm sorry, baby. I didn't mean to scare you."

"Jilly's not a baby." She pouted and swiped clumsily at her own tears with the back of one little pudgy hand.

"I know, sweetie."

Still frightened, still confused, they sat on the bed and held each other while Nick Russell pounded on the door. He'd said he was going to keep them there, and now Liza knew he meant it. It sounded like he was nailing the door shut.

She wasn't going to protest. She liked the idea of having more than a locked door between her and him.

"Wiza?" Jilly touched Liza's lips and drew back a finger glistening with blood. "You gotta boo-boo?"

It was only then that she realized she had a split lip. "I guess I do. Can you get me a towel from the bathroom?"

Jilly hesitated, glanced uneasily at the closed door, which failed to muffle the sounds of Nick Russell pounding on the other side.

"Why don't we get it together?" Liza offered. "You can help clean up *my* scrapes for a change."

They got a wet hand towel from the bathroom. By the time they got back to the bed, Liza's legs were shaking so badly she couldn't have stood even if she'd wanted to.

Jilly was frightened, too, but playing nurse for Liza helped take her mind off it. First Liza made sure the bleeding had stopped, and then she let Jilly do the rest. Clumsily, but gently, the little girl stroked the cloth over Liza's face. It must have been numb before, because until now it hadn't hurt that much.

Of course, the pain wasn't nearly as bad as the empty space in her heart. Liza felt as if her heart had simply disappeared. She didn't feel anything now, except this strange numbness.

"Wiza?"

"Yes, Jilly."

As she looked at her, Liza's heart melted. Jilly looked so sad, so confused, so frightened.

"Oh, sweetie, come here. . . ."

They fell back against the pillows and snuggled as close as they could get.

"Everything's going to be all right, Jilly." It was the first time Liza had lied to the little girl, and the first time in a long time she'd lied to herself.

Jilly slept fitfully for a couple of hours, and Liza wished she could, too, but she was afraid to close her eyes. Every time she did she saw Deke's head sinking below the bloodstained water.

Gone, she thought with a sob. And she didn't even know the man she was mourning. Was he a crook, as he'd admitted reluctantly, even bitterly, to her? Or was he someone who'd wrestled with his conscience and eventually decided that no debt was too great to pay to save his brother's life?

Or was he, as Nick Russell had accused him in those confusing moments on deck, some sort of agent sent to put Russell away?

It had always been difficult for Liza to believe that Deke was a criminal—at least an ordinary one. He simply didn't fit the mold. He had a conscience, a sense of right and wrong, and when he'd told her about his brother's addiction, the distaste he felt for the very drug he was helping

Nick Russell smuggle into the country had been perfectly clear.

No choice, he'd told her. He'd had no choices—at least no good ones.

Still, he'd obviously made one choice. He'd decided to make the trip, and he'd certainly beat himself up about it more than once.

A government agent would have had a choice, wouldn't he? And the agent wouldn't have felt the guilt that Deke had struggled with over doing the job.

So who was this man she'd given her heart to? Would she ever know?

Was he gone for good? Was that what this emptiness in her heart was about? Did her heart know more than her head? Did it know that Deke was gone?

Liza shivered in the warm bed and stared at the ceiling as her tears fell. The truth came to her then, though she'd known it all along. She didn't care who or what Deke was. She just wanted him back.

Finally, near dusk, they landed at the dock behind Russell's house. It had taken them about six hours to complete a journey they should have made in two. They'd traveled in circles most of that time, Liza believed. She'd spent the whole time behind the barricaded door of her cabin with Jilly.

"Here, I'll take her." Ellen, grim but determined, held out her hands to take Jilly from Liza once Russell had finally freed them after the boat landed. "You two need to go, tonight. I don't know what Nick's going to do, but you can't stay. It's not safe."

Russell had had a particularly difficult time deciding anything this afternoon, from what Ellen told Liza as she quickly gathered her things.

One minute he was convinced that Deke was working for the government, that he had a dozen more agents on his tail and more waiting for him at his house. The next he was equally as convinced that Deke was double-crossing him with his own distributors.

In a frenzy, he'd torn the boat apart, ripping open the special compartments that held the cocaine and dumping a good bit of it into the water to get rid of the evidence against him.

Then he'd remembered the money he'd paid for the cocaine. Not all of it was his, and if he showed up back home without the drugs or the money he was as good as dead. His partners would see to that.

In the end, Ellen said, he'd decided to take his chances of either getting past the authorities or beating whatever charges they brought against him, rather than risk certain death at the hands of his "business associates."

He wouldn't get away with it, Liza vowed as she made her way through the ransacked main cabin to the deck. *Nick Russell would pay for what he'd done to Deke.* She'd make him pay.

Tears filled her eyes again, and she stumbled as she followed Ellen and Jilly off the boat, up the stairs and down the long, narrow wooden dock that led to the house.

In the backyard, Ellen put Jilly down and returned to the boat for her own bags.

Jilly, happy to be off the boat and home, giggled as she ran for the big old tree that held her tree house. "Let's go up, up, up, Wiza."

"In a minute, Jilly." She kept walking toward the house, but Jilly stood there, hugging the tree, with her lower lip sticking out. "Okay, we'll go up for just a minute, but I need to put these in the house first."

Actually, there was no need to put the bags in the house, Liza decided. She'd agreed with Ellen that the time to leave was now. She'd promised to get Jilly out of the way, and she would. But she'd made another decision. She was going to take her sister with her, as well. And somewhere along the way she was going to figure out how she could make sure Russell paid for what he'd done.

She was almost to the house when she heard the noise—a loud, heavy popping sound that shattered the near-silence of the night and reverberated over the water.

Funny... Liza had only a split second for the thought, before making the connection. *It had sounded like a gunshot.*

Then she didn't have to wonder, because the noise—that same loud, heavy popping—suddenly exploded all over the place, one after another. It seemed to surround her, and she couldn't figure out where to turn to find its source.

Gunfire! With only one thought in her head, she took off running across the backyard.

"Jilly!" She screamed as she ran, praying that she'd get to her niece in time.

Everything was happening in a curious sort of slow motion now. Liza was running, as fast as she could, but it seemed to take forever. She was screaming Jilly's name, but she couldn't see the little girl, just the big old tree where she'd left her a moment before. The noise around her was deafening, and it seemed that it would never end, that it came from everywhere, yet Liza couldn't find its source.

She almost made it—just like before, she thought as she was hit from behind. Or was it from in front? She felt nothing but the pressure at first, the tremendous weight from behind that robbed her lungs of air and jostled the very thoughts inside her head. *So heavy,* she thought, as she waited for the ground to rise up and meet her. It was so hard and so heavy.

Then she felt the pain, a single burning pain that seemed to drill into her from in front, pushing her back against that heaviness behind her, flattening her between the two.

The ground came then. It was the last sight she could make out before the blackness descended. It fell from the sky, this thick, black cloud, and it took away the pain, the pressure, the worry.

She welcomed the blackness, would have gone happily into the fuzzy numbness, the absolute absence of sensation, if not for one thing.

That voice. His voice. In that last instant of consciousness, she could have sworn she heard Deke call her name.

She somehow found the strength to smile then. She hadn't lost him after all. She was dying, and she was going to be with Deke.

Chapter 21

In the midst of the smoky mist came the pain. A long, thin jab in her side that made her wince, made her unwilling even to try to fight through the curious fog that had settled around her.

It wasn't like the darkness—the last thing she remembered. This fog was white, thick, puffy and soft, too soft for anything to get through and hurt her.

She liked the fog, liked the way it seemed to shield her, to protect her, to hold her in its sheltering arms.

But it must be lifting, because she'd clearly felt the pain. And the—the voice, the same one, again. She puzzled over it.

She remembered now. The blackness wasn't the last thing she recalled from before. The last thing had been that voice, his voice.

He was calling to her from so far away. She struggled to open her eyes, but couldn't. She tried to call to him, but couldn't manage that, either. She wanted to rise up and run toward him, but her limbs were too heavy; they wouldn't obey her commands to move.

Liza felt a light pressure. Was that his hand? Had she managed to touch him somehow, to reach through the thick white cloud and touch him? She tried to close her fingers around him, to hang on to him and never let him go.

Deke! She cried his name inside her head as she slipped back into the fog once again.

A moment? An hour? It might have been days later—she couldn't have said for sure—when she did manage to open her eyes.

She was lying in a bed. She knew because she could see her right hand beside her on the blanket. Her empty hand.

How long ago was it that she'd imagined someone holding her hand, imagined her clutching at him, trying to hold him to her, trying not to let him drift away, trying to keep the mist from taking him?

Oh, Lord! She needed Deke so much, didn't see how she could go on without him, couldn't summon up any enthusiasm for doing so.

Why? she thought as she let her eyes drift around the drab green hospital room. Why would she find him, find love, only to have it so briefly and then lose it? For that was what it had been—what it was—love.

Liza tried to shift her weight to a more comfortable position on the bed. A mistake, she realized as the pain grew more insistent.

But it didn't seem so bad, not when compared to the pain in her heart. Grimacing, she experimented, eventually figuring out that the greatest pain was centered low on her right side, and she deliberately shifted her weight toward it. Pain shot outward from that spot, radiating in circles that grew and grew like ripples from a rock thrown into an otherwise calm pond.

The hospital sounds faded, the room started to spin, and then the blessed fog descended upon her again. She welcomed it.

"Liza?" Deke was at the window, staring into the predawn sky, when he heard her cry out in pain. Had her eyelids flickered for just a moment? Had her hand shifted on the mattress?

He settled himself in the chair by the bed to wait some more. Elbows on his knees, head in his hands, he offered up another desperate prayer.

He'd made a dozen rash promises to God. He'd had time, while he waited, to review each and every decision he'd made since he first found out Charlie was in trouble, and he could see clearly every wrong turn he'd made.

He'd thought of a thousand different ways to tell her just who he was, what he'd been trying to do, and why he'd felt he couldn't tell her, why he'd let her suffer so, thinking she was falling for a common criminal.

Mostly he'd begged to be able to take her place, but it didn't seem like God was making any deals today.

So he'd waited and wondered. Would she get through this? Would he survive if she didn't? Would she hate him for it?

Maybe, he thought grimly, but not nearly as much as he already hated himself.

He'd been so close—so damned close to getting her out of the way before the bullet had gotten her. He'd been there, waiting with the other agents for the boat to dock—they'd waited forever while Nick Russell had decided to take his chances and come on in as he'd planned.

Deke had actually started to relax once the Coast Guard boat docked at the house the FBI had rented just down the sound from Russell's house. From there, it should have been easy. They'd wait Nick Russell out, let him unload his cargo and call in his distributors, then move in.

But something had gone wrong. He didn't know what, and he didn't much care. All that mattered was that someone had started shooting, and Liza had been in the way. She must have been running for Jilly. That was the only explanation that made sense. It would be like her to worry about the little girl first and herself second.

He'd watched for a delayed instant—too stunned to move—as she'd raced across the backyard and straight through the barrage of bullets, before he'd taken off after her himself.

And he'd realized as he ran that, while the rest of his life might well be a total wreck by now, one thing was certain. He loved her. He always would. He might not be able to make it up to her for the pain he'd caused her or the danger he'd exposed her to, but he would love her until there was no breath left in his body.

It had all come so clearly in that seeming eternity he'd spent running across the yard while bullets whizzed past. It wasn't the danger or the close quarters or some here-today-gone-tomorrow kind of infatuation.

This was the real thing, the love he'd been waiting for, the one he'd never been sure would ever exist for him.

Then he'd reached her, had his arms around her, and had had her halfway to the ground when she'd been hit. He'd been so close behind her that he'd felt the sickening impact of the bullet as it ripped through her body.

Deke would never forget the instant of pure sheer terror, never forget the way the bullet had drilled into her, the way she'd stiffened, then gone limp before they even hit the ground. It had seemed to take forever, as he lay there on top of her, his body shielding hers, too late, for the shooting to stop.

He'd already started praying as he rolled off her and gently turned her over. The sight of the blood seeping through her shirt on her right side had turned him cold.

And there had been nothing he could do except hold her in his arms, cursing and praying at the same time, as he sat there on the grass and tried desperately to stop the bleeding with nothing to work with but his hands.

That had been sometime late yesterday. He'd stayed with her during the air ambulance ride to the Jacksonville hospital's trauma center, and had sat here for hours while they pulled a bullet out of her shoulder.

As far as shootings went, the wound was no picnic, but it was survivable, the doctors had told him. Then they'd started battling the damage done to her lung. A nick, they'd said at first, but a stubborn one. Fluid gathering there, an infection. Then, an hour or so ago, the lung had simply collapsed.

His heart had constricted, and he'd stubbornly refused to budge from her room as the doctors and nurses rushed around her.

She was so still, so pale. Half the time he felt compelled to put his hand on her chest, so that he could feel the slight rise and fall and be sure she was still breathing.

Come on, Liza, he prayed. Don't give up on me now.

Deke straightened, slowly, his stiff body protesting any and all movement now, the knife wound on his arm throbbing like a big bass drum as he stared down at his hands, still stained with her blood. He hadn't had time to wash.

It had been literally, at first—his hands being stained with her blood—but it would be figuratively forever.

She'd tried to tell him that what he was doing was crazy, that he couldn't have a reason good enough to justify risking his life helping Nick Russell smuggle his precious cocaine out of Colombia.

Well, he could risk his own neck. That was his decision to make. But he'd had no right to endanger her the way he had.

No right at all.

It was so clear, now that the damage was done, now that he couldn't take back the mistakes he'd made. He'd known from the beginning how dangerous it could be, and yet he hadn't fully acknowledged that danger to her. Or maybe he'd simply had a little too much confidence in his own ability to protect her.

And he'd certainly never counted on her coming to mean the world to him.

He was back when Liza opened her eyes again, but she knew now that she couldn't trust the sound of his voice or the sight of him there beside her.

Her mind was merely playing cruel tricks on her again.

She stared at him, then around the room, then down at her hand. Strange, she thought. It looked like her hand, but it seemed so heavy that she couldn't lift it.

So she hadn't seen him before, couldn't have touched him, couldn't have held on in desperation to keep him with her.

Deke looked like hell. He was brooding there in the dark, beside her. *Real* darkness, she realized, the kind that came in the night, not the blackness that had overtaken her in the yard after the shooting started.

She could see his features clearly in the dimly lit room. His head had fallen back against the chair, and he was staring out the window. She could see the tension in his face. It had worn little grooves around the corners of his worried eyes and pulled his jaw into a tight line.

She frowned at that. He shouldn't have to worry now, not anymore, not where he was.

Liza willed her hand to move, up off the mattress, across the abyss that separated them, so that she could touch him one more time. She wanted to find the strength to reassure him. She wanted him to smile for her one last time.

"Deke?" Her throat felt raw and sore, and she winced at the effort to speak.

He turned toward her, and some of the tension in him fell away. Slowly, cautiously, she struggled to stretch out her hand to him.

Then she felt his hand, so warm, so strong, as it guided hers back down to the mattress. He held on to it, with his fingers tucked into her palm and his thumb moving in little circles on the back of her hand.

Liza smiled at him, and he smiled back.

So real, she thought, happy to have just this moment. She could even feel the calluses on his fingertips.

"It's all right," she told him, and waited for him to vanish into the darkness.

"Yes, Liza. It's all right now. You're going to be fine."

She went still then, stopped breathing altogether, as she stared down at their joined hands.

Little circles, she could feel them on the back of her hand, drawn by his thumb. She could feel the warmth of his palm, feel the strength, the energy that radiated from him.

The fog had cleared completely now.

Yet he remained there beside her. He'd spoken to her, answered her back.

"Deke?" Tears gathered in her eyes, but she wasn't sure yet why they were there. Either, by some miracle, he was here, safe and whole, or God was even crueler than she'd imagined. "Deke?"

She held her breath as he got up from the chair and sat carefully on the edge of the bed. He carried her hand to his knee and used his other hand to brush her hair gently over to the side of her face.

"What are we going to do with this hair of yours? Seems like it's always in the way when I want to look into those beautiful blue eyes of yours."

Her tears welled up then, spilled over, and her vision blurred. Oh, Lord! Don't let this be a dream. His face came close, closer still, until she could feel his breath on her face, feel his lips, so soft and so sweet, as they kissed away her tears.

"No, baby, don't you dare cry. There's not much more than a wish and a prayer holding this lung of yours together, and Dr. Richardson would have my head if you started bawling and it collapsed again."

Fighting back the tears, she sniffed once, then again, stronger than before, and it was then that she felt the pain. She moaned.

He paled instantly. "Easy, Liza. Shallow little breaths, and no sudden movements."

He put his hand over the spot that hurt, and she concentrated on the warmth of his touch while she tried to do as he instructed.

"Better?"

Of course it was better. He was here, touching her, so nothing seemed that bad. He *was* touching her, wasn't he?

"Liza."

She waited, silence stretching between them. He was still there. He hadn't disappeared. Neither the blackness nor the mist had come to claim him.

"Are you—?" What was the proper question? she wondered. Are you real? Or, do I need you so badly that I've conjured you up in my mind?

"I thought I'd lost you forever," she said finally through a fresh mist of tears.

"I know, baby. I thought I'd lost you, too."

And it had hurt him dearly to think that. He might not tell her that—he wasn't a man for pretty words or hasty promises of love and devotion, or at least he hadn't been so far. But she could see the truth in his eyes. It had hurt him to think that he'd lost her. Warmth flooded her being.

He was trembling, too, as he sat there on the bed beside her, and those were tears in his eyes, as well.

Maybe there was hope for them after all.

"Hey," he smiled crookedly, the pad of his thumb sweeping away her tears. "Enough of this. Your doctor's dying for an excuse to kick me out of here, and if he sees you this upset, I'm gone for sure. So we have to calm down, okay?"

"OK."

"I need to call the doctor now, all right? He's been waiting for you to wake up."

"OK—but," she held onto his hand, with surprising strength, when he would have gotten up and walked away, "do you have to go?"

"Just as far as the door. Just to get the doctor. I'm not going any farther."

"OK."

"Let him look you over, and then we'll talk."

"OK."

She made it through the questions and answers, through the vital-signs checks and the explanation of what had happened to her. But the examination of the wound, on top of the fatigue she felt from simply keeping her eyes open and following the conversation, was too much for her. She drifted off again to somewhere between sleep and unconsciousness.

"Doc?"

Deke moved warily back into the room and saw the doctor leaning over Liza, stethoscope atop her injured lung.

Liza's eyes were closed, and he wondered if she was merely asleep or if she'd lapsed into unconsciousness again.

"Well?" He waited, somehow feeling sick inside and hopeful all at once, while the stethoscope moved slowly and deliberately around her chest and the man listened. "Well?"

"The lung's back up and holding. I'm not sure how, but it's holding."

Deke sank heavily down into the chair at her bedside as his knees simply gave out.

God, he'd come so close to losing her.

"She's going to make it?"

The doctor shrugged, and Deke knew what he was in for. More doctor-talk about probabilities and conditions, unknowns and anything-can-happens. He was in no mood for it. He'd endured enough in the past eighteen hours.

"Your gut reaction here, Doc. Is she going to make it?"

"I think so."

Deke exhaled long and slow, leaned his head against the back of the chair, and didn't know whether he was going to laugh or cry. So he'd get another chance. He'd make another chance for himself with her.

She'd be angry at him when she finally learned the truth—hell, she had a right to be—but anger burned itself out eventually.

Love endured.

Deke smiled for the first time in ages. "Thanks, Doc."

"Thank me by getting out of here. Get some rest and get cleaned up. You smell like a fish."

Deke did laugh then. He was still in the cutoffs he'd been wearing when Nick Russell had pushed him overboard. He hadn't been in the water that long before the Coast Guard had fished him out. They'd been following the sailboat at a discreet distance all along and had pulled closer once they'd picked up the radio message that had tipped Nick Russell off to Deke's true identity.

Someone on the Coast Guard vessel had loaned him a shirt and some shoes. Someone else had put a bandage around the knife wound in his upper arm. He'd forgotten all that until now, now that he knew she was going to be all right.

"Hey, I've got some pull in ER," the doctor said when he saw the way Deke was favoring his arm. "I can get you in without a lot of waiting if you're ready to have somebody look at that."

That wasn't such a bad idea, he thought, but then he remembered the two suits outside the door to the hospital room. Deke wasn't too sure whether they were guarding her or him or both of them. But he had a feeling that once they got him out of here, he'd have a hell of a time getting back in.

"I may take you up on that, Doc. Let me see where I stand with my friends out there in the hall first."

"Suit yourself, Mr. MacCauley. I'm sure you will anyway, no matter what I say."

Deke caught a glimpse of the two agents through the doorway when the doctor opened it and left. Suits they were. Underlings. The FBI had thousands of them, and they all seemed to own the same nearly identical, totally unremarkable blue suit.

Deke hadn't paid much attention to them since he'd arrived at the hospital, but he did know the men were none too pleased to have him here.

It was a damn shame, but Nick Russell seemed to have escaped injury in the firestorm set off in his backyard, which had apparently started when an overeager agent who couldn't distinguish between a real gun and a belching car had started shooting.

And once the firing had started, it had been hell to get it stopped.

The only person hurt in the whole mess had been Liza. Russell had walked away from it, and he was probably still sitting in a darkened room somewhere, sweating out his improbable explanation of his actions for Buddy Morris and the FBI.

Deke didn't remember a whole lot of what the FBI man had told him, except that the guy seemed more than anxious to get Deke out of the hospital or when he couldn't manage that, to get him out of sight, at least.

So Deke had stayed in Liza's room, with the two suits guarding the door, and they both seemed to be able to deal with that.

All of which probably meant that, just in case anyone was asking—say, some of the people waiting to help Nick Russell distribute his stash—Deke had gone overboard somewhere south of Jacksonville and no one had found him yet.

They must have gotten lucky in the confusion of the shooting at the house. Apparently Russell hadn't seen him, didn't know that Deke hadn't drowned back there where Russell had left him.

Deke decided he liked the idea of Russell sweating like a pig under questioning, wondering how long it would be before someone charged him with murder.

With something like that hanging over his head, it might not seem so bad to admit to a few lesser crimes, such as smuggling.

They wouldn't tell Russell that Deke was dead—that wouldn't fly with the courts. But they could ask, ever so innocently, just what had happened to the man they'd planted on his boat.

Nick Russell could draw his own conclusions.

Deke suspected that was just what the FBI and Buddy Morris were hoping. Trials were a risky business, expensive and time-consuming. There was no need to go through that unless they absolutely had to.

So maybe all he had to do to wrap this thing up was to wait for Nick Russell to confess and wait and make sure Liza was really going to be all right.

Then he could figure out how he was going to straighten out this mess he'd made of his life.

It seemed as if she'd waited forever for him to come back, although she couldn't be sure. Time had become distorted, either by the weakness that made it hard for her to stay awake or by the pain medication. She wasn't even sure what day it was, or how long she'd been in the hospital.

He finally returned, or, at least, he did in a manner of speaking. The man who came into her room that day had Deke's mannerisms, his voice, his face, but if not for those things, he might well have been a stranger.

He was so different now, in a crisp, dark suit that was no doubt tailor-made for him, a white button-down shirt and a red striped tie.

Funny, she thought, she'd never seen him in a suit. Had never even imagined him wearing one, yet he wore it with such ease.

"Hi." He said it cautiously, staying at least two feet away from the bed and not even trying to touch her.

She had a feeling she wasn't going to like what was coming.

"Hi," she said, just as warily as he had.

He lifted a hand toward her. It hovered in the air between them for a moment, and then he pulled it back and raked it through his hair. She looked, stunned, at the sun-kissed strands. He'd gotten it cut, short. Not a hair dared touch the collar of the crisp white shirt. And there was a little curl to it on top, now that it was shorter.

The hands went into his pockets then, and he turned, so she could only see his profile. He stood so tall and straight and strong that it seemed he was unbendable, untouchable, clearly a man in control.

Liza had a feeling, a sinking feeling, that she was finally seeing the man for what he really was. And he wasn't a boat captain or a criminal.

Which meant that he'd told her even more lies than she'd thought. Which in turn had her wondering if anything that had happened between them had been real. Had any of the feelings been genuine?

Or had the man simply been doing his job, whatever that was?

The thought hurt more than the bullet had.

"The doctor says you're doing better."

Now why would that make him unhappy? Liza wondered, detecting the underlying dejected tone. "I am better."

"Good. Then I guess we need to talk."

Talk? She looked at him intently. He made all the right motions to form a smile on his face, but Liza could tell he definitely wasn't a happy man.

Oh, Lord, she prayed. Strength. Give me strength. She realized, only then, that most likely she'd made a fool of herself over this man once already. She didn't want to do so again.

"How's Jilly?" She already knew the answer; she'd talked with Ellen herself. But she wanted a minute to brace herself for the hard questions.

"She's fine. Ellen is making arrangements for Nick's sister to come and get her."

"Ellen's okay, too?"

"Yes."

"And Nick?"

"Unfortunately, he wasn't hurt, either. He's in custody."

Damn. They'd run through the list much too quickly. "So... that just leaves me and... you."

"I'm fine. Nick didn't get very far when he tried to turn me into fish food."

He spoke so casually of it, about a man with a knife who'd threatened him, pulling it through his flesh and then pushing him overboard into shark-infested waters, leaving him to die.

Just the memory of that moment, the moment when Deke had gone overboard, was enough to send the tears pooling in her eyes. "I tried to get to you. I almost did, and then I tried to get him to turn the boat around and go back for you, but—"

"Sshh." He put his finger to her lips, and for just a moment she thought she caught a glimpse of the old Deke. "I'm all right, Liza. I wasn't in the water for more than fifteen minutes before the Coast Guard pulled me out."

"They were following us?"

He pulled back then, once again the stranger in the suit and tie. He pulled at it now, at the knot at his neck, but loosened it only a fraction.

"The Coast Guard and a whole host of federal agents, the whole time."

And so the time had come. There was nothing left to ask. He seemed to be dreading it as much as she was. Guilt, she reasoned. He must be feeling guilty about…about lying to her, about holding her, kissing her, making love to her, perhaps about letting her fall in love with a man who didn't exist.

"So—" she braced herself, though she already knew the answer she'd get "—I guess you're not really one of the bad guys."

He was facing the window and she couldn't see his expression. "I'm not so sure right now, Liza. Good, bad— Let's just say I wasn't really Nick Russell's partner. I was working for the government."

She shook her head back and forth and bit down hard on her lower lip to keep from making a sound. Oh, it hurt, almost as much as thinking he'd died there in the water. And no wonder. It seemed that the man she'd known, the man she'd come to love, was as good as dead to her. He had simply ceased to exist.

Her eyes clashed with his for a long moment. Then he dropped his gaze to the floor.

What was he looking for? she wondered. What kind of response? Did he expect her to rant and rave at him for lying to her? For allowing her to agonize over the idea that she had fallen in love with a criminal, when the whole time he was working on the side of the law?

Liza held on to the railings of her bed as the world seemed to shift beneath her. It tilted off center for good, then settled into an unfamiliar position. Everything had changed. Nothing was as she'd come to believe, and he was clearly a stranger to her.

A guilty one. Surely that was what she was seeing in this handsome stranger? Guilt?

He'd had a job to do, and he'd done it. So what if he'd played on her emotions, used the feelings she had for him? What did it matter to a man like him? Dimly she wondered how many different men, how many different roles, he'd played.

"I didn't enjoy lying to you, Liza."

She laughed a little at that. "I didn't particularly enjoy being lied to, either, but I guess it's just part of your job, telling lies, pretending to be people that you're not."

"No, it's not. I guess nobody explained it all to you. I'm not an agent. I'm an attorney, a federal prosecutor. My brother got into trouble. The cops had him cold on a drug charge, and when he tried to get out of it by cutting a deal with them, he just dug himself in deeper. I told you on the boat. I told you I was just trying to save my brother."

"Oh." She wondered how long this would go on, how long she could hold herself together, and prayed it would end soon. "That part was real?"

"Yes, it was real." He bit out the words. "I—I would have told you everything, I wanted to, but it would only have put you in greater danger."

"Of course." She didn't want to argue with him. She just wanted this to be over.

"Liza—" He stopped, swallowing hard. She wasn't reacting to anything he said. He could feel her slipping away from him. He *had* to make her understand. Desperation laced his voice as he continued, "You have the most expressive eyes, and I know Russell would have seen right through you from the start. And that wouldn't just have endangered me. It would have meant trouble for you, too, and I couldn't risk putting you in more danger than you were already in."

"Of course not."

"Look. Look at me," he demanded, his hands gripping her arms. "I'm sorry you got caught up in all this. I'm sorry I didn't do more to keep you off that boat, and I'm sorry you were hurt."

Sorry. At that moment she knew for sure. She'd been puzzling over the way he'd looked yesterday when she'd finally regained consciousness, puzzling and hoping that she'd seen more than she was seeing now. But she hadn't. There'd been concern, yes, but mostly guilt. Not love.

She felt tears, heavy and stinging, in her eyes, knew they'd spill over soon and run down her cheeks, knew that she couldn't bear to let him see that.

"I'm sorry, too—Dixon? Is that your real name?

"Yes."

"I'm sorry, too, Dixon." She turned her head away. "And now, if you don't mind, I'm really tired...."

He didn't leave right away. She felt his eyes on her and held her breath. What else was there to say? What did he want from her? To say that she forgave him? That she'd get over him?

Well, now *she* was sorry. Because she wasn't feeling generous enough to ease his guilty conscious by telling him any of those things.

So, he wouldn't be forgiven. The knowledge settled into Dixon's chest like a great weight pushing down upon him, pushing the breath from his lungs and leaving him unable to move.

Until that moment, he hadn't faced up to how very much he'd hurt her. He'd come seeking forgiveness, hoping for it, knowing it wouldn't come easy, but still hoping that it would come.

God, what a mess he'd made of it all. And he didn't know how to put it right again.

Chapter 22

It had to have been the longest four days of his life, Deke thought as he rushed down the hospital corridor toward her room.

He'd argued around and around with himself about this. She'd made it clear she didn't want to see him anymore. So what was he doing here? he asked himself bitterly. For the life of him he couldn't figure that out. The only thing he could conclude was that the woman was driving him crazy and he couldn't stand to go another minute without seeing her.

What was he going to say when he finally did see her. He hadn't decided yet.

What was he going to do with her once he found her? He hadn't figured that out yet, either, even though he was practically running down the corridor to her now. All he knew was that he had to see her again, needed to feel the warmth of her smile.

She was feeling better. She'd been moved to the top floor, to one of those nice suites the hospital had for its sick VIPs. The FBI liked having her there because it was somewhat isolated. She was still under guard. He was supposed to be himself.

Nick Russell's confession and plea bargain were still being ironed out, and as far as anyone knew, Deke Mac-Cauley was still floating in the Atlantic somewhere.

The FBI was still trying to round up some of Russell's distributors, and they were uneasy about everyone's safety until those loose ends were tied up.

Deke flashed her guards his ID from the U.S. attorney's office, and they let him pass. He'd have a few words with their superior later about the way they'd barely glanced at his ID.

He opened the door into a place that looked more like a fancy hotel room than a hospital room. The only thing that gave it away was the hospital bed—the empty hospital bed.

"Dixon?"

She was sitting in the corner, in an overstuffed chair, with her feet propped up on an ottoman. Liza, alive and well again. She didn't look sick at all, and just the sight of her sitting there was such a relief. Her hair was still damp from the shower, and she was dressed in a shiny, billowy floral-print robe. There was some color in her cheeks, a healthy glow to her tanned skin, and best of all, a hesitant smile on her face.

"Nice place," he said, discovering that he was more nervous than he'd expected to be.

"Still a hospital. If the needles and the middle-of-the-night vital-signs checks didn't give it away, the food definitely would."

Liza leaned back into the chair and closed her eyes. She was fighting like mad to keep her expression blank, but inside she was shouting for joy. He'd come back to her. Please, Lord, let it be that.

Liza had died a little inside when he'd left her that day. She'd had nothing but time while she was here, though, and it was time she'd used to think everything through as best she could. And she thought now that she understood.

Before, when he'd come to the hospital and finally told her exactly who he was and why he'd been working for Russell, she'd been too hurt to think straight.

She'd seen the guilt in his eyes and assumed the worst—Deke, *Dixon,* she reminded herself, felt guilty because he'd used her. And why shouldn't he? He'd used her feelings for him, used her merely because it suited his purposes, without feeling anything for her in return.

But then she remembered. Dixon had a way of assuming responsibility for other people's lives. He saw his own brother's cocaine addiction not as Charlie's responsibility, but as his, and had even risked his life to get Charlie out of trouble.

It wasn't such a stretch, then, to think that now he'd taken responsibility for her own life as well, for the danger she'd been exposed to, the gunshot wound she'd suffered. And also for the possibility of exposing her to even more danger should she be anywhere near him if he had to give the testimony that put Nick Russell away.

That was it, she told herself. That had to be it.

She fumed for a while once she'd figured it out. Damn silly man. He had a big, fancy law degree. He had a big, important job. And he didn't have the sense to see beyond his nose and into his own heart, let alone hers.

Well, she certainly wasn't going to make it easy for him now that he'd finally come to his senses. Lord, she hoped the man had finally come to his senses.

Surely he hadn't come back just to apologize to her again.

"Are you feeling all right?"

Small talk? She could manage that. "Still a little sore, but I suspect I should be."

"The lung?"

"Holding up fine."

"Good." He still stood there in the doorway. "I . . . saw Jilly yesterday. She got on a plane bound for New Mexico. Nick's sister came to pick her up. She seemed very nice."

"Yes, I talked with her and with Jilly on the phone before they left."

"Was Jilly worried about you?"

"Yes. I hope to get out there and see her in the next few weeks. Nick's sister invited me to stay with them for a while."

"Oh."

Silence then, and if Liza hadn't know better, she'd have sworn the poor man was nervous. She eased down to the edge of the chair and braced herself with a hand on either arm so that she could get up.

Deke raced to her side. He had this undeniable need to touch her, and he figured this was the best excuse he'd get to do that.

He helped her get up from the chair, then put his arm around her and carefully hugged her to his side, drinking in the feel of her. Trying to be casual about it, he inhaled deeply. God, he could get drunk on the mere scent of her.

"Easy," he said, coming back to earth with a start. She was looking at him strangely. "Lean on me."

"If you insist." Liza pressed her lips together to keep from smiling. Silly man, she thought as she let herself lean against him. He was still fighting it.

"Have you seen Ellen?" she asked, taking some pity on him as they walked slowly across the floor. She didn't need that much help to walk, but she didn't have to tell him that.

"Yes. She's . . . doing remarkably well, considering the fact that she's turned custody of her daughter over to someone else. If Russell doesn't confess, she's going to be the chief witness against him."

"I was afraid she might be in trouble with the authorities, too," Liza said.

"They probably would have tried to pin something on her, at least, to try to get her to testify against Nick, but not now, with all the help she's offered them." He released her but stayed close by, as they paused near the sliding glass door that led to the room's small balcony. "But that's not why she's doing it. I never thought she had it in her, but it seems she's finally going to stand up to him."

"It's dangerous for her, isn't it?"

"She's in protective custody, but, yes, it's dangerous. And if she actually provides the testimony that puts him and some of his buddies away, it'll become even more dangerous."

Liza looked up into the sky. The sun was shining brightly in the west, and clouds were gathering in the east.

"She's doing what I was supposed to do, Liza. She's saving me."

He was right behind her when she turned. She saw the shadow in his eyes, and her heart ached for him. Liza knew he would have a hard time accepting that, and he would never understand that it might be Ellen's duty even more than his. Unable to stop herself, she tried to explain.

"No, Dixon. She's saving herself. She's through letting Russell walk all over her. No more allowing him to endanger her life, her child's, mine, even yours. Putting him away is going to go a long way toward helping her look herself in the mirror again without being ashamed of the woman she sees."

It was obvious from the surprised shock on his face that the thought had never occurred to him.

"Tell me something," she said, and in that moment she believed she was seeing inside him more clearly than she ever had before. "Has anyone ever taken care of you? I mean, even when you were little? Wasn't there ever a time when you weren't responsible for yourself as well as for somebody else?"

She searched his eyes. They were puzzled. Sighing, she realized that she might as well have been speaking some foreign language. He was obviously lost.

If she hadn't been so mad at him for scaring her so badly by staying away for so long, she might have found it touching, the way he seemed to think that his brother's welfare, her own welfare and who knew who else's, were somehow his responsibility.

"My mother took care of me," he insisted.

"Did she?" Liza had serious doubts about that.

"Yes."

"I don't think she did a much better job of taking care of you than mine did taking care of me."

His hand came up to her back then. It rubbed little circles into the satiny material of her robe. Gently he turned her so that they stood facing each other in the pale light streaming in through the glass of the door.

"I just wish I'd done a better job of taking care of *you*."

"Oh, Lord, Dixon. I'm a grown woman. I'm not your responsibility." Exasperated, and more than a little frightened—this was not going at all the way she'd hoped—Liza deliberately tilted her head sideways and down toward the floor, so that her hair fell forward and shielded her eyes from his view.

Not this again, she prayed. Not the guilt. She wanted so much more than guilt.

His hand came up to smooth her hair back into place. Then he kissed her, softly, on her forehead. "I know I told you the other day, but I want . . . I need to tell you again. Liza, I'm so sorry. . . ."

Thunder clapped across the darkening sky then and drowned out his words. Liza stepped out of his loose hold, opened the balcony door and smelled the coming rain. A few minutes later it was falling softly on the balcony floor.

She stared up into the sky and wondered how she could make him see. And then she saw it, so clearly. The rain. Just what she needed.

"It's raining," she told him with a smile that he couldn't see because she was facing the open door.

She stepped out onto the balcony and let the drops fall on her upturned face and soak into her robe.

"Liza? Are you crazy? Get in here."

"I hate the rain, Dixon. It makes the day seem so dark and gloomy. I've had enough gloom to last a lifetime." She leaned her head back so that it sprinkled down upon her face. "Make it stop for me."

He stared at her as if she'd lost her mind.

"You seem to be responsible for everything else that goes wrong in the world. Well, it's raining, and I hate the rain. Why don't you make it stop?"

"Are you on any kind of pain medication? Should I call the doctor?"

Liza laughed then. At least she meant to. But she was afraid it came out more as a sob.

"Make it stop, Dixon. Surely that's within your powers—a hot-shot federal prosecutor like you."

"Come on, Liza. You're still recovering from a nasty gunshot wound. The last thing you need is to catch a chill."

Heedless of the rain and the expensive suit he wore, he walked out onto the balcony and stood there beside her. The rain gathered in the little curls on top of his head, curls she had never known he had, and it slowly ruined his blue suit.

"You can't do it, can you?" She was taunting him now. The rain soaked through the robe to her skin. But she wasn't cold. "You can't admit that even the weather isn't within your control? So just make it stop, Dixon."

"I can't, all right?" he shouted. "I can't do it. Is that what you wanted? Is that all I had to say?"

"No. Now I want to talk about your brother. You didn't get him started on cocaine, did you?"

"No."

"You didn't introduce him to Nick Russell and suggest the two of them start running drugs up the coast, did you?"

"No."

"And it's not so awful to make something of yourself, is it? To get out of the poor little town where you grew up, to get an education, a good job, an important one? Last I heard, that was no crime."

"Okay!" He threw up his hands in surrender. "Enough."

"No, it's not enough. We need to talk about me, too. You didn't bring me into this situation, and it wasn't your responsibility to get me out of it. I'm a grown woman, Dixon."

"I know."

"I can take care of myself."

"Now, on that point, I'd argue with you, at least while you're standing out in the rain."

She frowned up at him—or at least she tried to. But by this time, they were both soaked to the skin, with the rain still falling and no end in sight. It didn't seem like the best time to argue that she was a mature woman who was perfectly capable of taking care of herself.

"Please come inside," he said, gesturing for her to pass through the door and into the room ahead of him.

And then they just stood there, dripping on the carpet, watching each other and waiting.

"Well," he said.

"Well? You got Russell off the streets. You bought Charlie another chance. Jilly has a new home, a good one this time. Ellen may even clean herself up now. It didn't turn out so bad, Dixon."

"Maybe not for them. But what about you?"

Liza closed her eyes and wondered if he'd notice tears falling down her cheeks and mixing with the drops of rain already there. "I'll be all right."

"Will you?" He tipped her chin back, and she felt his gaze intent on her face. "I hurt you, Liza. Don't you think I know that? Did I—is it so bad that you can't forgive me? Not ever?"

She heard the catch in his voice, then the tremor. Cautiously she opened her eyes and looked out through the blur of the tears gathered there. "Was it all a lie, Dixon? Everything that happened between us?"

"Of course not." He grabbed her, pulling her to him and holding her close so that he could watch her carefully when she answered.

"It wasn't just you doing your job?"

"No." God, he'd never imagined she'd think that—that he'd used her like that. "Making love to you wasn't part of the job description. And it didn't do anything except complicate the situation even more.''

"Then what did it mean? What does it mean now that Russell's in custody and Charlie's off the hook? Is it all over between us?''

He closed his eyes and reminded himself of the position he was in. Nothing had been settled for sure. He still might have to testify against Nick Russell, still wasn't sure he could go back to being Dixon MacCauley, federal prosecutor, or whether he'd disappear somewhere inside the government's witness protection program.

He still didn't know whether he'd be safe, or whether anyone with him would be safe. That was the sticking point right now. He wanted her for himself, but most of all he wanted her safe. Having watched her fight for her life after she took that bullet had convinced him that he had to make her safety his top priority.

"God, Liza. Everything's still such a mess. I don't know when it's ever going to be put to rights, or how it will all settle out in the end.''

One deep breath. Then another, to brace herself. He wouldn't say anything more than that. Instinctively she knew that, even as she raged inwardly at that darned noble, self-sacrificing streak. Liza figured it was go-for-broke time. What did she have to lose, anyway? Her pride? It had already taken such a beating with this man that another blow or two didn't matter.

Maybe she hadn't known his name, his job, his reason for being there on the boat, but she knew the man inside, whether he was in a suit and tie or a pair of ragtag blue-jean cut-offs. None of those things changed the man inside.

"Look me in the eye, Dixon," she demanded softly, a telltale quiver in her voice. "Do it and tell me that you feel nothing for me.''

"I can't do that." Never in a million years, he thought.

"It's not over between us. Not for me. Not in my heart.''
She took his hand, opened it wide and pressed it against her pounding heart.

He sucked in a ragged breath and would have pulled away, but she caught him. She took her hand and spread it over his to hold it there against her. "I know what's in my heart."

It beat there between them. He could feel it picking up speed, feel the warmth of her body through the damp cloth, feel the curve of her breast beneath his fingertips.

"Damn it, Liza. I have no idea what's left of my life right now. I don't have anything to offer you. My name may not even be my own anymore."

"And I don't have anything to offer you except my heart, my soul, my body, all my love. It's yours. All you have to do is reach out and take it."

He swayed toward her, inexplicably drawn to her by a force that was stronger than any he'd ever known. But still he hesitated. "Look, I don't know what's going to happen with Russell's trial. I don't know..."

"Does anyone ever know what's going to happen, tomorrow or the next day or the next year?"

"No."

"It was real, Dixon. What was between us was real. It was for me."

"For me, too." Hope was rising inside him now. He felt an unfamiliar tightening in his throat, and he had to fight to get the words past it.

"Then none of those other things matter. I didn't fall in love with a man named Dixon MacCauley who earned his living putting crooks behind bars. You could strip all that away, and it wouldn't change the way I feel. I love you, just as you are, standing here beside me right now. Nothing but you."

He closed his eyes tight. Waited. Then opened them again—she was still there. She was real. She was his.

"Oh, baby, I love you, too. Don't ever doubt that. I just—I want you to be safe."

Liza's heart ached with joy and relief when she saw the unmistakable love at last shining from his eyes. She *hadn't* been wrong. He loved her! Swallowing the lump in her throat, she told him huskily, "I'd rather be with you."

He laughed out loud. "God, you're a stubborn woman. Do you always get what you want?"

"You tell me."

"Let's see." He pulled her close, and his lips came down to meet hers. "Do you want to get out of this hospital?"

"Yes."

He kissed her softly on the lips, because he liked her answer. "Want to run away with me?"

"Yes."

Another kiss, slower than the first. Another smile beamed right down into her beautiful face. "Want to marry me?"

"Oh, yes."

He opened his mouth to caution her again about the risks possibly involved, but he never got the words out. Her fingers pressed against his lips.

"No more objections," she said softly. "We'll be safe. I know we will."

* * * * *

COMING NEXT MONTH

Take 4 bestselling love stories FREE

Plus get a FREE surprise gift!

Silhouette Intimate Moments is proud to present: The SISTER, SISTER duet—Two halves of a whole, two parts of a soul.

Mary Anne Wilson's duo continues next month with TWO AGAINST THE WORLD (IM #489). Now it's Alicia's turn to get herself out of a dangerous bind—and into the arms of the kindest, sexiest man she's ever seen!

If you missed the first book in the series, *Two for the Road* (IM #472), about Alicia's identical twin sister, Alison, you can order it by sending your name, address, zip or postal code along with a check or money order (please do not send cash) for $3.39, plus 75¢ postage and handling ($1.00 in Canada), payable to Silhouette Books, to:

In the U.S.	In Canada
Silhouette Books	Silhouette Books
3010 Walden Avenue	P.O. Box 609
P.O. Box 1396	Fort Erie, Ontario
Buffalo, NY 14269-1396	L2A 5X3

Please specify book title(s) with your order.
Canadian residents add applicable federal and provincial taxes.

SISTER1

SAVE 30¢
ON THE PURCHASE OF ANY
SILHOUETTE SHADOWS™ TITLE

TO THE DEALER: Harlequin/Silhouette Books will pay 30¢ plus 8¢ handling upon presentation of this coupon by your customer toward the purchase of any Silhouette Shadows book. Any other use constitutes fraud. Proof of sufficient stock (in the previous 90 days) to cover coupon redemption must be presented upon request. Coupon is nonassignable, void if taxed, prohibited or restricted by law. Consumer must pay any governmental taxes. Coupons submitted become the property of Harlequin/ Silhouette Books. Reimbursement made only to retail distributor who redeems coupon. Coupon valid in the United States and Canada. Reimbursement paid only in country where product purchased. LIMIT ONE COUPON PER PURCHASE. VALID ONLY ON SILHOUETTE SHADOWS BOOKS IN THE U.S.A. AND CANADA.

IN U.S.A., MAIL TO:

SILHOUETTE SHADOWS
P.O. Box 880478
El Paso, TX 88588-0478

Coupon redeemable at retail outlets only.
OFFER EXPIRES AUGUST 31, 1993.

SHIU

65373 100695